MW01134378

THE LORD OF DREAMS

Also by C. J. Brightley

A Long-Forgotten Song:
Things Unseen
The Dragon's Tongue
The Beginning of Wisdom

Erdemen Honor:
The King's Sword
A Cold Wind
Honor's Heir

Fairy King:
A Fairy King
A Fairy Promise

C.J. BRIGHTLEY

This book is a work of fiction. The characters, incidents, and dialogue are drawn from the author's imagination and are not to be construed as real. Any resemblance to actual events or persons, living or dead, is entirely coincidental.

THE LORD OF DREAMS. Copyright 2017 by C. J. Brightley. All rights reserved. No part of this book may be used or reproduced in any manner whatsoever without written permission except in the case of brief quotations embodied in critical articles and reviews. For information contact info@cjbrightley.com.

ISBN 978-1542621267

Published in the United Sates of America by Spring Song Press, LLC.

www.cjbrightley.com

Cover design by Jenny Zemanek of Seedlings Design Studio.

Public Domain Works Quoted:

Blake, William. "Mad Song." *The Poetical Works of William Blake.* London, New York. Oxford University Press, 1908. 3:7-8. *PoemHunter.com.* Web. 1 March 2017.

Brontë, Emily Jane. "A Day Dream." *Poems by Currer, Ellis, and Acton Bell.* London 1846. I:7:1-4. *Project Gutenberg.* Web. 1 March 2017.

Carroll, Lewis. "Four Riddles." *Phantasmagoria.* United Kingdom 1869. 3:1:1-6. *Project Gutenberg.* Web. 1 March 2017.

Carroll, Lewis. "Jabberwocky." *Through the Looking-Glass, and What Alice Found There.* United Kingdom 1871. 5:1-2, 7:3. *Wikipedia*. Web. 1 March 2017.

Coolidge, Susan (AKA Sarah Chauncey Woolsey). "The Morning Comes Before The Sun." *Verses*. 1:1-4. 1880. *Project Gutenberg*. Web. 1 March 2017.

Gibran, Kahlil. "The Seven Selves." *The Madman: His Parables and Poems.* 1918. 2,4 *Project Gutenberg*. Web. 1 March 2017.

Gorges, Arthur. "Yourself the Sun." 1-2. Late 1500s. *Poets.org*. Web. 1 March 2017.

Lawson, Henry. "The Things We Dare Not Tell." *When I was King and Other Verses*. 1906. 4:1. *Project Gutenberg of Australia*. Web. 1 March 2017.

Lowell, Amy. "Summer Rain." *Pictures of the Floating World*. 1919. 7-10. *Poets.org*. Web. 1 March 2017.

Shakespeare, William. *A Midsummer Night's Dream*. 1595. Act V:4. *Project Gutenberg*. Web. 1 March 2017.

Sheard, Virna. "Kismet." *The Miracle and Other Poems*. Toronto 1913. 2:3-4. *Project Gutenberg*. Web. 1 March 2017.

Yeats, W. B. "The Stolen Child." *The Collected Works in Verse and Prose of William Butler Yeats, Vol. 1 (of 8) Poems Lyrical and Narrative*. Stratford-on-Avon 1908. 1:9-12. *Project Gutenberg*. Web. 1 March 2017.

ACKNOWLEDGEMENTS

Many thanks to my lovely beta readers JA Andrews, Francesca Forrest, and Elizabeth Maddrey, who generously read and reread this book and offered their time and talent to help me make it better. They are all wonderful friends and authors.

For my dad, who really deserves a co-writing credit but will be much happier with a dedication. All the clever ideas were his.

PROLOGUE

When Claire was seven, she had a very strange dream.

Impossibly tall trees towered above her, the sound of their distant rustling like whispers. The air in the dappled shadows was cool and still, broken only by a murmuring of unseen water. Claire looked down at her bare feet, skin pale against the deep green moss covering the earth. Static made her pink nightgown cling to her slim legs.

Where was she?

A fluttering overhead caught her ear, and she looked up, her eyes searching the shadowed branches. Nothing was visible, but the whispering of the leaves seemed to increase ominously. She began walking carefully toward the sound of water, chewing her lip.

What was this place?

Her feet padded on the moss as if it were thick green carpet, soft and cool against her skin. She made her way through sparse brush, the leaves parting before her invitingly.

Screech!

The sudden cry behind her made her start in fear, and she froze, looking back into the shadows. It was darker, as if the sun had not only disappeared behind a cloud, but descended to the horizon in a matter of moments.

Her heart thudded, and she whimpered a little. Another angry cry gave wings to her feet.

She flew through the brush, tiny twigs and leaves slapping her in the face and across the arms. She glanced behind her once, not sure what she expected to see.

Green eyes glinted in the twilight.

Claire cried out and stumbled when her foot hit a nearly buried rock. She fell headlong, her hands splashing into a pool of water.

"You aren't right. You're not what you're supposed to be!"

Claire looked up to see a boy of about her own age glaring down at her.

"There's a... a..." She pointed helplessly behind her, too terrified to look for the eyes of the creature that had pursued her.

"Yes. A cockatrice." The boy's blue glare intensified. His eyes were rimmed in red, and she had a fleeting thought that perhaps he had been weeping. "You should know better than to wake a sleeping cockatrice." His eyes flicked behind her with a frisson of fear, and he grabbed her shoulder. "Back you go, then." He pushed her into the pool of water, hurrying her deeper while glancing over his shoulder. A final shove sent her flailing, the water closing over her head. Her last glimpse of him was of his silver-white hair plastered down by water, one arm flung up against a beaked maw that struck with cobra-like speed. Claire screamed, water filling her mouth.

She woke, trembling and sweaty, tangled in her blankets.

PART I

CHAPTER 1
Nine Years Later

Icy rain gusted into Claire's face a full block before she made it home. She shrieked and ran faster, her backpack lurching awkwardly, the thin soles of her shoes slapping on the wet pavement. Damp tendrils of hair whipped across her face as she fumbled with her key.

She tumbled inside, grumbling about the storm and her wet feet, dripping water across the floor as she strode toward the stairs. "Anyone home?"

Silence answered her.

"It *would* be too much to ask. 'How was your day, Claire? Happy birthday, Claire! We made you a cake!' Or something, anyway." She scowled into the darkness of the kitchen, blinking in the sudden light as her fingers found the switch. "But *no*. They're out celebrating something else. Not me. Not on my sixteenth birthday. That would be too much. They probably forgot about it."

A folded piece of paper leaned against the vase of flowers in the middle of the table and she snatched it up, hope briefly lighting in her eyes before dying away. The flowers weren't for her; they'd been there for almost a week and had been for her mother from her father. But the card must be a birthday card!

Claire, we're out for dinner with Dad's clients tonight. I'm pretty sure I told you, but I wasn't sure if you remembered it was today. I'm sorry to miss your birthday, but this is important to your father and we can't miss it. Ethan's spending the night with Nate. There's frozen lasagna you can heat up. We can go out this weekend; you pick the place.

Love you Sweetie,

Mom

Claire wiped furious tears from her eyes. "Of course it's important. It's anything but me." She stomped to the freezer and yanked it open, seeing the foil tin of lasagna right on top, just as promised. "I hate lasagna."

She stomped upstairs and into her room, aware but not caring that she left damp footprints across the pale carpet. Scowling, she stripped out of her wet clothes and pulled on flannel pajamas, flopped down on her bed, and buried her face in her pillow. She screamed, muffling the sound not because she didn't want to be heard but because it felt more satisfying somehow. The warm, damp air filtered back onto her face as if in validation of her anger. The sound was louder inside her head than in her ears.

Claire flung the pillow across the room, where it hit the bookcase, dislodging several of her knickknacks. She gave a dramatic groan, then heaved herself off the bed and across the room, where she snatched up the pillow and threw it back onto her bed. She replaced the little resin figurines with more care, checking to make sure they hadn't been damaged.

"Stupid temper. Stupid me. Stupid expecting to be important for once. Stupid birthday. They don't care at all!" Tears streamed down her face. "Stupid me being upset by it! Who cares? It's just Claire. No one important. No one that matters." A pain in her hand made her glance down to find she was clenching a little resin fairy so hard that one of the wings had snapped, a jagged point digging into the soft flesh of her palm. "Stupid breakable fairies. I wish..."

A breath of air across the back of her neck made her shiver suddenly. She glared at the fairy figurine and put it back on the shelf with unnecessary force.

Claire, you're being ridiculous. Mom told you about dinner two days ago. She sighed and stood up, shivering as her wet hair slithered inside her collar. Maybe a hot shower would improve her mood.

HALF AN HOUR LATER, she slouched downstairs. She'd piled her dark hair in a messy heap on top of her head and clipped it, hoping for curls the next day, but she knew it wouldn't work. It never worked.

She stared disconsolately at the frozen lasagna and groaned. "I still hate lasagna." Instead, she pulled a box of cookies from the pantry and ate five of them, washing them down with a glass of milk. Then, feeling vaguely guilty, she picked up an apple and crunched on it as she wandered back upstairs.

Claire didn't have much homework, just a few problem sets for Intro to Physics and a section of reading for her Shakespeare class. She glared at it half-heartedly.

I hate being a teenager. I hate my temper.

Rain beat against the window, angry drops that matched her mood.

A crack of lightning made her jump. She stepped toward the window and looked out into the furious darkness. The streetlight near the end of the driveway glowed weakly through sheets of rain. The maple by the corner of the house whipped in the wind. There would be broken branches to clean up tomorrow.

She tossed the little paperback copy of Romeo and Juliet at her still-wet backpack and sniffled. "I don't know what Juliet's problem was. At least someone loved her!" She snorted. "Ok, Claire, even you know that's ridiculous." She glanced across the room at the little fairy figurines lined up along one shelf. She had a whole shelf of tiny fairies, resin and pewter and crystal, all different shapes and sizes. The shelf above it had other fantastical creatures: several unicorns of various colors and materials, a tiny pewter knight in shining armor, a variety of little goblins and gnomes with expressions ranging from sweet curiosity to diabolical mischief, a crystal griffin, a sphinx carved of blonde wood, and others.

"I wish…" The hair on the back of her neck stood up, and she shuddered. She looked around, with the suddenly uncomfortable sense of being under scrutiny. "That's stupid. There's nothing here."

She brushed her teeth and went to bed, snuggling with the ragged bear she'd loved since childhood. She knew it was silly; on her sixteenth birthday, she should be willing to go to bed without a stuffed toy. But tonight she felt lonely and sad. Abandoned. The anger faded, leaving only a childish grief and a longing for someone, anyone, to make her feel important.

As always, she told herself stories as she fell asleep, stories of fantastic adventure and extraordinary heroism. She was always the heroine, of course, brave and steadfast in the face of whatever phantasms her mind could conjure. Last summer she'd researched dreams, and she suspected she didn't really dream of adventure at all. Only the stories she told herself were adventurous, not the dreams themselves. Her dreams were quite ordinary, just disconnected images, fears, and memories of her perfectly boring life. Showing up at school only to find herself naked. Getting a D on her trigonometry test. The cute boy in English class laughing at her.

Yet in the stories she told herself, she was important. Sometimes beloved, sometimes shunned (always unjustly), but always important. She made her own way, carving out a place for herself among the heroes of whatever land she imagined. Often, she was a princess because they were her stories and she wanted to be a princess. Sometimes, she was the heroine, courageously standing against whatever danger threatened some helpless innocent. In her imaginary adventures, she focused on the dramatic climax and the triumphant aftermath, defying the villain with brilliant words and acts of valor, earning the accolades of her adoring subjects. She was always beautiful; her hair curled in perfect ringlets, sometimes blonde, sometimes dark. Never was her hair as it was in reality, a medium brown with waves but no curls.

This night she imagined a castle, neglected but still beautiful, all white stone with intricate arches casting shadows in the dying evening light. Perhaps the windows used to hold stained glass, but they were empty now, a cool wind curling softly around the worn stones, carrying a few dried leaves through the deserted courtyard.

She murmured into her pillow, "I wish... I wish I could be the hero."

Her window slammed open, wind howling inside with a flurry of rain. Claire shrieked, clapping her hands over her ears as she fought free of the covers.

Terror made her heart stutter.

A shadow stood between her and the window. It stepped forward, and in the strobe-like flash of lightning she saw his face.

He waved a hand, and the window closed behind him, the storm suddenly muffled.

With trembling fingers she flipped on her bedside lamp.

He tilted his head and looked at her, a faint, toothy smile lifting his lips. His clothes might have been leather, thick and dark, with a faint, unsettling texture across his chest. Tight, dark breeches were tucked into black boots. His hands were gloved in a similar dark material. His cloak (*who wears a cloak?*) swirled and settled behind him, the edges ragged, made of feathers or perhaps tattered cloth. The exaggerated collar spread around his angular face, making it appear narrower and paler. High, sharp cheekbones caught the light below glittering eyes of an indistinct color, blue and gold and silver all at once. His hair was long and white blonde; it stuck straight out and up from his head, unaffected by gravity, fine as dandelion fluff.

He let her study him, his smile widening slowly as he watched her fear rise until it nearly choked her.

"Come." He held out a gloved hand to her so dark it seemed to suck in the light around it.

Her breath squeaked, and she gasped, "Who are you?"

His teeth gleamed, sharp and predatory. "Your villain."

CHAPTER 2

"I ... I didn't mean it. I take it back."

"Come now. You can't believe it's that easy." He tilted his head the other way, the movement reminiscent of a cat considering the pleasure of ripping apart the mouse between its paws.

"Isn't it?" She found her voice but not the rest of her courage as she shrank away from him.

"What's said is said." His voice had an odd inflection, a hint of anger and frustration that made her skin crawl.

"I'm not going anywhere with you."

In an instant he was only inches away, the shadows slithering over his shoulders and flowing down his back like living darkness, so close she smelled him, frost and moonlight and ozone and bleached bone. "I didn't ask." He straightened, looking down at her, his pale hair catching the light.

Then she blinked, and in the space of her blink, the world changed. She felt a disconcerting bump and found herself sitting on the ground, staring up at him. Her bed and covers were gone, as were the storm and her entire world.

Beneath her was a drought-parched hillside, all dust and tufts of brown grass.

"As you wished." His voice was low and smooth, and it carried no hint of friendliness. His expression radiated pride, arrogance, and a predatory glee that made her stomach try to turn inside out. "There is a young fairy imprisoned in the deepest cell in the dungeon under the castle in the center of the city. Release him from his cell and escort him out of the city to this hill."

"Who is he?"

His smile grew more pointed, more dangerous. "Wouldn't you like to know?"

"What will happen to him if I don't?"

He bent to whisper into her ear, "Do you really want to find out?" His breath stirred her hair, the words laced with menace so profound that tears filled her eyes. She edged away from him; his chuckle sent a shiver up her spine.

Then he vanished.

"What?" she muttered. Then "What?!" more loudly as she stood, turning in a circle. "This is ridiculous! This has to be a dream."

She kicked the ground with one bare foot, grimacing at the bite of the grit. "Or maybe not." Once she'd read that if you questioned whether something was a dream, it generally wasn't.

The air was cool, though not cold, and she had the impression it was mid-morning. To her left stretched endless hills of yellow-grey rock scattered with faded bushes low to the ground. Wind gusted past her carrying the hint of smoke, and she turned to look the other way. A city spread out below her, but it wasn't like any city she'd ever seen before. The streets were cobblestone, the buildings all small and made of stacked stone or wood with dark slate roofs or wooden shingles. A few fires sent up smoke, but none were close to her. The city looked desolate and forbidding, despite the distinct lack of anything overtly frightening.

She turned again to squint at the nothingness of the hills behind her, and then began to pick her way down the slope, bare feet already stinging from the abrasive rock. She shivered. Her pajamas, thin shorts of a grey and pink heart print and an old tee shirt, comfortably threadbare, were entirely unsuited to trekking any distance, especially in the wind. She growled in frustration as she walked, glaring at the city and the barren ground around her. "I should have worn shoes for this," she grumbled. "This is a stupid dream! I want to wake up now."

Much to her own disappointment, she did not wake up, even after stubbing her toe on a sharp stone. She pinched herself, which didn't work either.

As she approached the city, the shadow of a wall grew above her, tall and obsidian. She glowered at it resentfully. "You weren't there before," she muttered.

For a moment, the thought gave her pause. The wall *hadn't* been there before. Such a huge edifice couldn't have simply grown up at her approach. Had it? Or had it been there all along, merely invisible?

There was a massive gate made of some unidentifiable metal embossed with intricate scrollwork and inlaid with blood red enamel. She banged on the door, hoping that somehow, miraculously, someone would open it for her. The sound died away into pregnant silence.

"TRYIN'A GET KILT?"

The rough voice startled her, and she whirled to see a tiny, irritable-looking man half her own height. He had a sharp, angular face and suspicious eyes. His hand rested on the handle of a long, curved knife at his waist.

"Who are you?" she breathed.

"No one." He grinned toothily at her, his eyes glittering with malice. "Breakin' into His Majesty's city is a good way to get skint." Then he looked at her more closely, and his eyes suddenly widened. "You're human!" he breathed. "Oh. *Oh!*"

Claire watched him cautiously. He glanced at the door, then at her, then back at the door. His stubby fingers caressed the hilt of his knife.

"You don't know what you're doin', do you?" he murmured at last. "Not a bloomin' hint of a clue."

"I..." Claire hesitated, wondering what she should tell him. Would he help her? *Could* he help her?

"Course you don't," the little man spat. "That explains a lot." He glanced at the door again. "You need to get in, don't you?"

Claire hesitated, then nodded.

"Come with me." He sprinted away, following the wall to the left. He glanced over his shoulder, and Claire belatedly jogged after him. She quickened her pace after a moment, realizing the little man was unexpectedly swift, and found herself panting, her legs burning, after only a few minutes.

A painful stitch in her side forced her to slow. "Wait!" she gasped.

"Hurry!" he barked, and she forced herself onward.

When Claire thought her heart was going to beat out of her chest, the little man stopped abruptly at an unremarkable spot beside the wall. He glanced back behind them, then up at the top of the wall. With a grimace, he flopped on his stomach and slithered beneath the wall.

Claire frowned after him. There didn't seem to be space for even a tiny person to shimmy between the stone and the wall. The wall was solidly planted in the stone; the foundation was buried deep within the earth.

The man's small hand emerged from the wall. He grabbed her ankle and yanked, and Claire fell to her buttocks with a painful jolt. "Duck," he muttered and jerked her feet first through an impossibly small hole.

SHE FELL SOME SIX feet to land in a jumble of a bruises and scrapes. "Ow!"

"No time for that. Sentries were coming." The little man's voice came out of the dark.

Claire caught her breath. "How did you... how did I fit through there? There wasn't space for you, much less me! And..."

"Not enough space? What... oh. You know even less than I thought. You see a wall and a hole of a certain size, like everything is physical or something. Right?"

She nodded slowly.

"You need to learn *everything*. A hole is, well, a *hole*. What goes through it has more to do with how much it wants to go through than the size of the hole or the size of the thing." He must have seen the look of bafflement on her face, because he muttered, "This is never gonna work."

"What are you, anyway? Do you have a name? Where are we?"

He huffed angrily. "I'm an imp. And because I'm not an imbecile, I'll not be telling you my name. Not my real name, in case *he* catches you, and not the one my friends use, because even a false name used often carries more power than I'd give you." He struck a match, and his eyes glittered an eerie green in the light. "You can call me Feighlí."

"Fayley? Like a girl's name?"

He gave her a withering glare. "Exactly."

"Can I trust you?" Claire's question stuck in her throat. In the flickering light, his green eyes looked wild. His teeth were too sharp. He clutched the hilt of his knife as if he ached to use it.

His toothy grin widened, and his eyes glittered. "Not my problem how you feel." He cackled softly. "I have my own reasons for offering my assistance."

"Where are you taking me?"

"To the dungeon under the castle at the center of the city, of course." He gave her a sidelong glance. "That *is* where you're going, isn't it?"

"Um… well, yes, but how do you know that?"

He smirked. "As if I'd be telling you that!" He shook out the match and grabbed her hand, his short grubby fingers unexpectedly strong. "Come on."

He pulled her through interminable tunnels.

If what he'd said about the hole was true, maybe she was right about the wall. Maybe there was a barrier, and she had perceived it somehow, but her mind only supplied a form that made sense when she got closer to it.

At last, when Claire had begun to wonder whether her eyes would ever see light again, he stopped. "Up we go." He scrambled up ahead of her while she fumbled around in the pitch black until she found a rickety wooden ladder. A splash of yellow light from above her lit the dusty rungs, and she blinked owlishly. She followed the imp's bony rump up the ladder, emerging just behind a tiny wooden hovel.

Feighlí closed the trapdoor through which they had emerged. He muttered under his breath, and the edges of the trapdoor seemed to waver and disappear into the bricks.

The imp turned and studied her. "Afraid, are you?"

Claire shook her head, pretending her heart wasn't about to beat out of her chest. He leered at her. "Not very good at lyin', that's sure. You'd think that'd be one thing a human would be good at. Maybe you're not a very good human." His eyes narrowed. "Don't lie to the chimeras."

He grabbed her hand with his strong, grubby little fingers and pulled her around the corner of the wooden hovel. They were confronted by a long, narrow corridor; both walls and the floor were brick, and the top was open to the copper sky. Feighlí hauled her forward. "Can't stay still in His Majesty's lands. Have to keep moving."

She jogged after him. He darted through an opening she hadn't noticed and sprinted down another long corridor, then a gap in the bricks so narrow she sucked in her breath to shimmy through, then another tunnel through a dense thicket of long thorns.

Her eyes were drawn inexorably to the thorns. They were two inches long, and each one seemed to have the tiniest, almost unnoticeable glimmer on the tip. She hesitated, and then raised one hand and put a finger out.

"Don't touch them!" Feighlí barked.

She jumped, and the imp grabbed her hand again. "No sense at all," he hissed at her, yellowed teeth bared. "Use the noggin you got, even if it's a bit slow for the task you been given." He jerked her out of the thicket and into a tiny stone courtyard, and shoved her away from the edge of the thorn bush. "These are *His Majesty's* lands. Don't trust nothin' in here!" He waited until she nodded, her eyes wide, then muttered, "'Specially not things with pointy bits."

A MOVEMENT ON THE OTHER SIDE of the courtyard caught Claire's eye.

She raised a trembling hand to point at the behemoth lumbering to its feet. "What's that?"

Feighlí glanced over his shoulder and made a strangled noise. "Rock thrower. Hurry!" He yanked her across the courtyard toward a wooden door in the stone wall to their left. The wall towered over their heads, spikes curving from the top of the wall down toward the ground, as if to keep the creature contained. The monstrous beast lumbered toward them. "*Run!*" Feighlí's voice cracked. He slammed his shoulder into the door, breaking the latch out of crumbling wood and careening into another stone corridor.

"That didn't seem very secure!" Claire cried as she sprinted after Feighlí.

"Magic barrier," the imp huffed. "His Majesty won't be pleased I broke it."

The immense creature lumbered into the corridor behind them.

Claire's heartbeat pounded in her ears. Feighlí flew down the corridor, short legs pumping. With considerable effort, she caught up with him and kept pace for a moment before edging ahead.

A rock the size of a softball hurtled past her head, and she flinched. She glanced back, and tripped on an uneven brick. She tumbled to her knees and scrambled up, her heart pounding with terror. The creature was upon her, one enormous finger barely catching the back of her thin tee shirt.

Then the imp screamed in fury. He plunged his dagger through the beast's foot and into the dirt between the bricks of the tunnel floor.

The rock thrower roared, swinging both enormous fists wildly. Claire stumbled away, barely out of the creature's reach. One fist hit Feighlí, throwing the imp into the air only to come crashing down beside Claire.

Her breath came too fast, fear rising in prickles of chill and nausea. She felt frozen, like in a nightmare, imagining her limbs unable to move in the face of certain death. She forced herself to look at Feighlí, his eyes wide and dazed, dark blood coming from his mouth.

Claire forced herself to reach for his hand, intending to pull him out of the rock thrower's reach.

The rock thrower grabbed Feighlí's ankle, and he cried out, twisting away from Claire's hand. The monster jerked him closer, his wide maw opening in a bellow of inarticulate rage. Feighlí pulled a short dagger from an unseen sheath.

"Run, you idiot human!" The imp's voice was almost lost in the rock thrower's roar.

Claire turned and fled.

THE DESOLATE BRICK TUNNELS twisted upon themselves so that Claire couldn't tell which direction she was running. The sun seemed to hang at the apex of its arch for hours, beating down from a cloudless bronze sky.

At times the wind seemed to gust above her, dry and cool, despite the harsh light. It carried odd sounds, a clashing of metal and a few unidentifiable cries. Once she heard a long, high-pitched wail above a lower roar from larger throats, as if a cat were being ripped apart by a pack of dogs.

What a horrible mental image! She frowned at herself, determinedly brushing the dried crust of tears from her cheeks. *It's Feighlí. The rockthrower is killing him.*

No! It's probably nothing. Just a fox or something. Foxes make strange sounds, don't they? She'd read that in a book once, and clung to the thought as if it would assuage her guilt.

The tunnel at last gave way to a grassy expanse with soft rolling hills spread out before her. She let out a sigh of relief.

Claire looked around, noting that the brick walls turned to stone at apparently random intervals to both her left and right. The grass was green but dry; the spikes pricked the tender soles of her feet. She began climbing the nearest hill, hoping to regain her bearings.

A small cluster of stone pillars and tumbled-down walls perched at the top of the hill, and she glanced up at it occasionally. The ruins seemed peaceful in this strange, desolate land. Something about them reminded her of a castle she had seen once in a book about Ireland. Or was it Scotland? Definitely somewhere far more interesting than the outskirts of Richmond, Virginia. She scowled at the grass as she walked, her thighs burning with the constant upward motion and her skin prickling with the chilly wind.

The climb seemed to take far longer than it should have. She stopped to pick spiky bits of grass out from between her toes several times, then clambered higher. Higher and higher.

Claire stopped, panting, and looked upward. How much farther could it be? The ruins seemed no closer than before, and she scowled at them. Then she put her head down and continued climbing. She was hungry, thirsty, tired, and cold, but focusing on the next step was easier than letting her mind wander.

Feighlí's scream echoed in her mind, and she pushed the memory away.

CHAPTER 3

Claire stumbled into the ruins, her throat parched, dizzy with exhaustion. She explored half-heartedly, the silence broken only by the faint song of the wind through the broken columns and fallen walls and arches. The stone was pale gray, and the edges were rounded with age, as if the wind had been tearing at the stone for uncounted millennia.

She found a corner in the lee of the wind and sank against the wall, letting her eyes close. *Will this ever end? When will I wake up?*

"What are you doing?"

Her eyes snapped open and she looked up at a dark silhouette. "Who are you?" she breathed. "There was no one here!" She pushed herself to her feet, shifting so she could see him better.

He looked to be no more than eight or nine years old, with pale silvery skin and white-blonde hair that stuck out from his head like dandelion fluff. His shirt was ragged and stained with dark rusty streaks. For some reason the stains made her think of blood. She pushed the disquieting thought away.

His lips lifted in an irritated smirk. "Wrong question. You should be asking 'where's a charcoal?'"

She blinked. "What?"

"Cats! You need cats." He produced a piece of charcoal without appearing to reach into a pocket. "This is not a place of safety." He sketched a hurried cat on the wall. "Draw." Command filled his voice, and he shoved the charcoal into her hand.

Claire found herself drawing a cat on the cracked stone wall. Her mind felt fuzzy with exhaustion, and she blinked again, studying the wall as she pictured the next cat.

"Draw! Now!" the boy barked.

She turned to him. "Why?"

He bared his teeth at her and snarled, and Claire stumbled backward, her heart thudding. He snatched her hand, his small fingers cold on hers, moving her hand in quick strokes to draw another cat, a massive beast with a maw filled with teeth. "Another!" He shouldered her down the wall and started drawing again, his hand tight around hers. "Faster!"

Claire was trembling. "All right!"

He stepped back. Claire tried to keep an eye on him over her shoulder, her cat drawings hurried and sloppy.

"More teeth," he muttered. "Give them teeth and claws. Think fierce thoughts!"

Claire swallowed. "Why?" Her voice was weaker this time, fear curling up her throat and nearly choking her.

He produced another piece of charcoal and began drawing on a nearby wall. His strokes were quick and sure, his cats huge and feral, more akin to lionesses than house cats. "Keep drawing!" he growled. "Cats and cats and cats."

Claire shuddered at the menace in his voice and drew again, the charcoal rasping in her fingers. Black stained her fingertips. "Who are you?" she whispered. The pale gray stone had become nearly black in the shadows, reflecting orange and pink in the fading sunset.

"Time's up." The words rang out, clear and sharp as a gunshot. "In here." One small hand on her arm, he hauled her bodily across the room and flung her into a cold, narrow space. "Lock the door. Be silent. Don't come out until the sun comes up." He pressed something cold into her hand. "Put this around your neck. Fierce thoughts!"

A heavy wooden door closed in front of her face. With trembling fingers, she found the hefty lock on the inside and let it fall.

The solid metallic clunk was lost beneath an unearthly screech that made Claire's every hair stand on end.

"What is that?" she breathed.

Her stone refuge was little larger than a coffin, a smooth marble rectangle three feet deep and six feet tall, perhaps two and a half feet wide. She trembled with her back pressed against the cold stone behind her. The angular pendant dug into her palm, and she hurriedly slipped it over her head. The pendant briefly caught on the neck of her shirt and then fell with a soft, comforting thunk against her chest.

There was an instant of silence, in which she remembered the disquieting stains on the boy's shirt. Why had she thought they were blood? They were a deep navy, not the rusty red-black of dried blood. Her eyes seemed to be playing tricks on her. She shivered.

A spitting, squawling, howling cacophony roared over her, the sound beating against her in waves of terror. The tone was *wrong*, the sounds too sharp, too sudden, too vicious for any natural animal.

How many creatures were there?

And what had happened to the boy?

Claire crouched, shaking, in the corner of her hiding place with her hands covering her ears. Her thoughts seemed to fugue from terror to terror, until her exhaustion made time stretch out into meaninglessness.

CLAIRE WOKE, SHIVERING, light streaming through a tiny crack in the door to light a stripe across her arm, catching the fine hairs and turning them to gold. She blinked, dazed, and felt her eyes crusty with dried tears.

The silence was absolute, the air heavy with an odd, musky scent. Claire was still thirsty, and finally forced herself to rise. The crack was too small to afford her a view, but she remembered that the boy had said not to come out until the sun rose. She studied the light on her arm, listening to the sound of her heartbeat in her ears. Then she swallowed her fear and cautiously pushed up the latch.

Peering out, she saw the dark shapes indistinctly at first, the brilliant light temporarily blinding her. A soft breeze ruffled her hair, carrying a metallic scent.

Blood.

She saw it first on the teeth of the charcoal-drawn cat nearest her shoulder. Then on its paws. A larger smear around the mouth of the yawning cat figure on the opposite wall, triangle teeth bared.

Strewn around the ruins were the torn, bloodied corpses of giant rats. The largest was the size of a small pony, the smallest the size of a labrador retriever. Sharp, curved teeth gleamed bright white in the sun. Blood puddles soaked into the dirt, and splashes of gore dried unevenly across the white marble floors and walls.

Claire vomited bile, her empty stomach rebelling against the horror.

THE SILENCE BROUGHT HER back to herself. Neither birdsong nor breeze nor distant insect chatter reached within the tumbled marble walls. Claire coughed, her throat raw, and gagged again at the taste, her mouth dry and sour.

She sighed and stood, then staggered, barely catching herself against a wall. The stone was cool against her forehead, and she waited for the dizziness to recede. Too long with little water and no food. *How long has it been? Only a day, I think, but it feels like forever.*

Eyes closed, she breathed in the coppery scent of blood and the musk of rat fur, and she imagined, for a moment, she heard a rustle behind her. She whirled to see the boy leaning wearily against a tumbled pillar, one elbow resting on the worn edge. His white-blond hair stood up like dandelion fuzz around his narrow face. "Don't lie to the chimeras," he said.

"What?"

He gave her a sharp look. "Pay attention! This isn't a game. Don't lie to the chimeras."

She turned the words around in her mind looking for some way in which they made sense. She didn't even know what a chimera was. "Why would I lie to the chimeras?"

"You're human. It's what you… well, it's one of the things humans do. Lies just spring out, even unbidden and unintended."

"We don't! Not all of us, anyway."

He seemed taken aback, and glanced at her. Then his lips lifted in a slight smile, and he gave a knowing nod. "Really? Can you name a human who hasn't lied?"

"Well…"

"That's precisely what I mean. You lie like you believe it, and make us believe you. We can't do that. But do it with the chimeras and … well, just *don't*. Watch your words. It isn't in your nature, but you *can* do it. For long enough, anyway. "

They stood in silence for a moment. The boy seemed older than his years, a dry humor glinting in his eyes as he watched her.

"You knew the rats were coming," Claire said at last.

"Yes."

She wrapped her fingers around the pendant on the chain around her neck. She had nearly forgotten about it, but now she studied it. The pendant was round with a raised design on it of three lines that almost converged at the top, spreading apart towards the bottom. The metal glinted in the sunlight. It was gold, or perhaps polished brass; she wasn't a good enough judge of metals to be sure.

"Why did…?" Her mind felt bleary and unfocused, and she stopped to frown at the boy. "Those monsters would have killed me."

"Yes. But they didn't."

"Was I brought there on purpose, or was it just chance?"

"Very few things are 'just chance' in Faerie. And when you say 'on purpose,' you must consider whose purpose. You wished. I also wished. The Awen might have a purpose of its own. Or perhaps not. You might be serving some purpose we know nothing about. Whose purpose—or purposes—are you serving, and whose are you thwarting?" He gave her a narrow smile. "The rats are Unseelie, part of what you might call the vanguard of the opposing forces. You have a unique ability to use a specific type of magic. You have no knowledge of it, of course, so I gave you a token that would activate the magic on your behalf."

Claire stared at him, growing more confused. "But how?" Then her confusion turned into anger. "You almost got me killed!"

The boy's brows drew together in innocent confusion. "This is your right and just service. I entrusted you with more responsibility and authority than you had reason to expect or deserve." His eyes flashed blue-gold-silver in the harsh sunlight. "Moreover, I risked much to ensure your safety and did not depart until I knew my trust had not been in vain."

Claire gaped at him. *Right and just service?*

His flashing gaze softened. "Besides, you have grown a little through the ordeal, have you not? Aren't you braver than you were before?"

"I just feel tired." Claire felt tears pricking at her eyes.

He smiled a little as he turned away. "Heroes rarely get to rest when they desire to."

Then he was gone, and Claire was gazing at empty rolling hills.

She closed her eyes and slid down to sit, her head resting against the cold marble behind her.

Perhaps she dozed off. Perhaps she merely wished to and let herself retreat into a dreamy haze.

When she came to herself again, the charcoal cat drawings were gone. The rat corpses were gone. The puddles of blood and gore were gone. The ruins were as clean and barren and desolate as she had found them the previous day.

Did I dream the entire thing?

Claire fled, her heart thudding unevenly as she flew down the hill, bare feet pounding on the grass.

CHAPTER 4

Claire ran without thinking.

The slope of the hill lent wings to her feet, and she followed the slope as long as she could, zigzagging through shallow troughs between hills until her legs burned and the protest from her feet was too insistent to ignore. She slowed to a gasping walk, tears sliding down her cheeks unnoticed, until finally she stumbled to her knees.

She sat back and let her tears fall, staring at her bare feet. The nails were crusted with dust and sweat, and there was a bit of blood under one toenail. The soles were red and pricked with blood spots from the grass. Claire brushed at her tears, examining the tiny wounds.

This was, in point of fact, a fantastic time to feel sorry for herself, and she almost reveled in the feeling for several minutes. But even justified self-pity couldn't comfort her for long. Feeling sorry for herself did absolutely no good at all.

This all started when I wished I could be the hero. The villain, whoever he is, even said it had to do with my wish. Feeling sorry for myself isn't really heroic. Maybe I need to do better, if I'm going to get out of this.

Maybe I won't be heroic enough, but if I don't even try, I bet things will be even worse.

She pushed herself to her feet, then sank back to one knee, spots wavering before her eyes.

"I'm dehydrated," she muttered in irritation. "You'd think that a dream land or fairy land or whatever this place is would have some water somewhere." She glared through the spots until they faded, and then pushed herself upright again.

She trudged forward, not sure of any direction but determined to keep moving.

TIME PASSED.

It was probably less than a day, because she didn't remember darkness or sleeping again. But it was definitely more than a few hours. Claire based this assumption on the fact that her mind wandered so far during this time; despite the dubiousness of this logic, she told herself it made sense.

Between one step and the next, the world changed.

She was held as if frozen, one foot suspended in the air.

Something was studying her.

Claire blinked and the image sparkled in her eyes, both too brilliant and too immaterial for her eyes to focus on. It was the afterimage of heat lightning, white hot, the memory of something she had not quite seen and could not quite recollect.

It shook its massive head, the mane of a lion sparkling like light on a bubble in the sun, simultaneously transparent and iridescent. To Claire's dazzled eyes, the creature appeared to be the size of a train car. The creature had a beak as long as she was tall, and its eyes glittered with sharp, terrifying intelligence. The lustrous fur of its mane cascaded over golden scales; the rear half of the creature seemed to be dragon, with a long tail and razor claws. Golden wings folded over a delicate crest of spines that started somewhere in its mane and ran down its backbone all the way to the end of its tail.

"What are you?" it purred into Claire's ear.

"I…" Claire licked her lips. "I'm a human."

A brush of air across the back of her neck made her stiffen. "I see *that*." A second voice chuckled softly from behind her ear. "A human child. But what *are* you?"

"I don't understand the question," Claire breathed.

"She speaks truth," hissed one of them, the sibilant sound raising the hairs on Claire's neck. "Why are you here?" The two terrifying faces were so close she could feel the faint heat radiating off their beaks. The second creature appeared to be the same species as the first.

Claire swallowed a lump in her throat, throwing each possible answer away until she came upon something that seemed safely true, but still uninformative. "I walked."

One of the creatures opened its beak and emitted a long, almost silent hiss. "Interesting," it murmured. "Has she been instructed, do you think?"

The other chimera stared at Claire with narrowed eyes. "What would you do if we let you continue?"

"I would continue."

A rush of air beat against her face, and she blinked against an iridescent thunder of wings and silky fur.

"She speaks truth." Claire couldn't tell which one had spoken. "We shall allow her to pass."

"Shall we?" The one on the left cocked its head sideways, edging its beak forward until it was nearly eye to eye with Claire. It clicked its beak suddenly, the sound nearly deafening so close to her ear. "I was of a mind to taste her heart. I've never eaten a human before."

The chimera to Claire's right shook its mane in irritation. "Like dust with a hint of starlight and too much salt in her iron blood. But she spoke truth, Sister."

Another hiss that sent terror curling through Claire's veins like ice. "As you say. Truth." It opened its mouth in a horrifying grin, the sunlight glinting on a row of needle-like teeth nestled inside the knife-sharp rim of its beak. "Pass, human."

The two chimeras withdrew a hairsbreadth. Claire found her feet on the ground again and stumbled forward, wincing at each step.

When she looked back a few seconds later, the hillside was empty.

CHAPTER 5

Claire walked, and she walked, and she walked.

Time drew out.

The sun shone down from the beaten bronze sky, the heat sucking the sweat from her skin until her thirst nearly drove her mad.

Claire stumbled into a street without realizing she had reached the edge of the city. She turned, momentarily disoriented, looking for the grassy hills and baked ground that she had crossed. Instead of what she remembered, she saw a dark forest looming high behind her, as if reluctantly ceasing its pursuit of her. She blinked and stared at it before shaking her head and trudging down the street.

Was I ever in the hills?

Was I in the desert?

"Why doesn't anything make sense?" she muttered.

A tiny voice beside her hissed, "Why *should* anything make sense?"

Claire flailed, startled, and the creature evaded her, laughing nastily.

"What are *you* doing here?" It grinned at her, tiny sharp teeth in a tiny human face. Humanoid, Claire corrected herself; the creature looked a bit like one of her fairy figurines, a bit larger and definitely not pink. Skin the color of new leaves glistened in the harsh sun, and its eyes gleamed like tiny emeralds. The wings behind its shoulders moved too fast for her eyes to see, but the vague shape of their movement gave Claire the impression that it had two sets of wings, like a dragonfly. The creature was about as tall as her hand, and disconcertingly androgynous. It wore a tunic belted around its waist that appeared to made of spiderweb.

"Ya!" It shouted at her. "Never seen a fairy before? Staring is rude!"

Claire swallowed, her throat raspy with thirst. "Sorry," she croaked.

"Of course you are." The fairy sneered. "Words don't mean much to your kind, though, do they?" It buzzed into her face to glare at her, nearly nose to nose. "Your kind lie and cheat. Can't be trusted, you humans."

"Can you be trusted?" Claire breathed.

The fairy bared tiny teeth at her in a smile that wasn't very nice at all. "Depends on how good you are at reading between the lines."

Claire felt dizzy with thirst, and she closed her eyes for a moment against the encroaching darkness at the edges of her vision.

A stinging pain on her lip made her cry out, and the fairy flittered back, laughing.

"Wake up, human child! It's not sleep time yet."

"What do you want?" Claire's voice cracked, and she swallowed a sob. She rubbed her lip, then stared at the minuscule smear of blood across her finger. "Did you *bite* me?"

"Ha!" The fairy waved a two inch long sword at her face, then darted forward to jab her cheek. "Sword's more fun." He laughed again as Claire flailed, then zipped forward to stab her earlobe.

Claire growled, then focused on the fairy hovering a few feet away. The laughter gave her the impression the fairy was male, a ha-ha-ha sound that tinkled like a silver bell.

She'd always had good reflexes. Her pulse thundered in her ears, and her anger pushed back the dizziness. Her cheeks flushed, and her hand trembled, but she smiled for a moment. "Oh, so you enjoy harassing innocent travelers, do you do?" She edged forward.

The fairy smiled, tiny white teeth glittering, eyes bright and hard. "Enjoyment has nothing to do with it."

Quick as a cat, Claire swatted him out of the air.

The fairy's tiny body crashed to the ground, tumbling end over end. He came to rest some feet away, sprawled facedown on a cobblestone.

Claire knelt to study him.

He was male, though his beauty was androgynous and strange to her eyes. As she had thought, his wings were as fine and iridescent as a dragonfly's wings. Now they were crumpled and broken. A tiny bit of blue fluid seeped from a crack in the leading edge of one of his upper wings. His body was thin and lithe, and, if fairies showed their ages as humans do, he was even younger than she was. His hair was the same spring green as his skin, and filled with dust from the cobblestones beneath him.

A blue stain spread beneath his head.

Claire's stomach twisted, and she swallowed guilt and horror.

Did I kill him? I didn't mean to kill him.

He didn't move.

Adrenalin made Claire's heart race, but there was no threat here. Just a tiny body broken on the ground, motionless and helpless.

She extended one finger and poked him gently in the side, suddenly conscious of her terrible strength in comparison to his fragility.

He didn't move.

Dizziness rose, and she pushed it back.

Please wake up.

She couldn't tell if he was breathing. Straining her eyes, she tried to see whether his back moved, whether the dust stirred in front of his tiny mouth.

I will never strike in anger again.

The fairy let out a soft groan and shifted a little, then fell silent.

Claire chewed her lip, feeling the tears well up and slide down her cheeks.

I don't want to be cruel. I'm sorry.

She couldn't tell how long she sat beside his limp body.

He groaned, coughed, groaned more loudly, and cried out as he tried to move.

"I'm sorry," Claire breathed. "I'm sorry. I was angry, and I shouldn't have done that."

The fairy made a desperate whimpering noise as he curled into himself. He lay on his side and wrapped his arms around his middle, gasping far too fast.

"Is there anything I can do to help?" Claire whispered. "I'm sorry."

The fairy closed his eyes and coughed, then moaned as if the coughing had caused unbearable agony. Perhaps it had.

"Why don't you step on me while you're at it? Put me out of my misery." The words were a bitter whisper, a tiny thread of sound that scarcely reached her ears.

"I'm sorry!" Claire cried. "I'm so sorry. What can I do to help?" She moved so that she could see his face as clearly as possible, and he could see her without moving his head.

His cold emerald eyes glittered at her. "Help? You wish to help *now*? A bit late for that, don't you think?" He coughed again, one small hand clenched into the spider silk tunic as if to keep himself from crying out.

Claire didn't brush away her tears, holding his gaze despite her trembling, despite the guilt and horror that made nausea rise to choke her.

The fairy's eyes softened a little, or perhaps Claire only imagined they did.

"Help me out of the sun. I'd rather die on my own terms than eaten by one of the dark lord's ravens," he muttered.

Claire used his tiny sword to cut a swatch from the lower hem of her shirt, then carefully helped him roll onto it. She lifted the fabric like a hammock, biting her lip as she heard him nearly hyperventilating in his effort not to cry out.

Would I be that brave?

At his direction, she found a pile of broken paving stones a short distance away. She pulled a few pieces of stone off the top, propped them up to make a sheltered enclosure, and then carefully slid the cloth inside.

"I'm sorry," she whispered again.

His voice barely reached her ears. "Don't eat or drink anything. Not *anything*. Got it?"

"All right."

He glared at her, a thin blue slime dribbling from his mouth. He coughed again. "Not even a drop of water."

"All right," Claire repeated. "I won't."

His eyes closed, and she waited, but he said nothing else.

THE ENDLESS WALLS GAVE Claire the sense of being stuck in some unending labyrinth, twisting and turning and leading her ever onward. She fled from an echoing, wolf-like howl; minutes later, as her footsteps slowed, she had the strange sense that she was being herded toward… something.

She looked up and found the tallest structure above the walls and distant trees.

Rescue the fairy imprisoned in the deepest cell under the castle at the center of the city.

She took a deep breath and continued walking.

CHAPTER 6

The structure might have been the castle; she wasn't entirely sure at this point. Everything was so different when she saw it up close, as if magic, distance, deception, or simple misperception made her vision completely unreliable.

The stone walls towered over her, rough and unpolished. The door in front of her was large but not fancy, hewn of rough wood dark with age. She imagined it was a servants' door, an impression borne out by the creatures that entered and exited at irregular intervals. Many of the creatures appeared to be some species of Fae, like the fairy she had so grievously injured but much larger and apparently flightless. They wore an interesting variety of clothes, and after nearly an hour of noticing the repetition in their attire, Claire realized that many of them were probably wearing uniforms.

One Fae wore rich gold fabric with a slithery sort of texture; it draped over his shoulders like a second skin, highlighting his sharp clavicles and finely drawn musculature. The cloth was drawn tight around his narrow waist with a belt of glinting silver set with clear stones that reflected rainbows. Claire wondered whether he was a servant or a prince, until he looked upward with a nervous flinch of his shoulders and hurried inside. She decided he must be a servant; no Fae prince would scuttle like a frightened mouse into the shadows.

Quite a number of the servants wore shapeless cloth tunics belted with rough leather. More interestingly, they wore cloths over their heads. A dark cloth was draped over the sides and back of their heads, and it was tucked under the edges of a soft, nearly featureless mask.

The masks were white with generous holes through which the wearer could see out. They appeared to be gently shaped to a vaguely humanoid shape, with a soft bump for a nose, rounded spaces for the cheeks, and dainty pointed chins. The mouth was a small circular hole in the mask itself; Claire imagined that the wearers were saying "Oh!"

What should she do? No one who had entered or exited the palace looked particularly human, but some of them were approximately her size.

She licked her lips and waited for her moment.

Finally a servant slipped inside, leaving the door to close behind himself, or possibly herself; Claire sprinted across the short intervening distance and slipped in just as the door closed.

The servant turned to her with a startled cry.

Panicked, Claire reached for the servant's face, intending… well, she wasn't quite sure what she was intending. Probably something ineffectual, like slapping a hand over the servant's mouth.

The servant stumbled backward, throwing a hand upward as if to ward off a blow, and Claire tripped on the long robe, falling forward. They landed in a tangle of limbs, the servant whimpering, flailing, trying to crawl away, elbowing Claire in the side of the head.

Sparkles erupted behind Claire's eyelids, and she flailed in response. "Quiet!" she hissed, grasping at the servant's robes. "I'm not going to hurt you!"

Her hand caught suddenly on the servant's belt, and she pulled, trying to keep the servant from getting away. The servant, small and lithe and terrified, thrashed like a hooked fish. Claire cried out as a pointed elbow hit her on the bridge of the nose. A sudden *clonk* thudded in her ears, and the servant abruptly went limp.

The servant had thrashed so hard he, or she, or it, had struck his head on the stone floor.

Claire carefully let her fingers relax, wincing at the pounding headache just behind her eyes. The servant didn't move, and now that the body was still, Claire felt how small it was, how thin and fragile, like a small-boned eleven year old. It was impossible to tell whether the motionless body was male or female without invasive groping, and Claire whispered, "Are you all right?"

Nothing.

The hallway, or tunnel, had some sort of faint ambient lighting from the top of each wall, but the sparks dancing behind Claire's eyes were much brighter. Her groping fingers followed the lines of the clothes upward to narrow shoulders, to cloth bunched around the neck, to the mask. Soft breaths came through the holes at intervals, which reassured her. She couldn't find any sort of attachment mechanism for the mask.

She hesitated, but then the thought of another servant entering the hallway and sounding the alarm helped her decide. She ran her fingers around the edge of the mask again, still unable to find any method of attachment. Frustrated, she pulled on the mask itself, one hand on each edge.

To her surprise, the mask came off in her hands.

The servant was still wearing a mask.

In the dim light, Claire squinted from one mask to the other, frowning. The servant looked exactly the same as it had a moment before, thin body sprawled helplessly on the floor, masked face upward toward Claire. She leaned forward, trying to look into the eyeholes, but the shadows made it impossible to see the servant's true face.

Claire had an odd thought, looking into the depthless black of the servant's eye holes. *Perhaps there's nobody in there at all.* She gasped in terror and sat back, her heart thundering.

She licked her lips and pressed her fear down, balled it up into a knot and tied it neatly, then put it aside. *I don't have time to panic right now,* she told herself.

She studied the mask in her hands. It was indeed made of some fine, soft cloth, and kept its shape by starch or magic or a plastic mask form beneath the cloth. Claire smiled, momentarily amused to imagine a fairy king using glue to stick fabric onto a plastic mask, but then the smile faded. The mask had no texture of starch, and no weight of plastic; it was as fine and light and featureless as air.

With a deep breath, Claire placed the mask over her own face.

CHAPTER 7

Despite the lack of any way to tie on the mask, it stayed in place. Claire felt it gingerly, careful not to dislodge it, feeling the edges resting lightly against her temples and her jaw.

Must be magic.

She looked down at the servant and felt... nothing. Why didn't she feel guilty or concerned?

A moment ago her heart had been pounding with a combination of the fear of discovery, worry that she had badly injured the fairy servant, and a general anxiety that seemed entirely reasonable, given her situation.

The servant's face was still hidden in the mask, the body sprawled bonelessly on the stone floor. She felt vaguely that she ought to care whether it (he? she?) was dead or seriously injured. The worry was there, but distant; as long as no one realized she was responsible, the incident seemed almost irrelevant. Claire rested her hand on the figure's chest, feeling cloth and a faint warm solidity beneath her fingertips, moving softly with each breath. At least the servant was alive. Whether it recovered or not had nothing to do with her.

Claire took a deep breath and let it out slowly, feeling the mask move with her skin as she grimaced. It was surprisingly comfortable, and she ran her fingers over the smooth surface again.

She wondered whether the mask was suppressing her terror, and whether it would do more if she wore it too long. The thought wasn't as terrifying as she imagined it ought to be.

In fact, she wasn't terrified at all.

That should be unsettling.

If the mask were responsible for her feeling—or rather, *not feeling* anything—like this, then surely suppressing feelings was not the mask's only purpose. Perhaps it was intended to make the servants compliant. If so, even if it helped her blend in, she should take it off.

She tried to remove it, her fingernails digging into the mask edges and pulling as hard as she could. No matter where she gripped the mask, she could not get it off.

Claire paused and thought. At least there was some benefit to not being able to be terrified. The mask suppressed her feelings, but she could still think. Suppressing feelings alone wouldn't really control someone, so something else must be coming.

I can't take off the mask, so what should I do?

I don't care.

Oh! That's how it controls the wearer. If I don't care about anything, then I won't have any troublesome tendency to do what I want. I will be left with whatever I'm told to do, and I won't mind doing it.

Well, I won't let that happen to me. Even though I don't really care, I remember what I was supposed to do.

No, what I should *do.*

Her mind was still her own, so that's what she would use.

Claire stood and crept down the hallway as quietly as she could. The soles of her bare feet stung, and she shivered in the cool air.

For a time she encountered no one as she walked an endless maze of hallways. At each intersection, she chose her direction at random, finding corridors of red carpet and gold-papered walls, then flagstones and brick, and later flagstones and rough stone walls. She grew so confused that she stopped in the middle of a hallway, trying to remember whether she'd turned left or right when she entered it. She looked behind herself, and found an endless straight corridor stretching for what seemed like miles.

The halls were shifting around her.

She thought vaguely that this ought to be frightening, but she was not frightened.

The hallway came to an intersection and she did not know which way to go.

She stopped to consider the decision.

It might have minutes or hours later when she realized she had been standing still for a long time. She didn't care which way she went, so she had been simply standing and waiting for instruction.

No! I must decide. I can decide with no feelings. And I must hurry, because this might get worse.

She flew down the hallway, careened around a corner, and ran headlong through several more corridors. She stopped abruptly when she heard voices.

Despite her lack of fear, she knew voices meant danger. Claire froze, unsure what to do, and the speakers turned the corner.

"Oh. Another one." A Fae woman turned up her nose at Claire. The Fae was white-blonde and as beautiful as a snowflake, all sharp angles and frost. Her voice tinkled in the air like dulcimer music.

"I think he likes the masks on them." The male Fae eyed Claire contemptuously. "Makes them interchangeable."

Claire shrank to the side of the hallway, glancing down in horror to realize that her pajama shorts and threadbare t-shirt were as distinctive as royal dress in this land. Why didn't they remark on her clothes? Perhaps the strange attire merely looked exotic to them. Or maybe they didn't notice at all; the woman's expression had not shown any surprise.

The Fae man was gold; he was sun-kissed brilliance; he was fire. His eyes were a green-gold that glinted with irrepressible mirth. His hair fell in luxurious ringlets around his face, his teeth glinting white as he grinned at Claire. He licked his lips, his eyes sliding down her body, lingering on the curve of her breasts through her shirt, on her slim waist, on her scratched and dirty legs, all the way down to her bare, bleeding feet. As the Fae woman began to turn impatiently toward him, his gaze lingered and caressed like a physical touch, lecherous and unwelcome, far too intimate for any friend, much less a stranger. His gaze reached the necklace, and the Fae woman tugged on his arm. His eyes fixed on the pendant for an instant and widened. Then he turned away.

The Fae woman strode on without giving Claire another glance, and she almost breathed a sigh of relief. Then the man glanced over his shoulder and gave Claire a wink.

Something snapped at her, catching her a stinging blow to her right thigh, and she bit back a cry.

They didn't even look back at her; the Fae woman's sparkling laugh echoed as they turned down another hallway and out of sight.

Was that hall there before?

Claire was sure it hadn't been, and she glared at it while rubbing her leg. She glanced down to see a bleeding welt across her thigh. "She whipped me!" Claire muttered, seething with indignation.

The feeling, or lack thereof, wasn't exactly anger; there was less emotion and more a sense of injustice. The Fae woman was casually cruel for no reason other than her own amusement.

The indignation gave her new resolve, and she held it close as she hurried onward.

She found a stairwell and followed it down, down, down an endless stone staircase.

Claire frowned, her bare feet curling against the frigid stone. Distant torches cast faint, flickering tongues of light up the walls, glinting on the worn granite beneath her toes.

Unease curled within her. *I shouldn't be here. I should go back up.* A desire to leave crystallized within her. The feeling was *wrong*. It was not her feeling; it could not be, because she had no desires of her own.

So the feeling of wrongness, the desire to flee, must be forced upon her, as it would be on anyone wearing the mask.

That probably meant she was heading in the right direction.

She shuddered and crept ever downward, following the spiraling staircase into the depths of the earth.

CHAPTER 8

At last Claire came to a door. The stairs curved away to her left, silent and cold.

How do I know this is the right door?

She didn't. But it felt wrong, as if she should back away. She should go any direction but through the door.

She pushed it open.

The door swung open with an ear-splitting creek.

Claire gasped.

The fairy prisoner was bound, hand and foot, with heavy brass manacles that looked obscene on his fine-boned frame. His face was pale and sharp. He glared at her, baring his teeth in a bitter smile.

"Have you come to gloat?" he murmured.

"I've come to rescue you." Claire's voice shook. His youthful beauty struck her as terrible and profound, his bright eyes gleaming like sapphires in the dim light. He looked innocent and dangerous, his golden-blond hair tangled with spiderwebs and dust.

"You've what?" He tilted his head and stared at her.

"I've come to rescue you," Claire repeated. "Not that I know how. I'm pretty sure I'm lost. The hallways turn on themselves like spaghetti, and I think I hurt someone in the hallway." She leaned dizzily against the rough stone wall at her shoulder.

I'm going into shock, she thought distantly. *It's about time, too.*

The fairy's eyebrows arched in an aristocratic expression of skepticism. "Oh, is that what you're doing? I thought you were about to swoon."

"I hadn't planned on it," Claire whispered, her heartbeat thundering in her ears.

"Well, you may have chosen the fastest way to convince me you aren't one of Them. So now, if it's all the same to you, I'd prefer it if you'd get these chains off before the guards come back."

"I don't know how." A few slow deep breaths pushed the dizziness to the back of her awareness, where it lurked like a shadow at the edges of her vision.

The fairy laughed, his voice like the plucked strings of a harp, pure and perfect in the dank air. "Oh, you are an innocent, aren't you? Here." He pushed his hands to the extent of the chains. "You've a mask on. I think everyone with a mask has authority over prisoners."

"What do I do?" Claire stared at his hands. They were as small as a child's hands, narrow and white and strong beneath a thick coating of grime. Dark blood crusted the edges of the manacles where they had dug into his thin skin; the wounds were both old and new, as if every movement for weeks or months had injured him anew.

"Just pull them open. It's magic." His sharp eyes swept over her masked face.

She put her hands on the metal and pulled, feeling the hinges open without a hint of resistance.

"Thank you." The fairy winced as he flexed his hands. "And the ankles, please."

His trousers appeared to have been torn off just above the knee, leaving his lower legs and feet bare. Claire winced in sympathy as her fingers brushed his bony ankles, bloodied and torn by the rough metal.

The instant the last bond was free, he snatched her hand and raced out of the cell.

He pulled her up and up, round and round the spiraling stairs. Claire's legs flew beneath her, but she still stumbled as she tried to keep up. He was too fast and too strong. She cried out as his hand tightened on her wrist as they rounded a corner, and he stopped abruptly.

"What is the problem?" He glared at her. "Why are you so slow? Do you want to be caught?"

"No! I just can't keep up." She gasped for air, panting, unable to catch her breath. The mask seemed to suffocate her, and she tore at it.

"That's no use," the fairy muttered. "It *was* a rather stupid thing to do, wasn't it? Helped get the chains off, though, and might come in handy again... if you can keep your mind your own a bit longer. How are you doing that, anyway?"

"I can't get it off!" Claire wept. Tears dampened her eyes, and she pulled at the edges of the mask frantically. A fingernail tore, and she cried out in anger and frustration.

The fairy caught her wrists in his too-strong hands and hissed, "Silence!You won't get it off that way. It's going to require the one who owns the mask to release you, or someone with a *lot* of power to take off a mask that you put on voluntarily. Better to run and hope we make it out before *he* catches us... or until you give in to the mask and betray us both."

"What would *he* do?" Claire sniffled. Her chest felt constricted, her breath uneven as panic clawed at her.

"You really don't want to know." The fairy pulled her on through the maze of hallways.

THE FAIRY KEPT A vise-like grip on her wrist and led her on without stopping for rest, but he did slow his pace to something she could manage without too much strain. Her breathing slowed, and the tension in her shoulders began to fade.

She let the fairy lead her, knowing there was nothing she could do.

Why worry? We'll get caught or not, but either way, I'm sure everything will be fine.

No, that wasn't true!

Terror and defiance burst through her apathy. This calmness was not natural. It must be the mask, or the magic behind the mask, trying to make her a mindless slave. She *should* be feeling terror!

She would fight this. She had to, if she wanted to survive as herself.

But how?

Panic would be counterproductive, and she wasn't sure she could muster strong emotion anyway. The terror and anger at the mask were already slipping away.

After facing the chimeras, she had decided that the way to be brave was to behave as if she were not afraid, even though she was. So her plan was simple: keep her goal in mind, and work towards that goal regardless of her feelings or lack thereof. Perhaps this might be easier. She felt no panic, so all she had to do was stay on task, despite apathy or distraction. Her conscious will had to master her wandering or lethargic thoughts.

She took a deep breath. *It's no different than writing a term paper while internet videos beckon. Just like studying, Claire. Focus.*

The fairy started around a corner but abruptly reversed course, crashing into Claire and forcing her backward before she got more than a glimpse of massive wooden door and a formation of—well, not men-at-arms, exactly, since they were clearly not men. But they gave that impression, being dressed in uniforms and brightly polished bronze armor and carrying bronze-tipped spears and swords. Their hooves and hairy legs implied they were something like minotaurs. She stared for a moment, coming to the conclusion that the horns were not part of the helmets but rather part of the heads under the helms.

The fairy turned to her and whispered, "They had to hear something. They will send someone to investigate. And anyway, we have to get through that door." He looked doubtful. "Are you still with me? Can you think for yourself?"

Claire nodded. She was actually heartened to feel a thrill of fear flow through her; perhaps she was a little better than before. Maybe she was figuring out how to fight the mask. Maybe her plan was working, and she was rejecting the mask's magic. Or maybe she would ordinarily have been incoherent in terror and was now only slightly unnerved. *Whatever, I'll take it. Pay attention,* she told herself.

"Very well, we have no choice anyway. Normally if a servant wearing a mask is leading a prisoner, the prisoner is under the same spell as the one wearing the mask and simply obeys. You will have to lead me, as if I am under that compulsion and you have charge of me. We need to go through the door. Anyone with a mask is presumed to be unquestionably loyal, so they will believe you, but they won't expect me to be able to speak. Can you speak?"

"Of course I can speak. You've heard me." Claire frowned at him, feeling the mask moving as she spoke.

The fairy raised his eyebrows. "You're holding up well."

Approaching footsteps sounded something like a horse walking on cobblestones, except the gait wasn't quite right. Perhaps it was because the guard had two legs instead of four.

The fairly quickly placed her hand on his wrist. He wiped all expression from his face, looking almost as blank as if he were wearing a mask himself.

The guard stepped around the corner.

Claire barely stifled a cry of alarm at the portions of the creature's face she should see through the gaps in the helmet, which seemed to be designed to be put on from the front rather than from the top. Perhaps that was required because of the horns. Or perhaps the helmet was a sort of mask, like the one she wore, but for a different purpose?

Claire managed to stand quietly for a moment, then walked calmly (at least she hoped it looked calmly) directly toward the guard. He stepped aside to let her pass and fell in behind her as she walked toward the door.

The fairy allowed himself to be led by the wrist as if he were sleepwalking. Claire wondered how much he could observe without glancing around and if he was strong enough to fight the guards if necessary. He was strong and fast, but she had no idea how strong and fast the guards were, not to mention that the guards had weapons and armor and outnumbered them six—no, eight—to two. Eight to one, if she were honest, since she didn't imagine she would be much help in a fight.

As she approached the door, one of the guards said, "This passage leads Outside. It is to be opened only to one with authority to leave the palace. You may not pass."

CLAIRE SAID, "I HAVE such authority. Open the door." Her voice didn't shake at all, and she felt a tiny shred of confidence, of defiance, threading through her veins.

She had the impression that the guards were confused, though she could not have said how or why she got that impression through the masks and alien body language.

"But… the door is to Outside?" The guard's voice carried a questioning note.

"I have my instructions," Claire said firmly. "Open the door. I must take my prisoner to where he should go."

The guards looked at each other.

One pulled at the door handle, and there was an audible *clunk* as whatever mechanism or magic that had sealed the door yielded to the guard's authority. The door opened smoothly. The guards stepped aside as Claire led the impassive fairy through their midst, and then the guards closed ranks again.

As they stepped through the door, the guard closed it behind them, and there was the same clunk as it sealed again.

Claire paused and looked around. A path led straight from the door and directly away until it passed over a hill and out of sight. To the left—actually, that would be north, and the road ran to the east, as she could tell by the shadow of the castle cast by the setting sun—were carefully tended fields and pastures. To the right, south, was a broad lawn bordered by a dense forest. She whispered to the fairy "Which way should I lead?"

No response.

She looked at him; his face was still blank. She shook his wrist and whispered, "Give me a hint, here!"

He did not react.

She released his wrist and watched his face carefully. He seemed to slowly wake, as from a deep sleep. When he was aware enough to realize where they were, he snatched her up, tossed her over one shoulder, and ran like a deer for the woods.

Though he ran smoothly with little jouncing, his shoulder was like a bony knife blade and far from comfortable. But she had to admit that even being dragged by his powerful grip she could not have managed such speed, and she did not complain.

A few yards into the forest, the fairy abruptly changed direction. He did so again some distance later. After what had to be a mile or two, and several more changes of direction that left Claire completely disoriented, he paused and put her down. The mask was less strongly influencing her than before. Maybe its power depended on her being in the castle. She didn't understand, but nonetheless she could feel panic rising, just below the surface.

He looked carefully at her and asked "Are you all right? Do you understand me?"

"Of course I do!" she snapped.

"What happened? How did you deal with the guards and get us outside?"

"You were there. You probably understand what happened better than I do."

"I saw nothing after you took hold of my wrist. It was as if… wait. I did see a little. I had… forgotten?" He frowned thoughtfully. "I remember you walked to the door and told them to open it. They did." He looked at her sharply "How did you do that? Tell me! It may be important."

"You said they would assume I was loyal. I acted as if I were doing what I was supposed to, and told them I needed to go through the door. They believed me and opened it. That's it."

"But… The mask is working! That's proved by what I felt while you held my wrist! I cared for nothing and had no thought of anything! So how did you continue? Does it not work on you?"

"I knew what I was feeling was not what I wanted to feel, and so I did what I thought I should. And, either it's getting weaker as we get farther from the castle, or it's working less and less well as I try to ignore it. Either way, I'm scared half to death right now, and I don't know what to tell you. Do you know the way back? Can we make it from here without being seen?"

"Yes. To both, I think, though I can't promise we won't be seen. It depends on when they discover I am missing, and whether—or rather, how long it takes before they think to look outside the castle. But, I think nothing more is required of you other than you keep your composure until we reach our side." He took a deep breath and pressed his lips together, bright, hard eyes searching her face. "I think my king will do what he can for you, and he should be able to remove the mask if you can hold out until then."

THE REST OF THE ORDEAL was a blur. She followed the fairy through what seemed to be several more miles of forest, though the sun didn't set. She couldn't tell whether the day was eternally long, or whether her sense of time passing was entirely confused.

Her mind was occupied with fighting the effects of the mask. For a while, she felt that she was succeeding; her fear seemed to flutter at the back of her mind, distant but still present. But at some point, the mask seemed to change its attack, letting go of her mind and trying to stifle her breathing. It pressed against her nose, closing her nostrils, and the hole through which she breathed and spoke began to shrink.

She pulled at it as she walked, her fingers unable to get a grip on the smooth edges of the mask.

"It's trying to kill me," she gasped.

"Hurry, then!" The fairy pulled her forward, and she stumbled over something and pressed on.

Someone must have found the servant she had left in the hallway. Or perhaps someone had noticed that the fairy had escaped, maybe even received a report from the guards they had passed. In any case, someone must have realized that someone wearing a mask had managed to ignore or defy its compulsion. Now the mask was simply trying to kill her.

Her attempts to get her fingers under the edge of the mask never seemed to work, but she kept trying.

She sucked in great gulps of air through the tiny hole in the mask.

I'm not going to die, you stupid mask! I won't. I'm not giving up, no matter how much you want me to.

Whoever controlled the mask must have been concentrating directly on her rather than relying on a general spell, as they had before.

I'm not giving up.

CLAIRE STUMBLED TO HER KNEES, blindly reaching for the edges of the mask again. "Have to get it off," she gasped.

Warm hands pushed her fingers out of the way and removed the mask without effort.

She sobbed on her knees, her hands over her face, feeling desperately for her own familiar skin, the feel of her nose, the edge of her jaw. Then she saw his boots, and she looked up.

He towered over her, cloaked in shadow and terror, the wind caressing his cloud of white-blond hair.

"You succeeded." His voice was coldly neutral.

She swallowed fear and forced herself to stand up. Her worn pajamas made her feel exposed and helpless, entirely unprepared to face this nightmare villain. "I did." She raised her chin. "So I'm a hero, now, is that it?"

"Evidently." Tightly held anger flickered in his eyes, but his voice remained even.

He glanced at the mask in his hand and back to her, and pressed his lips together.

He gestured to the fairy. "Rise, Fintan."

Claire glanced over to realize that the fairy had been kneeling, silent and still. Now he straightened and bowed toward the dark king with obvious respect. "Your Majesty, your generosity has been proven yet again. I thank you for my life and my freedom," he said in a low voice.

"It was not without cost," murmured the king. He held out a hand, palm upward, and a tiny scene appeared appeared on his palm.

Claire watched in horror as the miniature image of Feighlí was nearly crushed by the rock thrower, and her figure fled, leaving Feighlí to his fate.

The king gestured and the scene shifted, this time showing her confrontation with the tiny flying fairy.

Fintan gasped. "Your Majesty, I request…"

"It has already been done," the king said, his voice hard. The scene shifted yet again, showing the confrontation in the darkened hallway. Claire watched herself puzzle briefly over the duplicate masks, then put the second mask on her own face.

Why was I so stupid?

The king abruptly clenched his fist, making the magical scene vanish. He stared at her for a long, tense moment, his eyes bright and hard and cold. Then he said, in a voice like shattered glass, "Your wish has been granted. You have been the hero."

"I'm an awful hero," she whispered.

The king closed his eyes and turned his face away.

The world shattered.

CHAPTER 9

Claire woke in her bed. The clock on the nightstand said it was midnight, meaning she'd slept for only an hour.

The strange dream was entirely too vivid and unsettling. She went to the bathroom and guzzled water, feeling it soothe her parched throat. She sat on the toilet and inspected the bottoms of her feet for cuts and thorns, but found nothing.

She lay in bed for hours, replaying the most awful moments in her mind.

When she went to sleep again, she imagined that she'd seen silver tears glinting on the king's cheeks as he turned away.

PART II

INTERLUDE

CHAPTER 10
Three Years Later

A distant rumble caught her ear. Her heart stuttered, knowing, with a prey animal's instinct, that danger was coming. Hooves thundered, and above them she heard deep-voiced cries of animals she could not identify. Words, though not in any language she could understand, sang out from inhuman throats.

She turned and ran.

Lungs burning, she crested the hill and started down the other side just as they cleared the forest. She heard a tiny, whimpering sound as she ran, and realized that she herself made the noise. Stark terror flooded her veins, and she flew down the hill.

She wasn't nearly fast enough.

The first centaur passed her with barely a glance, fully occupied by shooting arrows over his shoulder at impossible speed.

She gaped at him, taking her eyes from the rocky ground in front of her for a split second. She tripped, flailing through the air before skidding to a stop, hands outstretched and bleeding. Another centaur and a creature she could not identify leapt over her, focused on their opponents.

Claire gasped, trying to catch her breath. Should she run? Stay still and hope she wasn't stepped on? The noise was deafening.

She couldn't think! It was so loud, so fast. Panic scraped at her throat, trying to break free in a scream.

She had an instant's impression of the nightmare king's face, pale and shocked, looking directly at her from a great distance. He was at the very back of the company, running as fast as the centaurs in leaps and bounds no human could match. He glanced over his shoulder and made a motion with one hand; a cry of agony from some unseen enemy went keening into the sky, all smoke and fury and despair.

Then he was before her, hands on her upper arms. "Get out," he growled.

CLAIRE GROANED, STRETCHING LUXURIOUSLY, the soft cotton sheets caressing her bare arms. She blinked at the ceiling, then frowned. She'd been dreaming.

About what?

She closed her eyes. Smoke, though very faint. Terror; she remembered the feeling, but not what caused it. Nor did the terror seem to affect her now. Normally, the emotion of a nightmare would bleed into her waking moments, dissipating slowly in the familiar comfort of her room. This dream's terror had remained inside the dream, leaving her only curious and confused. Centaurs? Her mind found a glimpse, just a split-second image of a body flying over her, as if she were lying on the ground looking upward.

How strange.

If she thought very hard, she could almost remember a face, but the more she tried to remember the features, the more the dream dissolved into mist.

PART III

CHAPTER 11
Six Years Later

"Claire?" Her mother's voice floated up the stairs. "Could you get Ethan from soccer practice? I'm about to start painting."

Claire sighed. "Sure, Mom." She put aside her book and stood up, stretching her stiff shoulders and neck. She slipped on a pair of bejeweled sandals that set off her summer tan and hurried down the stairs before poking her head into the dining room.

Her mother glanced over one shoulder as she ripped a piece of blue painters' tape off the roll. "Thanks, sweetie."

"I was going to help with that," Claire said. "I like painting." She pushed down a vague resentment that her mother had started without her.

"You can help when you get back. Thank you, dear." Her mother's curly head bobbed as she stuck the tape to the trim.

"All right. See you later."

The school practice fields were only a few miles away, and Claire sang along with the blaring radio, thumping the steering wheel with her thumbs in time with the music. The air was still warm at the end of summer, but the hint of crispness promised that autumn was only a week or two away.

Practice was over when she arrived. Gravel crunched under her shoes as she got out of the car and walked toward familiar crowd of parents and players.

The boys crowded around the piles of bags, guzzling water from plastic bottles, sweat darkening their shirts. They tore into granola bars and oranges as parents and siblings waited tolerantly.

Ethan pulled off his shin guards and cleats and slipped on sandals while she waited, then they headed toward the car.

Ethan flopped tiredly in the seat.

"Don't get sweat all over my car!" Claire teased.

"Coach ran us hard," Ethan groaned. He upended his water bottle and sucked at it, then sighed. "I'm out, and still thirsty."

"You can survive until we get home."

Claire left the windows rolled down as they drove out of the parking lot and down the street. She turned the music up and hummed along, ignoring her brother's rolled eyes. The sun was setting and shadows stretched across the road. Her hair blew in the wind, and she flipped it with one hand, luxuriating in the feel. Sometime in high school, her hair had become curlier, exactly as she'd wanted when she was younger. *I look like a movie star.*

Ethan leaned forward to change the radio station. She slapped his hand away. "I'm driving! I get to decide on the music."

He grinned and reached forward again, and she pushed his hand aside, stomping on the gas in irritation.

"You're going a little fast, don't you think?"

"When you can drive, you can critique my driving," she shot back, glaring at him.

Something flashed in the corner of her eye. She jerked the wheel, seeing the white of a deer tail disappear into the underbrush beside the road.

The car fishtailed, and she stood on the brake.

The car spun. One tire dropped off the edge of the shoulder into the soft loam, and then the whole vehicle seemed caught in a blender. Claire would have screamed, if she'd been able to catch her breath, but something hit her head and everything went dark.

A SPACIOUS VAULTED CEILING soared overhead. Both walls and floor were stone, lending the air a vague hum of almost-lost echoes of every sound. The walls to her left were covered in tapestries depicting words she could not read. She wondered for an instant whether it was because she didn't know the language, or whether it was because she was dreaming. She'd read once that it was impossible to read in dreams.

She'd found the idea fascinating, and always wanted to try, but in her dreams she either couldn't find anything written, couldn't find a writing implement, or couldn't remember that she'd wanted to try at all.

Ethan stood just beside her. His eyes were wide as he looked over the room and its occupants.

Beds stretched along the left wall, each some few feet apart as if in a long hospital hallway. About half the beds were occupied. All but one of the occupants looked more or less human, though something unidentifiable about them struck her as odd. Five figures seemed to be tending the patients; they were similarly humanoid but slightly strange in a way she couldn't identify. They moved from bed to bed with quiet efficiency; Claire couldn't tell what they were doing for the patients. Their clothes seemed strangely foreign and old-fashioned, not at all similar to the medical scrubs she might have expected. Their shirts were dark burgundy, their sleeves rolled up to their elbows beneath dark leather vests. Their trousers might have been black or perhaps charcoal grey, and were tucked into dark boots.

Sconces and chandeliers flooded the room with light.

The right wall of the room was lined with tall, pointed windows like those of a chapel. The glass in them was clear and filled with graceful arcing patterns of what she assumed to be leading. One window was open, the glass swung inward on invisible hinges. Outside a storm raged; thunder rolled overhead and the rain on the pavement sounded like ocean waves, shifting with the wind.

Their entrance did not seem to have been noticed, but then Ethan took a deep breath and one of the doctors looked up.

The quiet murmuring vanished, and all the figures appeared frozen in momentary disbelief. Then the doctor stepped forward, motioning the others to continue their work.

He strode toward them, stopping some four feet away. He was pale and dark haired, with bushy eyebrows over brilliant green eyes. A dark cloak fell from his shoulders to his waist. Gemstones glinted on both sides of his collar.

"Who are you?" His voice was musical and resonant. "How have you come into my lord's house, and for what purpose?"

Ethan's eyes widened and he stood up straighter. "You talk like a king in one of my books!"

The man's eyes flicked between their faces. "You have not answered the question. Is that an innocent breach of courtesy or is it by design?" His fingers flexed as if aching to reach for the sword hung at his hip.

"Um... We're kind of here by accident," Claire ventured. Her voice sounded small in the vast space.

With a rush of cold air and raindrops, of wind and storm and power, something—*someone*—flew through the open window, dark wings folding up behind him.

Everyone turned toward him. Those on their feet bowed, leaving Claire and Ethan standing, shocked and awed.

He barked something in a language they didn't understand, and everyone sprang into action.

He wore black, an unsettling pattern of shadow that shifted and resolved into a shirt and dark trousers tucked into black boots. A cloak hung behind him; it might have been made of tattered cloth and raven feathers, but as she blinked it slithered up his shoulders and vanished, leaving only an impression of dark pinions folded up and equally vanished. His cloud of white-blond hair was plastered to his head by rain, and he shook a spray of water from it with an irritated gesture.

His arms were full, and it took Claire a moment to decipher the shape of the figure he held. The boy was black as night, skin and clothes and hair; not the dark of a human boy from Africa, but the black of coal, the black of India ink. The palm of one hand, hanging helplessly downward, was not pink or warm brown but ink-black.

Ethan shifted closer to her. "That's not a human, is it?" he breathed.

The king's eyes snapped toward them, flashing blue and gold and silver. He said nothing to them, only murmured something under his breath to the man who had confronted them first.

The doctor prepared a bed for the boy, and the king laid the boy down carefully, watching with sharp eyes as the doctor bent over the child.

The boy was clothed in what appeared to be black feathers (*or was it ragged cloth?*), and his inky hair was as fine as down, the dripping strands splayed across a cream colored pillow.

The Fae king strode to the window and closed it. The roar of the storm outside was suddenly muffled and distant.

The floor was wet; the king was drenched and dripped water with every step.

The head doctor, or so Claire assumed he was, approached the king with a bow, indicating Claire and Ethan with a graceful gesture and began to speak in a low voice. She imagined he was asking what to do about them.

The king studied them over the doctor's shoulder. His eyes were dangerous; Claire felt her insides turning liquid as she tried and failed to meet his gaze. Her pulse pounded in her ears.

"Why are you here?" He stood in front of them, power and authority and magnetism. His voice reverberated in her bones, threading her veins with light.

How did I not feel that before? Was I so young and stupid I missed that?

Claire had to clear her throat before her words were audible. "I don't know." She frowned, trying to think. Something about autumn, and driving, and perhaps Ethan's soccer practice. "I… I don't know how we got here."

"Do you often travel between worlds unintentionally?" The dry humor in his voice made Claire glance up.

The king's gaze flickered over her face, lingering on her pendant for an instant before meeting her frightened gaze. "Perhaps… yes." A strange light appeared in his eyes, something like hope, or the memory of hope. "The mask came off much too easily. You were rejecting it, and had almost entirely succeeded. And you functioned well enough, even with it on. There is more to you than there seems." He let out a soft breath. "But I fear there is not enough time."

Ethan, apparently having missed the humor of the king's first words or the gravity of his latter comment, said, "Is this some stupid prank?"

The king's eyes flashed. Terror shot through Claire, and she put a hand on Ethan's shoulder, digging her fingers in. "Don't make him angry!" she hissed into his ear.

"Why not?" Ethan's voice rose.

"Indeed. Why not?" The king raised one elegant eyebrow, blue-gold-silver eyes flashing like heat lightning.

"I… I just don't like it," she whispered. *Don't turn him into a newt! Or eviscerate him. Or whatever you do.*

The king turned away. She couldn't read the expression that flickered over his face; she was trembling, and her stomach felt sour with fear.

"What's up with him?" Ethan whispered as the king spoke with the doctor or servant or whatever he was. Her brother twitched his shoulder against her grip, and she loosened her hand a little.

"Just don't be rude," she breathed. "This is serious, Ethan."

"Fine," he muttered. "I get it."

I don't think you do, she thought.

The king spoke over his shoulder. "I will send you back where you came from after I have addressed some more pressing concerns." Blue drops dotted the floor around him, smeared by water and footsteps. He stared at the ink-black boy on the bed while the servant spoke quickly to him in low, urgent tones, then nodded once. He turned toward Claire and Ethan.

Ethan had, apparently, just began gathering his courage and youthful impertinence. He straightened his shoulders and raised his chin. "Who are you, anyway?"

The king gave a slow, dangerous smile, showing teeth that glinted white and sharp in the lamplight. Claire realized with a shudder that there was *blood* in his teeth. *No! I'm imagining that!* she told herself frantically, but she knew it was a lie.

"I'm the villain," he murmured. He twitched two fingers in a slight, graceful gesture, and Ethan gasped. He had barely begun to turn to Claire, his mouth open in a soundless cry, when he faded, growing ethereal and then invisible in a breath.

He was gone.

"What have you done?" Claire cried.

The king raised one eyebrow at her, a thin, mirthless smile playing over his lips.

"You monster!" She wanted to slap him, to punch his supercilious face in, and force him to bring Ethan back. But she felt frozen, caught in grief she had no strength to endure.

The king's gaze grew distant for a moment, and then focused on her, his lightning eyes flashing. His eyes flicked to her necklace, and he twitched his fingers again.

Claire tried to scream as the world shattered into a hundred thousand bits of spiraling chaos.

CHAPTER 12

Claire groaned, tears springing to her eyes at the all-consuming ache that gripped her body. Pressure and pain were indiscriminate, and she tried to control her ragged breathing.

"Good. Very good," an unfamiliar voice said reassuringly. "I'm sure you're in quite a bit of discomfort, but you're a very fortunate young lady. Please don't try to move yet."

The bright fluorescent lights seemed to beat through her closed eyelids. "Where am I?" she croaked. Or tried to croak; the words weren't as clear to her ears as they were in her head.

"Oh honey, don't worry about it now." Her mother's voice was soft. "Everything's going to be fine."

"What happened?" She imagined that her words were more clear, stronger.

The unfamiliar voice said, "You're in the hospital. You were in a car accident. Your brother is fine. He has a broken collarbone but he's recovering very well. No one else was hurt, except for you."

"Is he okay?" Claire whispered.

"He's fine, Claire. It wasn't even a bad break." Her mother sounded like she was on the verge of tears, and Claire forced her eyes open.

"Mom? Are you okay?" Her voice sounded raspy and strange.

Her mother choked out a laugh. "I'm fine, dear. You'll be fine too."

"It will take some time, though." The voice belonged to a nurse wearing cupcake-patterned scrubs. She smiled down kindly at Claire. "Your car rolled twice and hit a submerged piling in the ditch. Your side of the car, and you, managed to take most of the damage. We got you stabilized, but you had some pretty serious surgery to go through. We induced a coma and you've just come out of it. You'll feel strange, but you're healing very well. If you continue this way, you should make a full recovery.

Claire frowned. Everything seemed hazy, both her eyesight and her sluggish thoughts.

SHE WENT HOME A week later, home being her parents' house and not the apartment she'd been planning to move into when she started graduate school. A broken collarbone, three broken ribs, a collapsed lung, a cracked pelvis, some internal injuries that she mentally summarized as "liver and stuff got squashed," and, the most serious, a traumatic brain injury. The swelling had been controlled only with a medically-induced coma lasting just over a week.

Her mother had taken a month off of her job at the boutique to take care of Claire, and after a week being pampered at home, Claire insisted that she could go back.

"I'm fine, Mom."

Her mother studied her worriedly. "Claire-bear, you look like you got run over by a truck. You're so pale, and you're barely eating. And don't pretend that you aren't hurting."

Claire grimaced weakly. "The drugs make me blah. But Ethan's here to fetch me the remote and snacks. I can go to the bathroom by myself. There's no need for you to stay stuck at home every single day."

"No more than an hour of television."

"I know." Claire wasn't even tempted to watch more; she'd pushed the limit once to try to finish a movie. Not long before the end, the headache rose like a great, throbbing ocean of pain, drowning out any other thought. "I'll be fine. I'll lie on the couch and veg."

After a kiss on her head, and a chat with Ethan, her mother felt reassured enough to drive away for a half-day shift.

Claire closed her eyes, trying to decide if she felt up to reading or whether focusing on a book would be too much. Maybe a nap would be better.

"Did you have any weird dreams while you were in the coma?"

She opened her eyes to see Ethan staring at her from where he sat on the oversized ottoman.

Claire considered the question. She did have strange memories, but it was hard to piece them into any sort of logical narrative. There was the king, all shadow and danger and malevolence. A boy clothed in black whom the king had carried. Blue ink spots on a marble floor.

"I think there was a crow-boy," she said finally. "And a nightmare king who disappeared you."

Ethan's grew wide. "And he flew through the window like a bird of prey," he whispered.

Claire closed her eyes, suddenly aching and dizzy. "It was just a dream." She toyed with the familiar pendant on its chain around her neck.

"I've never had a dream like that before," Ethan said. "Lots of dreams feel real, but that one felt important. Like I was supposed to understand something but I don't get it yet. You remember it, right?"

"I don't know if what I remember matches what you remember."

"How long was it for you in the dream after he disappeared me?"

"A few seconds."

Ethan frowned. "Dreams are so strange," he muttered. "I was only out for a few minutes. I woke up right as the ambulance arrived." His voice changed, and Claire opened her eyes to see him brushing away tears. "It was really rough, Claire. There was blood and everyone was shouting and I was so scared."

"I'm sorry." The words seemed inadequate, and she reached out to put her hand on his arm. "I wish I'd been more careful." Her throat closed with emotion. *I almost got my little brother killed.* "I'm so sorry, Ethan." She rubbed the side of her thumb against the edging on his sling. "Does it hurt much now?"

Ethan's eyes widened. "It's fine, Claire. It was scary to see *you* like that!"

Claire smiled faintly. "Yeah. I'm sorry about that too."

CLAIRE WAS MORE OR less mobile six weeks after the accident, but she was hardly up to moving by herself. Graduate school started in two weeks. She'd been reluctant to postpone entering graduate school for an entire semester, so after some serious discussions with her parents and with her doctor about recovery, she had decided to attend this autumn semester, despite the lingering headaches and fatigue. She'd picked out a studio apartment by looking at pictures online; technically her mother had done most of the searching and just presented her with a few options, since she wasn't supposed to look at a computer screen for more than an hour a day yet.

Everything hurt, but she was off the painkillers aside from the occasional over-the-counter ibuprofen to push the aches aside long enough to fall asleep. She was nearly bald. An arc of fresh, red scar tissue edged by the dots of staples marred the left side of her head just behind her ear; that was from the longest laceration from the car window. The surgeon had used the same wound to drill into her skull to relieve the pressure on her brain. They'd shaved her entire head to stitch up the other lacerations, so now she looked like… well… she wasn't sure what she looked like. Not a punker; she was too shy and boring for that. Not a cancer patient; the fuzz they'd left over the rest of her head was too dark and thick. But she didn't look like *herself*, or what she imagined she ought to look like.

After all the pain and discomfort, it felt ridiculously unfair to have to look in the mirror and see someone else. Someone with her features, though her eyes were still shadowed like those of a raccoon from the two black eyes she'd gotten from the air bag, and her cheeks were still slightly swollen from the fluids and the possibly-cracked cheekbone. Someone who looked tired and a little frightened, someone with no hair and a big red scar on her head, someone who looked… older. More serious.

Her friend Beth came to visit before school started. They sat on the back deck in lounge chairs with tea and fresh scones Beth had brought from the Java Jim's. Eating hurt. Chewing hurt. The bright autumn sun beat down on Claire's newly shorn head, stinging the tender skin, and she'd finally had to move the chair into the shade.

"You're really lucky, Claire." Beth stared off into the distance, not looking at her friend. "You haven't seen the pictures of the car, have you?"

"No."

"I'm honestly surprised you're alive at all." Beth took a slow bite of her scone. "Maple cinnamon. You should eat more."

"I'm not that hungry."

Beth studied her. "What's bothering you, aside from the obvious?"

Claire rubbed her thumb over the rim of her cup. "I don't like being bald." Her throat closed with unexpected, unwelcome emotion, and she muttered, "It's probably stupid. But I really don't like it. My hair had finally gotten a little of wave, and it was pretty. I don't have the cheekbones to pull off a pixie cut, much less a buzz like this."

Beth snorted. "You're *alive,* Claire. Hair grows back. Don't worry about it. And you have gorgeous cheekbones."

Claire raised her eyebrows skeptically. "Says who?"

"Says me! You want me to shave my head too?"

Claire blinked at her. "What? No!"

Beth pulled her golden curls forward with both hands. "I'm serious. I'll do it if it would make you feel better. We could be baldies together. I'll buy us matching bandanas." She grinned. "No! Little old lady hats with flowers on them!"

Claire giggled, then groaned. "Ouch. Don't be ridiculous. Cutting off your luscious hair won't make mine grow back faster."

"But would it make you feel less alone in your baldness?" Beth met her eyes seriously. "It's not about the hair. Claire. We'd make a cute pair with our heads bare… um… because I dare and I care!"

Claire laughed, then groaned more pathetically. "Oh, Beth. Don't make me laugh." She tugged on the pendant on her necklace, feeling the familiar ridges and bumps. It was comforting, and she was both surprised and grateful that it hadn't been lost in the accident or the hospital stay.

When she let go of it, she forgot it again.

THE SUN FELL BELOW the trees. Claire shivered, the air a little too crisp for her to feel comfortable. Beth had left, having promised not to cut her hair off in solidarity with her friend but having made plans for another visit in three days. With some effort, Claire dragged herself into the house, juggling her paperback and the empty cup and plate with crumbs from the scone. With some effort, she had managed to eat the entire thing, and now doubted she'd be able to choke down much of dinner.

Two days after Beth's next visit, Claire would be on the road to Charlottesville, Virginia, land of racehorses and wine and beautiful old brick buildings with lots of character. It was a lovely, albeit expensive, place to spend the next few years. Fortunately she had several scholarships; the awards wouldn't cover all her costs, but a part time job would cover the rest. Her parents would help move her into the little studio apartment she'd leased.

She slid into the hot shower, letting the water soothe the lingering aches.

A WEEK LATER, HER parents slept on an air mattress on her living room floor after moving her few things into the apartment. Ethan slept on her couch. Her apartment was on the second floor with a lovely view of one of the many grassy areas around campus, edged by an old brick wall that exuded historic charm.

Claire felt, if not entirely healed, at least able to face the walk across campus to her classes. She didn't have a car yet and didn't want to drive anyway.

"Are you sure you're all right, dear?" her mother asked for the hundredth time.

"Yeah, Mom. Thanks." Claire smiled reassuringly. That had gotten easier over the weeks.

Ethan hugged her gingerly. "Have you had any more weird dreams?" he whispered in her ear.

She shook her head, glancing at him. "Have you?"

"No." He studied her face, then glanced away. "But I keep wanting to."

Claire frowned. "Don't. I can't imagine anything good could come of that."

"What are you two whispering about?" her father said cheerily.

"Nothing!" Ethan's voice squeaked, and Claire grinned at him, watching him blush. He was all gangly teenage limbs and floppy hair. Only a hint of little boy roundness remaining in his face. The thought of him in the wreck brought sudden tears to her eyes, and she wrapped her arms around him again.

"Love you, little brother."

"Love you too, big sister." He smiled at her. "Next time I see you, I'll be taller than you. So enjoy it while it lasts."

CHAPTER 13

Claire survived her first week of classes and even made a few new acquaintances who might turn into friends with a little time. Someone asked about the pink scarf wrapped around her head like a turban, and she explained about the accident and the resulting scar and shaved head. She hadn't wanted to feel vulnerable so soon after meeting these new people. Unwelcome tears sprung in her eyes, and their sudden sympathy and kindness felt both surprising and comforting.

Friday, after her long morning class, she went back to her new apartment and made a cup of tea in a free mug from one of the groups advertising on campus. Then she sat at her little breakfast table that doubled as her desk when she didn't want to sit in front of her computer. She pulled out the syllabus and found the book for the first assigned reading. *A Brief History of Modern China.* It thudded on the table.

Something in the corner of her eye flickered, and she spun in her chair.

It was *him*.

Claire sprang to her feet, glancing around frantically for some sort of weapon.

He stood several feet away, not moving, though his very stillness was terrifying. His cloak was that same midnight black she remembered from her adolescent nightmare, shadows crawling up his shoulders like living void, subtly shifting in a wind she could not feel. His hair was still a white-blond cloud around his narrow, hard face. He had high cheekbones and a thin, expressive mouth that showed not a hint of friendliness; the overall effect gave Claire the impression of haughty, unyielding arrogance with a thread of cruelty.

She blinked, and she remembered that strange dream she'd had in the coma after the accident.

"You look different." Even Claire herself wasn't entirely sure what she meant by the words. He looked every bit as terrifying as he had in that childhood dream, even if perhaps now she realized how excruciatingly beautiful he was.

He had always been controlled before, elegant and aristocratic. Now there was a hint of desperation in the sharp lines of his face.

He tilted his head a little, eyes sharp on her face. "Even my kind can change, though not as quickly as humans do." He took a step forward, and she shrank back against the wall just beside the fireplace. His lips lifted in a tight smile, showing his too-sharp teeth. "I once gave you a gift. I need it back."

"You've never given me anything that could be called a gift."

His eyes narrowed. "Call it a loan, then. Or if you insist, I offer full recompense for its value."

"I don't even know what you could possibly be talking about." Her groping hand found the iron fireplace poker. Her fingers curled around the handle.

He stared at her, eyes bright and hard, glittering with malice. "You always were so eager to hate me. I had forgotten how much it hurt."

"It's not like you care! You're a nightmare I had in a coma! And now you want to take something back that you never gave me. You're impossible!"

He straightened, the withdrawal almost imperceptible. When he spoke again, his voice was all cool disdain. "I didn't come to parley with you. Let me take it and be gone."

"I don't have anything!" She swung the iron rod at him fast and hard.

He danced back out of the way, teeth bared in a mocking smile.

"Go away!" she growled.

She swung the rod at him again, and he would have avoided it easily with his disconcerting grace and impossible speed, but he stumbled at the edge of her carpet, his boot heel catching in the thick pile. He caught his balance with a twist of his lithe body, throwing his hand up to block the rod from hitting him. He dropped it with a hiss of pain.

He backed up, cradling his hand, his face tight and furious. "I should annihilate you for that."

"I'd like to see you try!" She advanced on him, then hesitated. The end of the rod was smoking, bits of flesh sizzling on the metal. Horrified, she looked back at him.

For a split second, she saw two versions of him, the images superimposed over each other. In one, he was as she had seen him before. Indigo silk shirt, high collared black cloak, tight breeches of dark leather, knee-high boots, hair an impeccable moonlight-pale pouf. He was predatory, feline grace and impossible beauty; he was seduction and fury and the longings of her teenage heart. His eyes shone with anger even as his lips lifted in a disdainful smile.

The other version made her pause. Dark blood was matted into his ridiculous hair on one side; it had crusted on his temple and in a long line smeared by a careless hand swiped across it. He wore different clothes of some dark fabric coarser than silk; blood had soaked through his shirt in several places, and she could see lighter fabric beneath the torn edges. He favored his right leg, standing there with his wounded hand cradled in the other, smoke still rising from his palm. His lips were similarly lifted, teeth bared, but the impression was subtly different; pain and sorrow rather than fury. He'd been lean before, but this vision of him was too thin, cheeks a little too sunken, dark shadows under his glittering eyes.

She trembled, the rod dropping just a little. "What are you?"

"I have not the pleasure of understanding you," he growled. "Nor is the question relevant."

She shivered. His voice carried so many layered emotions. Irritation, anger, desperation, condescension, boredom, hunger, weariness, tenderness. It was velvet and gravel, chocolate and lust and dark promises.

He stepped forward again, hands low and unthreatening. "I once thought..." His eyes swept over her, down and up, the weight of his gaze pressing upon her. "It doesn't matter. Give it to me and I'll be gone."

She kept the iron rod between them, pointing it at him in what she hoped was a threatening manner. "No. Tell me. What are you?"

"Your villain!" he hissed. "As always, I am what you make of me. You're the hero. *You win!* Banish me, then, after this. But give me back..." He hesitated, both superimposed faces blinking.

He shook his head, and for an instant, the more imposing image of him flickered. Faded. The darker image looked dizzy, eyes glazed.

"What's happening? Are you using some kind of glamour on me?"

His eyes narrowed. "You've always seen what you wanted to see. Why ask that now?"

She glanced at his hand. His fingers were curled, not quite touching his palm. The tendons stood out on the back of his hand, the pale skin too thin. Her heart gave an unsteady little lurch. "Let me see it," she whispered.

"No."

"For once be honest with me!" she cried. "Please. Let me at least try to understand. Then I'll... I'll consider doing what you say."

His mouth twisted, eyes boring into her. Then he opened his hand, turning it toward her. His palm was scorched black on the edges of a furious burn, raw flesh and fine bones open to the air. "You chose your weapon well," he murmured. "I wish my words were half as effective."

Claire's stomach rose, and she turned away, the rod dropping from her fingers. "I'm going to be sick."

"None of that," he snapped. "There's no time."

She'd never been able to control nausea the way the heroines in the books seemed to. The feeling rose, her skin suddenly flushed and sweating, chilled and burning. She vomited on the beige carpet, the raspberry yogurt and coffee from breakfast stinging her throat. Hands on her knees, she couldn't look at him, didn't care if he took whatever he'd been demanding.

Her pulse roared in her ears, ka-thump ka-thump, and the sweaty heat turned to a clammy chill.

She swallowed the sour taste and focused on the texture of the carpet, trying to quell the roiling nausea. The edges of her vision faded a little with each beat of her heart. *I'm going to pass out.*

A touch on her shoulder made her heart leap into her throat.

"Come now. Didn't I say there was no time for that?" He drew her away, his hand on her shoulder surprisingly gentle but inexorable.

She trembled, breathing too fast, and he pushed her toward her worn sofa. She collapsed into it and sank into the cushions.

"Sit." He stood above her, his eyes bright on her face. "Don't you think it's a bit silly to be so concerned about the pain of a monster you both hate and despise?"

She stared up at the two images of him overlaid upon each other, polished and brilliant, worn and faded, bright and hard, thin and wounded. "Are you even a monster?" she whispered.

He sighed, and the more imposing image of him faded further. He blinked, then shook his head, as if he were dizzy. "I don't believe it matters." He focused on her again. "Besides, it all depends on your point of view, doesn't it?"

"Are you real?"

"Of course I'm real!" He flexed his injured hand with an almost hidden wince. "Will you not give it back to me?" His voice had a strange, terrible inflection that she couldn't decipher. It was as if she, or perhaps he, were fading out of reality, as if the sound traveled a thousand miles to reach her ears, drawn thin, the layers of seduction and danger stripped away to leave only the question itself.

Claire's vision blurred in time with her pulse, and she closed her eyes. "I don't know what you're talking about."

Perhaps she fell asleep, or perhaps she fainted; afterwards she couldn't be quite sure. The clock on her microwave told her that four hours had passed since her class had ended, but she couldn't remember when the nightmare king had arrived, nor could she even begin to guess how long she had spoken with him.

The time he had been present felt strangely separated from the rest of the day, both real and unreal.

Her iron fire poker lay on the floor near the fireplace, not where it was supposed to hang on the stand. It was devoid of any signs of the tiny sizzling gobbets of flesh from his hand, but it was not where she had left it. There was no sign of vomit on the floor, but the sour aftertaste of it was in her mouth, entirely real and not imagined. Or so she thought.

She managed to put the incident behind her with a shower and dinner. Her parents had stocked her refrigerator with fresh fruit and vegetables, pre-seasoned meats, and frozen dinners. She used her new cookware and put together a simple meal of roasted chicken with rice and steamed vegetables. Then she sat and stared at the food, wondering if anything was real.

That night she dreamed of nothing, or at least nothing she could remember. In the clear light of Saturday morning, the nightmare king's visit seemed like a dream caused by her overactive imagination or perhaps some lingering aftereffect of her head injury. But her brother remembered the same dream. And there was the iron poker… but that could explained by her mind playing tricks.

She tried to forget him.

CHAPTER 14

Three weeks later, Claire tugged on her pendant as she walked out of the library. Graduate school was harder than undergraduate by an order of magnitude, and she knew she needed to focus on this paper. These professors would not take the fluff that had carried her so easily through her first four years.

She relished the challenge, and realized that for years she had been *bored*. Busy, but bored. The busyness had prevented her from realizing how very bored she was, how unchallenged she was, and how desperately she wished to do something that mattered.

Once I wished to be the hero. She still wished it, if she were honest with herself. This degree wouldn't exactly make her a hero, but she thought it might give her some tools to work with. Organizations needed people with analytical skills. Surely she'd be able to do something heroic. Maybe she'd work at a nonprofit doing… something. Helping children in poverty stay in school, or get medical care, or something equally altruistic.

It did seem rather vague, when she thought about it. *But isn't that why we're all in grad school? Because we don't know what to do yet with our lives, and we're stalling. Or maybe that's just me.*

She walked home through the cool twilight, letting her mind wander. *I wish I could do something that really mattered.*

Entering her apartment, she tossed her keys on the counter and wearily slung her backpack to the floor.

The thought of making an "adult meal" seemed overwhelming. PB&J, then. *At least it's better than cereal.* She poured herself a large glass of milk and drained it. She pulled pieces of bread from the bag, then spread one thickly with peanut butter. Knife still in hand, she opened the jar of strawberry jam and slapped a generous portion of pink sugary sweetness over the other bread.

A flicker in the corner of her eye caught her attention, and she whirled to face the mirror in the hallway.

She gasped.

Feighlí stared out at her, dark eyebrows drawn down in worry. "There you are," he growled. "We need you."

"What?" Claire couldn't seem to find her voice. "I thought you were…"

"Dead?" Feighlí gave a mirthless chuckle. "Not quite. I got over it." A flash in his dark eyes made guilt twist inside her.

"I… yes. Or maybe you were a dream." Claire couldn't take her eyes off him. His face was just as she remembered it, sharp and suspicious, eyes gleaming with irritation.

"Don't you think if you were dreaming, you'd dream someone prettier than me?" He smiled nastily at her.

She made a soft, offended noise, and he waved a hand dismissively.

"You're human. You see what humans see. It doesn't matter. What matters is that we need you now. His Majesty is gone."

Claire blinked. "His Majesty?"

"We're at war. We need him. You are the only one who can find him. Ergo, we need you." The corners of his mouth turned down. "It ain't fair and it ain't what anyone wants. I argued against you being brought into it. But the wish holds, and there you have it." He extended his hand toward her.

"I… I…" Her heart thudded irregularly in her chest. "This isn't real, is it? I'm dreaming now."

Feighlí's eyes bored into her. "Will you come?"

Her mouth felt dry. "Shouldn't I pack a bag or something?" *I'm stalling. Surely this can't be real.*

Feighlí's expression grew bleak. "It took seven months to reach you through this portal. If I lose sight of you, it could take another seven to reach you again." He stared at her, neither pleading nor relenting. "Will you not help us?"

Claire swallowed. "All right," she whispered. "What do I do?"

He indicated his outstretched hand, and Claire, feeling as though she were dreaming, put her hand in his.

She stepped through the mirror.

She stumbled, and Feighlí's strong hand caught her. "You look pale. I hadn't noticed that through the magic." He studied her, his sharp eyes taking in her shaved head and the long scar without additional comment.

Her mouth felt even drier than before. "Are you going to go with me?"

Feighlí frowned faintly. "I don't think so."

Claire glanced over her shoulder to see a large, ornate mirror standing against one wall. It reflected only the room in which she stood. The floor was covered in a deep blue rug, and a massive fireplace covered most of one wall. A row of windows lit the room with warm golden light. A third wall was covered in book cases filled with thick, leather-bound volumes. The fourth wall was lined with layers of maps pinned atop each other; they appeared to have been made by an exquisitely skilled cartographer, colored in delicate watercolor washes and labeled in a precise, flowing hand. "Where are we?"

"His Majesty's study."

The space looked so intellectual, so cultured. Claire's eyes roamed over the room, taking in the worn, elegant desk and the equally worn velvet-cushioned chair behind it. The top was empty but for a quill pen beside an inkwell.

"Does he really write with that?" she wondered.

"When he's here." Feighlí nodded her toward a door she had not noticed. "Come. The others will be glad to learn my efforts have at last succeeded. Perhaps there is hope after all."

The hallway was tiled in white marble; Feighlí's small boots clicked authoritatively as he led her into a larger room a short distance away. At his entrance, the dull roar of conversation abruptly died, and Claire's gasp of surprise sounded deafening in the resulting silence.

Half a dozen Fae stood just to her left. They were tall and fair, their angular faces reminding Claire uncomfortably of the nightmare king. To her other side was a pair of smaller creatures that appeared to be made of dense smoke twisting sinuously in place. At her awed glance, one of the clouds formed a mouth and hissed at her. Other creatures of various types she could not name spread out before her, some appearing to have just stopped conversing with their neighbors. A flock of smaller fairies hovered in the air above, their wings buzzing almost inaudibly in the echoing silence.

"Peoples of the Seelie court, our long search is at an end. Behold, I have brought Claire Delaney, who will rescue His Majesty the king."

The room erupted into agitated murmurs.

Feighlí glowered. "I thought they would be more appreciative." His grumble was nearly lost in the heated arguments that filled the air.

One of the Fae stepped forward, and the murmuring abated a little. He addressed Feighlí with barely a glance at Claire. "You said you could bring a hero to find and rescue His Majesty. This is nothing but a thin, weak, wounded child." His voice rang with scorn. "Your judgment has always been suspect, but even I did not expect this."

Feighlí glared up at him. "She will do it."

The crowd had begun growing louder, arguments beginning in earnest.

"She is doomed!" a voice cried. "This is ridiculous, Lord Faolan! How can you send a pathetic child into the dark lands? She will die, and she will cost us everything."

Who is Lord Faolan? Claire wondered.

Feighlí said more loudly, "I am not mistaken in this. She is the hero and *she will do it.*"

"I object!" another voice rang out. "It is wrong to send a defenseless child into the very heart of the dark lands. No human and no child should bear such a burden!"

"Is this not the human who freed Fintan?" The thin voice rang out from somewhere in the back. "I think it is. Perhaps there is a little hope."

"No! That was different! Fintan was..." The words were lost in the growing clamor.

Someone close by grumbled, "Even if it is the same one, I see no reason to trust her."

"I don't see a hero."

Claire closed her eyes and sighed. Everything had a sense of unreality to it. Her stomach growled, and she thought longingly of the peanut butter sandwich she'd left sitting on the counter. Then, with some surprise, she realized the butter knife was still in her hand. It still had quite a bit of jelly and a thin layer of peanut butter smeared over the metal. With a mental shrug, she raised the knife to her mouth and licked the peanut butter and jelly from the blade.

Silence fell over the room just as Feighlí roared, "SHE IS CHOSEN!"

His words echoed as everyone stared at Claire.

"What are you doing?" one of the Fae asked in a strange voice.

Heat rose in her cheeks. "Sorry. I was hungry. I hadn't eaten dinner yet."

The Fae's eyes flicked over her once before going back to the knife.

"By whom was she chosen?" another voice asked.

"By His Majesty." Feighlí did not blink.

That can't be possible. Are we even talking about the nightmare king, or is there another one? Surely I've gotten confused somehow. They can't be talking about him, can they?

"Then so it shall be." The Fae bowed formally to Feighlí. "I was not aware that His Majesty had chosen her. I withdraw my objection. I see there is more to her than there first appeared."

"So it shall be."

CHAPTER 15

Although it had been evening in Charlottesville, it was only mid-morning in Faerie. *Or whatever this place is.*

Blue-gold light streamed through the windows. Claire stood on the balcony and gazed out at the alien landscape. Verdant green hills receded into the distance, the color broken occasionally by the gleam of white stone beneath the lush grass. Low stone walls snaked over the hills, penning in sheep and cattle.

The room was spacious and beautifully decorated in shades of blue and gold. Rich blue and gold rugs layered the floor, giving the room an unexpectedly bohemian air. A luxuriously quilted bed stood in one corner of the room, canopied in heavy indigo velvet. The walls were covered in intricate drawings; Claire thought it looked as if someone with an obsession with swirls and whorls had been given free rein for a very long time with a fine point marker.

A Fae girl knocked and curtsied in the doorway. "Time is short. You must depart."

"Where am I going?"

The girl did not answer, only shook her head with a doubtful frown.

"What's on the walls?" Claire asked impulsively. *I want to understand one thing before I leave. Just one thing!* "The designs?"

The Fae girl's face brightened. "Oh! The patterns are an old magic. Although he was but a child when he formed them, His Majesty was already quite powerful. The designs were an assignment from his father for protection for travelers. This room is used for visiting dignitaries, such as the regional kings and provincial lords who owe allegiance to His Majesty."

Claire turned to look at the walls again, stepping closer to study the patterns. The patterns did not look like the work of a child; the strokes were too sure and precise, the design too intricate. The lines circled back upon themselves, entwined in endless twisting knots arranged in a symmetry that she could only begin to see with her eyes half-unfocused.

"Is he a good king?" she asked curiously. She didn't know what kind of answer she expected.

The girl gave a soft cry. "What a horrible question!" Her wide, golden eyes swept over Claire's face in sudden disapproval. "He is ours, and we are his."

Claire opened her mouth, then closed it again helplessly. "I didn't mean…"

The Fae girl frowned fiercely. "Without him we've lost thousands to the Unseelie in the past months. When he fought for us, we lost only three centaurs and a dryad in the previous five years. He shields us from them with his power." Her brows drew downward. "Even he cannot stand alone against the Unseelie in these times. Not without… That is why…" She pressed her lips together. "I shouldn't speculate."

Claire tilted her head, wondering at the godlike powers ascribed to the villain she pictured.

The girl continued, "The only reason he is gone now is to prevent an even greater catastrophe."

"What would that catastrophe be?" Claire asked cautiously.

"No one knows. But he told Lord Faolan before he left that this was the only way to prevent it. He knew his effort would go badly, or at least suspected it, and had made preparations."

FEIGHLÍ SEEMED TO BE in charge of preparing Claire for the task before her.

"His Majesty is being held somewhere we cannot reach him. We believe he is likely held in one of the Unseelie king's dungeons at a remote stronghold."

"Have you tried to rescue him?"

"Well…" The imp frowned. "It's a bit more complicated than that. He's been *captured*, you see. Well and truly captured."

"Yes, I think you said that already."

Feighlí's frown deepened, as if he knew she didn't really understand. "Not all of the Unseelie are entirely loyal to Taibhseach, so we are not entirely ignorant of the situation. His Majesty is guarded with great force, and scouts and spies keep watch over all approaches. Small forces are to be let in to search for the king's prison as long as they continue to move deeper into Unseelie territory, but only small forces; our stronger forces have been repelled at the border." His voice was tight.

"So I could be walking to my death?" Claire's voice was flat.

Feighlí hissed out a soft breath. "I think such an outcome is certainly likely but not inevitable."

"Why would they let in small rescue parties?"

"I have a suspicion. It would explain why His Majesty did all this. If I am right, there is great risk, and not only to you. You endanger us all by going, but it may be our only chance. His Majesty seemed to think so."

"You're going to have to explain better than that."

The imp gave her a sidelong look. "No, actually I think that would be a grievous idea. Might ruin everything, in fact. Also might not be possible, and dangerous to try. For me, at least. No, we'll just have to chance that I'm right, and the king was not too mad."

She pondered that. *Not too mad. I wonder what he means by that?*

"We believe he is held in a stronghold in this region." He pointed on a map, and Claire studied it with interest. "This is only a small portion of His Majesty's domain. Even His Majesty's subjects can be dangerous to humans, though they are not evil and wish no ill toward your kind. The border is here." He pointed to a long river which cut across the map diagonally. "Once you cross it, if you come to any road or path, follow it to the east or north and it will either lead to the stronghold or pass within sight of it."

Mountains spread across the far corner of the map, but that did not appear to be an area she would cross. Several smaller rivers snaked across the map. Much of the paper was covered in a faint, pine-green watercolor wash, which she understood to mean that the area was wooded, but there were areas of lighter green that might have indicated clearings or other features.

"If somehow you succeed in freeing the king, the guards will not stay to fight; they will send word to Taibhseach. He will come to take you both before you escape. So your only hope is to flee as quickly as possible, before he overtakes you. It's unlikely you can move fast enough, but that's what you have to do."

Claire let out a breath. "So it's a trap?"

"Of course it's a trap, but not for you in particular. It's for…" he hesitated. "Taibhseach's orders were for the scouts to let an individual or small party approach until they attempt to free the king. He hopes they succeed."

Claire narrowed her eyes. "That doesn't make sense."

Feighlí made a *hm* sort of noise that gave Claire the impression he was not impressed with her intelligence. "It won't be possible without… never mind. If you can do it, you will be allowed to do it. And then you must flee. If you cannot, then no one can, and all is lost either way."

"Have you sent anyone else to even try?" Claire's voice shook a little with anger and fear.

"His Majesty was quite clear that you were the only one who had a chance of success."

"I'm not particularly confident in that chance, Feighlí."

He glanced at her with a mirthless smile. "Neither am I." He sighed heavily. "I suppose it depends on the definition of 'success.' I think there is a good chance you will reach the king unmolested by the Unseelie. I think there is a chance, quite slim, that the king will somehow be freed, although I dare not imagine how. There is an even smaller chance you will escape Taibhseach's pursuit for more than a few hours. Beyond that… I still see little hope.

"Yet, if he is to die, he would rather die free and fighting for his people than in prison, receiving the news that all is lost and there is no more reason to keep him alive."

The air seemed too heavy upon Claire's shoulders, the weight of responsibility she had never wanted and did not know how to carry. "I can see why you think it's better for *him*. I don't really understand why you think me trying is better for *you*, but I imagine you have a reason that makes some kind of sense. But I was safe in my world. I don't understand why this is a good idea for *me*."

Faolan shrugged, his gaze suddenly colder. "Oh, that's the easy part. If you don't want to do this, then you are clearly not supposed to do it and have no hope of succeeding." Then he frowned. "No, *want* is probably the wrong word. I don't mean that you think it will be enjoyable, but in the sense that you feel you *must* do it. If you are supposed to do this, you will go, even if I wanted to stop you."

"He'll die if I don't go?"

"Oh, he'll die either way. We all do, you know. It's only a question of when and how. But yes, he is certain to die soon if you don't go. He is almost as certain to die just as soon if you do go, but in a much preferable manner." His voice was flat.

"So this is really mostly about choosing the manner of his—of *our* deaths, and what we do before we die."

"Well, yes. That's pretty much what all of life is, all the time, isn't it?"

Claire let out a tremulous breath. "I'll go."

CLAIRE WAS GIVEN A knapsack full of food, most of it relatively familiar: a few apples, a stack of soft flat breads, a generous chunk of cheese wrapped in a waxed cloth, a smaller sack of strips of dried meat, and something that looked like a bronze cookie tin full of fresh snap peas. Feighlí strapped a belt around her waist and then clipped a heavy leather scabbard to it.

"Put your knife in there," he said.

"This?" Claire held out the butter knife. "Why? I didn't even mean to bring it. It's just a butter knife. I was making a sandwich."

Feighlí leaned away from her. "Careful with that. You know not what you carry."

Claire eyed him curiously. "What do you mean?"

"Use it only at great need. Don't touch His Majesty with it. And don't eat *anything* but what has been provided for you. Nor drink the water."

"Why not?"

He gave her an incredulous look. "This is Faerie. Most things are dangerous and little is as it seems. You're human. If you ever want to go home, don't eat or drink anything."

"Where did this food come from, then?" *The little fairy told me that before, too.* Guilt pressed upon her as she remembered him, a weight she had not shed in the intervening years.

He opened his mouth, and then seemed to think better of what he was about to say. "If I tell you, it won't work." His worried frown deepened. "You'd best get on your way."

Claire let him walk her to a door. "You said you didn't want His Majesty to catch us before. But now it sounds like you want him back."

He shook his head. "I was talking about Taibhseach, the Unseelie king, before. We were in his lands. Saying his name would've caught his attention, and… well, then we would've been skint, quartered, and hung up for decoration." He glanced up at her, frowning in puzzlement. "Did you think I was afraid of my own king?"

Claire opened her mouth, then closed it again without saying anything.

SUNLIGHT SPILLED ACROSS THE gardens like molten gold.

Several hundred Fae of many species gathered to see her off. The assembly was silent but for faint whispers that hushed whenever she looked over the group. Centaurs, like those in her dream—*was it really a dream?*—stood solemnly in the back of the crowd, their broad shoulders tanned bronze. Before them stood a contingent of pale Fae, all dressed in silk that draped lightly over their slim, elegant bodies. The one who had challenged her in a dream, the one she had imagined might be a doctor, stood in the front row, his green eyes solemn and his expression grim.

"Who is he?" Claire whispered to Feighlí, nodding toward him as discreetly as she could.

"Declan, the royal physician." Feighlí nodded courteously to the taller Fae. "He's been busy of late."

"Why?"

The imp glanced up at her. "We're at war, human child. But one way or t'other, it will end soon." His voice lowered until she could barely hear his next words. "Long live the king."

CHAPTER 16

Claire walked for hours. The land reminded her of what she imagined Ireland might look like, all lush green grass and craggy hills, ancient stacked stone walls and distant stone ruins. The sun warmed the air, and the grass beneath her feet gave off a sweet, spicy scent.

The knapsack made her shoulders ache, but otherwise she felt better than she had since before the accident.

She stopped and squinted at a spark in front of her. It glowed softly, glittering and spinning so fast her eyes struggled to follow it. It darted ahead, then back toward her, stopping to hover a short distance away. Then it flew on again.

What are you? She wondered whether it was friendly and whether it had a consciousness at all.

She'd read once of will-o-the-wisps and wondered whether this might be one of those mythical creatures. Was it even a creature, or was it a natural phenomenon like the northern lights or a shooting star?

She followed it.

The spark led her up a long hill and down the other side, up another hill, and down again where she found a small brook burbling cheerily. It was perhaps six feet across, with rocky banks covered in moss on both sides.

The water was clear and fast-moving, though it couldn't have been deep, given how narrow the creek was. Each little wave and eddy threw glittering drops and reflections into the air.

Claire glanced at the spark, which seemed to be dancing in the air over the water, as if encouraging her to continue across. She looked at the craggy hill on the opposite side, and wondered where the spark was leading her.

She took one long step back, gauged her distance, and then leapt across.

Her foot hit the mossy stone and flew up in front of her, sending her flailing into the water.

The knapsack dragged her deeper, the water pounding her with unbearable force. She fought upward, but the water pressed her down, beating upon her still-bruised bones, tumbling her deeper and deeper into the abyss. *I need air!*

An icy hand caught her wrist and belt and dragged her to a stop. The water's assault seemed to relent, though it sped darkly past her eyes just as quickly as before. A pale face rose before hers.

Claire opened her mouth in surprise, letting out a few bubbles. Her lungs did not protest. *Do I not need to breathe air at the moment? Am I breathing water? Maybe I'm already dead.*

The woman smiled, showing sharp, needle-like teeth. "What are you?" Her voice was low and melodious. Her round eyes glinted silver-blue in the water, bright as fish scales.

Claire didn't want to speak, but she didn't seem to be drowning yet, so she ventured cautiously, "I'm a human." The words bubbled in her ears, surprisingly clear despite the water pressing against her.

"I see that. But why are you here? I haven't met a human in a millennium." Her smile widened. "And a young one, too. The last one was old and too stringy."

"I'm not for eating!" Claire pulled against the inexorable grip. "I'm... I'm... I have a thing I have to do." She wasn't sure whether it would be wise to tell this creature of her mission.

"Oh?" The water woman raised her eyebrows mockingly. "And what would that be?"

"I'm..." She hesitated. "What are you?"

The creature laughed; the sound was like water burbling over pebbles. "What a question! No human has ever lived long enough to ask that." She frowned slightly and studied Claire. "Is it only the old ones who cannot breathe under water? Or perhaps only the males?"

Oh. So she isn't letting me breathe. How am I breathing then?

Claire licked her lips, feeling the water pressing upon her, marveling at how she could see clearly and continue breathing. "I don't think I should tell you that," she said finally. "Don't you think trying to eat me would be a silly way for someone so old and powerful to die?"

The water woman drew back a little. "You could be bluffing." She showed her needle teeth again in a slow smile. "You probably *are* bluffing. You're a young human girl with no power at all."

"I could be bluffing," Claire agreed easily, hoping that the sound of her panicked heartbeat couldn't be heard through the water. "But I could *not* be. Do you really want to risk it?" She smiled as carelessly as she could.

The water woman hissed something unintelligible. A huge tail flashed green in Claire's eyes and the creature disappeared.

Claire found that she could move again. The water monster was nowhere to be seen, and Claire swam toward the surface.

Despite the long swim upward, the pressure did not hurt her ears and she could still breathe comfortably. Her head burst through the surface and into the sunlight air, and she heaved a great breath of relief. She looked around and headed for the nearest shore.

She had surfaced in what appeared to be a small lake in the middle of a forest clearing. The trees were set back a little from the sandy shore, leaving the sky clear for the sun to shine through, glittering golden on the water. Her shoes dragged at her feet, but she didn't kick them off, knowing she was unlikely to obtain another pair.

Her toes touched the sand, and a moment later she slogged her way up the sandy slope. She sat down a short distance from the water to catch her breath.

Her backpack was gone, along with all the supplies it had contained. She still had the knife on her hip, though it wouldn't be much use outside of a kitchen. The afternoon sun beat down on her with comforting warmth, slowly drying her sopping clothes.

She closed her eyes.

THE NIGHTMARE KING SAT at the desk she had seen in the palace.

He glanced up at her, appearing not to be surprised. "Good evening," he murmured.

She frowned at him, not daring to say a word. He wore an exquisitely ornate jacket of midnight blue embroidery that set off his moonlight-pale hair. The edges were trimmed in gold that glittered as if it were liquid rather than thread, outlining the high collar and the wide cuffs of the sleeves. He spread one elegant hand over a piece of paper on the desk.

The king pulled the quill from its stand, dipped it in the inkwell, and wrote quickly, still without looking at her. He put the pen aside, blew softly on the ink, and stood.

He strode toward a doorway she had not noticed; she wondered whether it had really existed in the palace or whether it was a feature only of the dream.

"Are you real?" she whispered.

"This is Faerie," he murmured, as if that explained anything to her. "There are layers upon layers upon layers. Don't be deceived by appearances."

He stepped out the door, still without looking at her.

Claire went to the desk. The writing was elegant, so beautiful it reminded her of the calligraphy on a wedding invitation rather than a warning.

Always carry a piece of charcoal.

CLAIRE WOKE TO A soft sound a short distance away, a gentle snuffling sort of noise that made her smile drowsily.

She sat up to see a pony grazing in the turf between the sand and the trees. It was white and delicately boned, with ears that pricked up when she called softly, "Well, hello there."

The pony watched her with limpid eyes as she stood, then ambled toward her, bits of grass stuck to its dark lips.

"I'm sorry. I don't have any sugar or apple or anything."

It tossed its head and whickered, as if dismissing the objection.

The pony's mane was wet, and long strands of something dark appeared to be stuck in the luxurious white hairs.

"That's odd," murmured Claire. She reached out to pat the pony reassuringly before plucking the kelp from the its mane.

Her hand stuck fast against the pony's shoulder.

She tried to pull away, but her hand would not come free.

The pony snuffled contentedly and turned toward the water, his steps quickening.

Suddenly she knew he intended to walk all the way in, dragging her beneath the surface.

Claire cried out in frustration and rising fear, jerking frantically on her arm, but her hand would not come free. Then she remembered the knife; maybe she could pry her hand free. Even if she left some skin on the horse or some horsehair remained on her hand, it was better than being dragged back into the water.

Stumbling, she twisted around, trying to reach the knife as the pony's steps grew faster. Her fingers brushed the handle once before she got a grip on it. She raised the knife, unsure what to do.

The blade flashed in the sunlight. Shiny as it was, she knew it was as dull as … well, a butterknife.

She'd be lucky if she could work the blade between her hand and the pony's hide, and she had no idea if the knife was even strong enough to pry effectively.

She stumbled again, and her feet splashed in an inch of water.

Panic rose in her throat, and she pressed the flat of the blade against the pony's shoulder. Maybe she would saw at the creature's hide if prying didn't work.

As soon as the blade touched the pony, there was a sizzling sound. The smell of burning hair filled her nostrils, and a scream split the air.

Claire's hand came free and she fell backward, scrambling away from the water.

A handsome young man stood where the pony had been, his face contorted in pain. He reached toward his back with one hand, yet lunged toward her, reaching out with his other hand.

She scrambled backward awkwardly, struggling to rise to her feet, but he was faster. His grasping fingers just grazed her ankle when she thrust the knife toward him threateningly.

The young man snatched his hand back. He edged a little to the side, as if contemplating how to reach her while avoiding the knife.

"Tarbh! Have a care. Leave her." The words rippled through the air like water. The water woman waved a languid hand.

The kelpie froze where he stood and glanced at the naiad. The naiad's gaze locked onto Claire face. "It seems you were not bluffing after all. That is good to know."

Sunlight glittered on the water, the peaceful lapping of the wavelets against Claire's feet belying the danger.

The young man stepped back. He appeared to be trying, unsuccessfully, to look at his own back and simultaneously keep a wary on Claire.

"Is he yours?" Claire asked. "Did you send him to test me?"

"No. Just a neighbor. I've known him for centuries. We get along and sometimes… share. I was coming to warn him about you, but I see I was a little late. I arrived just in time to see you burn him." She bared sharp, pointed teeth. "That was unexpected. You are merciful. You could easily have killed him with that weapon, but you only warned him." The naiad's gazed slid over Claire again. "There is more to you than meets the eye."

"Um, well… yes. I thought it unnecessary to kill him." Claire glanced at the kelpie. He had, apparently, lost interest in his wounded back and focused his attention on Claire. His limpid brown eyes were fixed on her - no, on the knife - and he had somehow backed up another twenty feet or so without appearing to have moved.

The naiad said softly, "We will both remember this. If you pass this way again, you may find us more friendly. Or at least more careful." She smiled, either unaware that this was not reassuring, or perhaps knowing it full well. She disappeared into the lake with scarcely a ripple.

When Claire looked back at the handsome young man, he gave her a slight, careful bow without taking his eyes off her, and slipped quietly into the water.

SAND CRUSTED CLAIRE'S SHOES as she made her way over the shore to the lush grass. She glanced over her shoulder at the water, narrowing her eyes suspiciously at the glints of bright sunlight on tiny wavelets. There was no sign of the kelpie or the naiad, and she let out a tremulous breath.

Everything is dangerous.

The imp had seemed surprised that she saw the wall as a physical wall, and the hole in it as a hole through which she could not fit. *Things are not as they seem.*

She walked across the grass into the edge of the forest. The shadows were not as deep as she'd feared; sunlight filtered down through the canopy of tall, stately trees and dappled the layers of fallen leaves and loam beneath her feet. Her shoes squelched as she walked, shedding sand over the leaves, and her sopping jeans and shirt stole the heat from her body.

The air wasn't exactly cold, but it was certainly "brisk," as her father would say, and she shivered as she walked.

An odd, unpleasant sensation of being watched crept over her.

A fox, or something like a fox, peeked out at her from a thicket, and she breathed a sigh of relief. The creature, though vulpine, was quite small and not particularly frightening.

Then it glanced up at a bird, who studied Claire with bright black eyes before taking flight.

The fox disappeared into the underbrush.

Claire had the sinking feeling that, improbable as it seemed, she was being spied upon by animals. *That's ridiculous! Well, everything else about this is ridiculous. I bet they really were spying on me.*

She hurried through the forest more quickly.

At the tree line she paused, studying the landscape.

A short distance away, a track of packed earth crossed from her right to her left, then snaked away from the forest and between two low hills, the first of what seemed to be miles of hills covered in grass and heather. The wind rustled the tallest reeds softly, carrying the scents of pine, unfamiliar grasses, a cold, wet scent of rotting plant matter that reminded her of a swamp, and a faint, unsettling whiff of acrid smoke.

A few miles away, she could see a squat stone tower perhaps forty feet high atop one of the grassy hillocks.

She took a deep, tremulous breath and stepped out of the forest.

CHAPTER 17

No Unseelie monsters accosted her as she approached.

Smaller turreted towers stood some forty feet from the main tower, perhaps only twenty feet high. No guards were visible. The defenses seemed entirely unmanned.

After studying the edifice for some time, Claire decided to simply approach confidently. *There's not much else I can do,* she thought. *It's not like I have a weapon or would know how to use one even if I had it.*

Perhaps the guards were merely staying out of her way because they were looking for someone else more intimidating. *They expected a great warrior or a powerful rescue party. Ha! No wonder they don't bother stopping me.*

She wasn't sure if the thought was reassuring or terrifying.

The southern guard tower loomed over her as she drew closer. The stones were cleanly hewn but not polished, set atop each other with well-planned precision in lieu of mortar.

Her shoulders tingled with the sense of being watched as she passed by the nearest stone guard tower. There might have been movement behind her, or it might have been only a shadow as the clouds shifted, making the shadows dance across the grass.

The door to the main structure was perhaps ten feet high, made of heavy wood and crossed by dark bronze straps. It stood open.

Claire stood outside for a moment, glancing over her shoulder again at the guard towers, expecting some danger to present itself at any moment. The room was lit by the sunlight streaming in over the threshold. The floor was of thick-hewn slabs of stone and appeared empty but for a bit of rotting straw in one corner. An air of desolation hung over the place; the air in the room was somehow colder than that outside, with a faint, moist foulness to it that made Claire wrinkle her nose.

A bronze key hung on a hook on the wall across from the door, just beside the entrance to a dark hallway.

With a last, cautious glance behind her, Claire slipped inside, leaving the door open behind her. When her hands touched the key, the room darkened.

She whirled to see the door closed firmly, the room lit by a single lantern on one wall that she had not noticed earlier.

How can that be?

The silence was like a living thing, a dark presence waiting and watching while she tried to suppress her fear. The door had made no sound as it closed, no grinding of wood against flagstones or squeaking of neglected bronze hinges.

Perhaps the door was never open at all.

It's like the wall when Feighlí pulled me through the hole. It's only the idea *of a prison, and what I see is just as much in my mind as in reality.* She squinted at the stone walls, trying to imagine what else a prison might look like, but could see nothing unexpected. For a moment she fervently wished it was possible for her to see things as they were rather than through some filter her mind constructed, and for an instant she saw overlaid upon the stone a complex set of diagrams, seemingly drawn in the air in chalk and charcoal, a few in what seemed to be fire, and others in some blue liquid. The stone was translucent, only a result or representation of the diagrams that were reality. She mentally recoiled from this and saw the stone again with a sense of relief.

The dancing light of the lantern illuminated the hallway a few feet, and she peered down the hallway cautiously. Seeing other lanterns lining the walls at intervals, she crept forward with the key clutched in one hand.

The corridor seemed to twist and turn nonsensically; it turned left four times in a row, so that she was convinced it must have circled back and overlapped itself, but she passed no intersections with other hallways. Once, she stepped around a corner and saw a long, unending hallway, then looked back at the way she had come to see only a short hallway behind her, with no exit visible. She narrowed her eyes in irritation, then looked toward the way forward, which now turned again to the left.

It's herding me like a mouse through a maze. She hissed out a frustrated breath. *Does that mean they know I'm here, or is it always like this?*

Although she refused to try to see the diagrams again, some memory of them remained. If she concentrated, she knew which turns led onward and which to a trap.

Finally she reached a door at the very end of the corridor. The door was of heavy wood and solidly reinforced with bronze straps like the exterior door.

She hesitated, and then turned to explore the rest of the corridor, hoping there was a way out.

There wasn't. All the exits had disappeared, leaving a feeling of desolation and unnatural silence.

Claire stood in front of the cell door with a sense of trepidation. This wasn't normal fear, with her heartbeat pounding and a chill sweat between her shoulder blades. This was something else, some sense of danger unknown and unknowable, perhaps not meant to be known.

What if he's not in here?

What if he is?

She turned the key in the lock and pushed the door open.

CHAPTER 18

The lamplight fell on him, and he flinched away, hiding his face.

His hair was matted and longer than she had ever seen it. The white-blond strands were dark with dirt and grime. The smell was appalling, a mixture of excrement, urine, and sweat that filled her nostrils and made bile rise in her throat. His wrists and ankles were bound with manacles that appeared to be made of crystal or clear glass which had cut into his pale skin, dried blood layered atop half-healed scars. He crouched at the furthest extent of the chains, his arms upraised to hide his face.

"What have they done to you?" she whispered.

His head snapped up. "You!" he breathed.

With soundless speed, he lunged at her, his face contorted in rage.

Claire screamed and stumbled backward. Her foot caught the edge of one of the flagstones, and she fell. He fell atop her, his hands scrabbling frantically, dirty fingernails clawing at her. She hit him with an elbow to his jaw; his head snapped sideways, then back.

He bit her shoulder, teeth cutting into her skin, and her scream of terror turned shrill with pain. He writhed against her, his arms somehow wrapped around her waist and shoulders in a bizarre mockery of affection. The long fingers of one hand pressed against her jaw, pushing her face toward his. His teeth snapped, and he made a strange sucking sound, as if he meant to simultaneously drink her blood and kiss her.

The pendant on her necklace slid heavily over her neck. She gripped it in her right fist and twisted to hit him as hard as she could. The metal made a sickening thwack as it connected with his temple.

A burst of light behind her eyes blinded her.

ALL FOUR WALLS WERE covered in chalkboards.

The floor and ceiling were white, and there appeared to be no door through which she might exit this strange prison.

Claire spun slowly on her heel, studying each wall.

The king stood in the space she had looked first, which had been empty a moment ago.

He looked different, though it was hard to say exactly how. His eyes were a clear, brilliant blue-gold-silver that sparked in the fluorescent lights. His face was thin and hard, his mouth set in an expression she couldn't read.

"Well. Here you are," he said finally.

She studied him, neither of them moving.

He looked so strange partly because he was wearing an old-fashioned straightjacket of thick canvas. Both arms were contained, the buckles fastened securely. Beneath the straightjacket, he wore white and blue striped pants that looked like they had been issued by a hospital. His feet were bare, and his bone white toes curled against the chill of the concrete floor.

"Where is this?" she asked.

"A dream, of course."

"But you're here too. I didn't imagine you here, did I? You're really here."

He turned to look at the walls, his eyes flicking over the blank chalkboards. "I'm not *really* here at all. Neither are you." He shot a sharp glance over his shoulder at her. "You'll have to do better than that."

"All right. *Why* are we here?"

He shifted his arms slightly, indicating the straightjacket. "Isn't it obvious?"

"You tried to kill me."

He frowned. "Don't you think you'd be dead if I wanted to kill you?" He turned away. The bones of his shoulders stood out sharply beneath the rough canvas, and unexpected pity twisted in her heart. "Not even that much faith in me." The murmur barely reached her ears. "I must not have played my part well enough."

She stepped closer, studying his profile. Surely it would be safe here, in a dream. "Why are you wearing a straightjacket? Are you insane?"

"Mad as a hatter." He gave her a sideways look, then bared his teeth at her in a soundless growl.

She skittered backward, heart racing. "Were you always insane?" she whispered. "Or just recently?"

"It has been a rather long time, I think, although it is difficult to judge the passage of time when one is… bound… as I have been." He arched an eyebrow at her and turned away. He paced slowly around the room, studying the chalkboards, floor tiles, and ceiling with unhurried grace. "This is quite an improvement, I must say. Thank you." He glanced over his shoulder at her, a smile lighting his face.

The spark in his eye made her heart twist uncomfortably within her breast. "What do you mean?"

"It's like a palace," he murmured. "Spacious. So clean and bright, so richly appointed." He spun on one bare heel to take in the entire room. "Such enchanting company." He grinned at her, his eyes glittering with madness. "Though you don't belong here. You shine with the light of a thousand suns in the void." He swayed as if in a wind, bare toes clinging to the tile.

Her mouth felt dry, and she murmured, "They sent me to free you."

"Is that so?" He looked around again, his eyes wide and wondering, teeth pulled back from sharp, white teeth. "Which *they* do you mean?"

"Fayley and the fairies of your court, I think."

He snorted softly and looked around the room again. "Feighlí, you say?"

The silence drew long, and the king turned slowly, his eyes flicking over the walls.

"Fire in your blood," he said under his breath, not looking at her. "Always been there but never lit before."

She didn't know what to say, and after a moment, he gave her a calculating glance, just a quick flash of blue from beneath his white-blond lashes.

"To free me," he murmured. "Did you have a plan to get me out, or did you jump headlong into this ridiculous scheme?"

"It's not *my* ridiculous scheme," Claire muttered.

The king smiled, as if her irritation amused him. "Of course not," he said gently. "You always plan things in such precise detail."

She studied his face, trying to determine if he was being sarcastic or not, and he looked away, studying the walls anew. He shifted his shoulders against the confining canvas and glanced at her again.

She cleared her throat. "I have no idea how to break you out of here."

"Nor I, or I would have done so already. The first step would seem to be the breaking. I'm broken already. Breaking the prison is difficult… but I may be able to do that, now that you're here. Perhaps afterward the 'out' part will be more evident." His eyebrows drew downward. "I think you won't break, no matter what, but you might squash, which would be bad. So soft and fragile, despite the flame and steel. Untested. Perhaps…" His eyes flicked over her, lingering for an instant on her chest, where the pendant rested. "You'll have to stand close."

"To you?" Claire's voice cracked.

A strange, terrible mirth shone in his eyes, and he murmured, "Very close indeed."

Claire edged closer, then stopped a little more than arm's length away. "Or what? What will happen if I stay this far away?"

"Nothing whatsoever," he said mildly. "I won't break anything."

"I'd wake up. And so would you."

"Probably." He turned his head, looking at her slightly sideways. "Eventually."

"What would happen if I just left? Could I do that?"

He seemed, to her eyes, to grow a little more pale. There was an eternally long silence in which Claire wished wildly she could take back the words. *I didn't mean to be cruel! I could never leave him in that hole, no matter how much he terrifies me!*

"I leave that to your magnificent imagination," he said, his voice flat.

The words seemed to twist around inside her, cutting away some shred of anger, leaving regret in the bleeding space where she'd harbored her resentment.

"I'm sorry," she whispered.

He closed his eyes, and something in his face, so hard and cold and alien, seemed to soften. That almost imperceptible change gave Claire courage to step forward.

"Closer," he breathed, a tiny hitch in his voice.

Claire edged forward until she was so close she could feel the warmth of the air around him, smell the frost and ozone scent of his skin. He leaned forward, his wild, moonlight-pale hair just brushing her cheek.

Then the world broke apart.

CHAPTER 19

Something pressed upon her, angular and limp. It must be him. She strained to push him aside, and he flopped bonelessly to the stone floor. He was unexpectedly heavy, and she realized why when she heard the thunk of stone sliding off him to the stone floor, along with the soft sound of stone dust and smaller rocks tumbling from his back.

She fumbled for the lamp, feeling dirt and rough stone beneath her bruised fingers. There were rectangular stones too, and gradually she came to the disconcerting conclusion that the room had collapsed around them. Shattered bits of glass sliced her fingers.

She couldn't tell how badly they were bleeding in the darkness.

A faint breath of cold air told her where the exit was, though she couldn't guess whether the hallway was still standing or whether the air came from some collapsed portion of the wall.

The lamp was useless, and she resigned herself to feeling her way through the dark toward the air. The hallway was more or less intact, and a faint glow of light at the end hinted that the exit might be accessible.

She carefully made her way back into the collapsed prison cell.

She shrieked when her questing fingers touched the nightmare king's standing form. He stood swaying in the darkness, and he flinched at her touch.

That tiny movement gave her the courage to say, "Come with me." She wrapped her fingers around his wrist, the manacle cold against her skin. She tugged him forward gently.

He stumbled after her.

She didn't look at him, focusing on finding the enormous stones littering the floor before she tripped over them. He followed blindly. His wrist felt horribly thin beneath the thick crystal of the manacle; her fingers grew sticky with blood.

They rounded a corner, and she continued without looking back.

At last they emerged from the dusty darkness of the tunnel into the star-swept darkness of a breezy midnight.

Claire breathed a sigh of relief and turned, with some reluctance, to face the nightmare king. She dropped his wrist, facing him from a distance that still felt too close.

His expression was lost in shadow.

"I don't know what to do next. Only I think we should probably get away from here." Her voice shook; the sound of her fear, the raw edge in her voice, caught her by surprise. *I thought I'd at least sound brave. But I just sound terrified and exhausted.* He frightened her as much as anything else she had faced. Now, atop a desolate hill under a million unfamiliar stars, battered and bruised and thirsty, she wasn't even sure whether she had done the right thing in freeing him.

He said nothing for so long that she licked her lips, wondering whether she should say something else.

Then he crumpled forward into the grass with a thump.

Claire listened for sounds of pursuit. The night was quiet but for the faint rustle of the wind in the grass and the distant trees. The rubble shifted with a low rumble and then the sound died away into silence again.

The nightmare king lay awkwardly, his face mashed into the grass. One arm was beneath him, the other by his side, as if he had not attempted to break his fall. She knelt beside him, holding her breath until she could hear a faint, disturbing rattle in his exhalation.

At least he's alive. I think *that's a good thing.*

Exhaustion swept over her. The starlight shone down cold and clear and merciless, silvering the blades of grass beneath her. The blood smeared across her palms and between her fingers looked nearly black. She looked at the king again, at his matted hair thick with stone dust and crusted dirt, at the blood dried dark behind one ear. His shirt was worn threadbare across the shoulders and at the elbows.

She couldn't think; the day had been a thousand years long and her body and mind rebelled against another demand. She couldn't very well carry him, she didn't know where she was going, and she was too tired to stand up anyway.

So after one last, cursory look around, she curled up a short distance away and closed her eyes.

THE NIGHTMARE KING SAT in the corner of the chalkboard room, still wearing his straightjacket. He leaned his head back against the wall, his strange blue-gold-silver eyes following Claire as she walked slowly around the room.

Old writing was barely visible on the chalkboards, as if it had been vehemently erased but not actually washed with water. Claire tried to read it, but nothing was legible; faded swoops of elegant writing blended with what might have been mathematical equations.

"Is this your mind?" she asked.

The king did not immediately answer, and she glanced at him. He was staring off into the distance.

That's what they call a thousand-yard stare. "What did they do to you?" Claire whispered.

The king's gaze did not waver. His mouth was set in a tight, narrow frown that seemed, to Claire's eyes, to be either angry or regretful. Perhaps both.

"Can you hear me?"

His gaze flicked toward her, then away. "Sometimes." His voice echoed strangely, as if the chalkboards flung back the lowest tones with greater force.

"Is this your mind?"

"Not exactly." His narrow, bony knees were drawn up in front of his chest, and he looked down, studying the thin fabric drawn tight over them. "But I made it, and it is mine, and I let you in." He did not look at her. "We sprung the trap. We'd better leave soon."

"The trap?"

He thunked his head hard against the cement behind him, once, and again, and then a third time even harder.

Claire cried, "Stop it!"

Again and again in a rhythm that made Claire's insides turn upside down.

What if he dies while I'm stuck in this nightmare? Will I die too? Will I be stuck in this room with his corpse forever?

She screamed as he did it again and lunged across the room to grab his head with her hands, straining against his convulsive pounding.

Claire was reminded that it was a dream when her hands slid into his hair. The white-blond strands were fine and soft, the back of his head matted with crusted blood. *How did I not see that before? This is an old wound.* She hauled him away from the wall, pressing her knee into his shoulder to keep him from thrashing free.

The back of his neck showed the strain of wiry muscles through paper-thin skin. The canvas of the straightjacket had rubbed the skin raw in several places.

Abruptly he stopped moving altogether. She froze, wondering what he was doing, whether he was dangerous even now, whether she was helping or hurting him. He shuddered, as if her touch were unbearable to him, and she pulled away.

Claire watched him warily as he sat motionless.

The silence drew out for long minutes.

Finally Claire said softly, "Your head is bleeding."

His gaze slid toward her, fixed on her throat for a moment, then slid away. "Is it? I hadn't noticed." He smiled as if thinking of something long past. "I didn't think you would come."

"I didn't want to."

His lips tightened. "I imagine not."

The silence was like a living thing, coiling around Claire's heart more tightly with every passing moment, until she thought she would weep.

Finally he looked up, and the blue-gold-silver of his eyes meeting hers felt like a spark through her body. "They'll be coming. We sprung the trap."

CHAPTER 20

Birdsong floated on the air like dandelion seeds, carrying easily in the clear, cool breeze that rustled the lush grass. Sunlight warmed Claire's cheek.

She sat up, looking for the nightmare king.

He was gone.

A crack shattered the peaceful air.

The rubble of the collapsed prison tower spread over the hilltop. Claire could not identify the tunnel through which they had escaped the night before; no part of the structure seemed intact enough to walk through. Huge pieces of granite were tumbled over each other like so many discarded building blocks.

How did we survive that?

It must have been magic. No human body could possibly have escaped uncrushed, and even if, by some miracle, she had survived the initial collapse, she should have remained trapped beneath a thousand tons of stone.

A second crack rang out, and Claire began to circle the remains of the building. She rounded the edge of a wall, still half-standing though mostly buried by stones from the upper portions of the structure, and found the source of the noise.

The nightmare king put his left wrist against the edge of a rectangular stone and pushed the manacle so that the crystal ring lay on its edge on the stone. He twisted his left hand out of the way as much as possible, raised a sharp stone, and then brought it down with stunning force upon the edge of the crystal. It appeared to be completely unmarked, though the bits of crushed stone testified that the king had been at this for some time.

Claire stepped closer. "Is it working?"

The king froze without looking at her. He stared at his hand, at the crusted blood on his bone-thin wrist and on the manacle. "Need the key. Don't have it," he muttered.

Claire approached cautiously. He looked like a live wire spitting electric danger into the air. He glanced at her sideways, just for an instant, and Claire froze again. "Sorry. I'll stay away if you want."

He straightened. His fingers let the stone drop, as if removing the bonds no longer interested him.

She watched him warily. The soft light of morning was warm and forgiving, far kinder than the harsh mid-day glare. She half-expected violence again and balanced lightly on the balls of her feet, ready to flee if necessary.

The king merely stood there, swaying slightly as if the breeze threatened his steadiness. He stared blankly down at the stone in front of him. The breeze pressed his shirt to him, outlining his too-thin torso, wiry strength burned away to bone and sinew. He trembled a little; Claire wondered if the wind chilled him. The silence drew out, minute after minute, until Claire imagined she would scream from the tension.

"What do we do now?" she whispered.

His magnificent eyes turned to her, and they were empty.

Yes, they were still a shocking blue-gold-silver that defied description, but there was no *spark*, no magic, no life behind them. They were empty as the eyes of a mask, devoid of feeling or comprehension.

"You don't know either, do you?"

He tilted his head as he looked at her, eyes narrowing as if trying to decipher her words.

"Do you even understand me at all?"

He looked back at the stone.

She took a step closer, then another step. "Can I help?"

He didn't react, didn't appear to have heard her at all. Another step, and another, and then she was almost face to face with him.

He was quite tall, as she remembered from her dreams. His shirt had once been black but was now thick with light grey stone dust atop the more disgusting stains, some of which might have been blood. His sleeves were rolled up to his elbows; his arms were horridly thin and stark-white beneath a thick layer of grime. The manacles around his wrists gleamed bright in the sun, unmarred by any scratches. His trousers had probably once been close-fitting, like those he's worn in that first dream (*or nightmare, or whatever it was*) but were now too loose, and his feet were bare and dirty beneath the tattered hems of his trousers.

"How long has it been for you? How long were you captive?"

"How long is a piece of string?" he muttered, lips twisting in a snide grimace that vaguely resembled a smile.

"What do you need?" She studied him, the way his shoulders were somehow hunched slightly, as if hiding some pain, and yet more upright than most men ever stood, as if he couldn't remember how to slouch. "Are you hungry?"

He frowned faintly. His eyebrows were so pale she might have thought he didn't have any, except that the dirt on his face made them visible. "I don't remember." He shot her a sharp glance, as if he wondered whether she were responsible for such a memory lapse. "You don't have anything to eat, though."

"I lost my bag."

"Careless of you." He turned to look over the grassy hills. "I don't like this place."

"I imagine not," Claire murmured, still watching him.

"Smells like a trap." He cast his gaze over the landscape again, then took off down the hill, long strides eating up the distance. Claire jogged after him, startled at his speed.

"Where are we going?" she asked.

He looked toward her suddenly, eyes blank and uncomprehending. "How should I know?" he snarled.

"Then why are we in such a hurry?" she puffed.

He slowed a little, and she imagined it was only to let her keep pace with him. His face contorted for a moment in a rictus of pain and frustration, but he said nothing.

They reached the edge of the immense forest some time later. The king plunged in without a pause, and Claire followed him more cautiously. He followed no path, and the branches he swept effortlessly out of his way flipped back into her face. After a particularly sharp thwack in the cheek, she snapped, "Could you possibly be any less considerate?"

He stopped and turned on one bare heel to look down at her. "Probably not. I didn't know you were there." His voice had regained the supercilious air she remembered from the first dream. He tilted his head and studied her face without acknowledging her glare. "I know you," he murmured at last.

"Well, I should hope so!"

He frowned faintly, his eyes flicking to the chain around her neck and back to her face. "Where did you get that necklace?"

"I don't know. I've had it for years." She tugged on the pendant self-consciously. She never really thought about the necklace; it was just hers, familiar and comforting. Why would he ask about it?

His eyes narrowed. Claire took a step backward, half-expecting him to lunge after her, teeth snapping and fingers grasping. *He's insane.*

"Come on, then," he growled, and turned to continue striding through the forest.

MIST GATHERED IN THE shadows between the trees.

The king slowed to a cautious walk. Claire realized, somewhat belatedly, that for the past few hours he had been holding the branches aside for her rather than letting them snap back into her face.

"Thanks for not smacking me in the face with the branches," she said, her voice sounding loud in the immense silence of the forest. He didn't acknowledge her words, and she added, "I'm getting hungry. Can you magic us some dinner or something?"

"No."

The word had a dull finality to it that gave her pause.

She jogged a few steps to catch him by the arm. At her touch, he stopped as if electrified. She could feel him trembling beneath her fingers, and she pulled back. "I thought you were magic," she said. "Feighlí said you could do practically anything." *Except rescue yourself and get those manacles off,* she corrected herself.

He raised a hand in a gesture that clearly meant *quiet,* and his empty eyes flicked to the left, then ahead of them. "Come," he murmured.

"What is it?"

His steps quickened, and her jog turned into a sprint, and still she could not keep up.

Branches slapped her face as they ran headlong, and his hand was on her arm, dragging her with impossible speed, faster and faster. Her legs flew and she stumbled, unable to keep pace. The king caught her in his arms, and for a moment she felt his wiry strength speeding her away.

Then he made a strange, strangled sound and she was tumbling down a long slope. Stones and grass and sand, pine needles and oak leaves and beech bark flashed by in a tumult.

ORANGE TONGUES OF FLAME flickered in a vast stone fireplace. The nightmare king sat in a worn velvet chair just to Claire's left, dirty boots beside his sock-covered feet. He shifted, put his head in one hand, and stretched his feet toward the fire.

"Is this a dream too?" Claire asked.

"In a manner of speaking," he murmured, his voice scarcely audible over the crackling of the fire.

"Does that mean I'm unconscious?"

He sighed softly. The shadow of his hand hid his eyes. "I can't tell you much. It would… complicate things."

Claire studied the line of his jaw as the light played over him. The soft, dark fabric of his shirt looked refined and aristocratic rather than threatening. His wild hair looked… well, it seemed to fit him.

"Why would it complicate things?" she asked finally.

"Paradoxes are risky at the best of times." He straightened and turned toward her. His eyes *sparked*, the blue-gold-silver flashing in the firelight. "This timeline is…" He hesitated, his lips twitching as if he were considering words and then discarding them. "It's complicated," he said at last, with a bitter little smile.

"So you travel through time?" Claire felt more comfortable with this version of the king. He seemed less like a nightmare king and more like a fairy king, the air around him crackling with magic. "Time travel is impossible."

"Why?" He tilted his head and smiled at her.

For a moment his smile took her breath away; it was moonlight on water, lightning in the clouds, the scent after a summer rain.

"Because of, well, physics, I guess." She felt herself mentally flailing, scrabbling for some handhold of rationality in which the conversation would make sense.

"You understand physics?" His eyes sparkled a little, as if he wanted to laugh but knew it would be discourteous.

"Well, no. Because of paradoxes, then. You know, accidentally killing your own grandfather or something."

"Ah. But a paradox is not impossible in a dream. Dreams can be crammed full of paradoxes." His smile was sunlight. "And as for time, haven't you ever dreamed of the future? Or the past? Certainly you've dreamed of things you could not know except in your dream. Or dreamed an epic journey but woken to find that only a few minutes had passed. Or perhaps you've dreamed of doing something differently in the past?" His gaze intensified, and Claire had the feeling that she was falling into the depths of eyes. "Time exists in dreams, but of course it's much more pliable."

Claire shook her head, shook off the hypnotic beauty of his eyes and the seductive layers of his voice. "Still, that's only in dreams. It's not real!"

"Do you believe dreams are not real? Why?" He tilted his head a little, his eyes sweeping over her face.

"Well..."

"As for paradox, how about 'you must become who you have always been'?"

She froze, staring at him. "Care you explain?"

"Now that *would* be a paradox." Affection lit his smile.

CHAPTER 21

Damp moss pressed into Claire's cheek. She took stock of her injuries slowly, carefully moving each aching part and evaluating the pain before she pushed herself to her feet.

Claire's head ached, and she raised a hand to gently run her fingers over the scar. Her fingertips were cold against her scalp, and she shivered. Her hair was growing out, a soft dusting of dark brown hair that felt like velvet.

The ravine stretched to her left and right, with a friendly little stream burbling at the bottom. Tall hills rose behind her and before her; worn rocks poked their heads through the thick layers of moss and fallen leaves in a few places.

Thirst made her mouth dry. The water looked clear and devoid of any obviously hostile inhabitants, but she still studied it carefully before reaching out to cup some water in her hand.

"Don't!" the king barked from behind her. He snatched her wrist and jerked her roughly away from the water.

"I'm thirsty," Claire snapped. "There's nothing here! It's fine." She pulled away from him.

"Is there not?" The king gestured invitingly toward the water.

A ghostly stain spread through the water, apparently unaffected by the ripples and eddies. A face appeared and grinned at the king. "So possessive."

"I should have known," Claire muttered. "It probably bites, doesn't it?"

"Most things do in these lands," he said in a low voice. "Come away from the water."

She stepped back carefully, noticing that he edged between her and the water even as she retreated. *He can be chivalrous.* The thought made her warm a little toward him.

Then he turned and strode away without looking at her, following the creek upstream. Claire followed, frowning at his back.

"There's something on your shirt," she said.

He stopped and glanced back at her. "Blood, I presume."

She blinked. Yes, of course it was blood. It was rust-red. But for an instant, the smear had appeared blue, right at the edge of his worn collar, where it smeared into his white-blond hair.

What an odd trick of the light.

"It looked strange for a moment," she muttered. "Actually, I should be asking if you're all right."

"Irrelevant."

"Where are we going?" Her voice followed him as he turned to continue walking. "Because I'm going to need water eventually. Also I don't see how asking if you're all right is irrelevant."

He didn't answer immediately, though his steps slowed. "South."

"Why south?" She caught up to him and glanced at his face. He stopped and put a hand to his head, his long, thin fingers covering his eyes. "Are you dizzy?"

"The loss is disorienting," he murmured. He staggered, and she caught at his arm. He flinched away and then stumbled to his knees, pressing both hands against his temples.

CLAIRE STRETCHED HER FEET toward the fire. The room was cool, and the warmth was welcome.

The nightmare king appeared to be half-asleep in the opposite chair.

"Why am I here?" Claire asked. "When is this, anyway? Why would I be dreaming of something that hasn't happened yet and won't ever happen?"

The king made a series of intricate gestures with his left hand, leaving a trail of faintly glowing sparks in the air.

"You insist on speaking as if dreams are not real." His voice was softly seductive, velvet promises and sunlit mornings.

"They're not. They're just… dreams."

He glanced at her, his eyes sparkling with hidden mirth. "Just because in your experience dreams and what you call 'the real world' do not often interact does not mean that one is more real than the other. Nor does it mean they *cannot* interact. You know this." His thin lips lifted in a faint smirk, as if her confusion were darkly amusing to him. "You dream of things that affected you in the other world, and sometimes what you dream affects how you think and act when you are not dreaming."

She studied him, how the light glittered in his dandelion-fluff hair, how his long, pale fingers rested on his knees. His hands were not as relaxed as his posture would imply, nor as his voice seemed to convey.

"Yes, that's true." She watched his face. "But that's because dreams are just thoughts. They only exist in my head. Just because they *feel* real doesn't mean they *are* real."

"You have no reliable basis for that opinion. You formed it based on your experience, which I suppose is logical enough." A sardonic smile flickered around his lips. "But your experience does not include magic, and you interpret everything as if time were a line, with you moving steadily along it with no way to change position other than by waiting, no way to skip ahead or jump back, or even to truly see any point other than where you are." He gestured gracefully. "This is so far from reality that we might compare it to someone who believes in a flat earth because it agrees with what they see… or at least, they think it does."

Claire felt her heartbeat quicken in anger, and pushed the feeling down. This was a *dream*; besides, at least the nightmare king wasn't threatening her.

"Do you enjoy making yourself feel superior?"

He raised his eyebrows at her. "Is that what you think I'm doing?" The smile on his lips flickered and faded. "Oh, you do." The spark in his eyes flashed oddly, and he looked toward the fire. "Very well." One narrow hand tightened on his knee, and then he murmured, "The best men die of a broken heart for the things they cannot tell."

"Are you dying of a broken heart?" She couldn't keep the skepticism out of her voice. "Forgive me if I don't believe that."

"I forgive you everything." His words were nearly inaudible. "Not that you'll believe that either."

"What have I ever done to you?" She frowned, genuinely curious now. *This version of him is delusional as well.* Then guilt assailed her, and she muttered, "Other than burn the palm of your hand off, I mean."

A soft chuckle startled her. She hadn't imagined that he *could* laugh, much less that it would sound like music.

"I'd forgotten that," he murmured. He seemed to be looking at the fire, but she caught a flash of blue as he glanced at her. "You were magnificent, you know. So brave and furious. You had no idea what you were doing."

"I didn't mean to hurt you."

He gave a full-throated laugh that made the very air tremble with mirth. "Oh yes, you did." His smile held no trace of bitterness, and he glanced at her as though they were sharing an especially funny joke. "Of all the pains I have suffered, that is the most trivial of unpleasant memories. I console myself with the memory of your eyes blazing in righteous anger, your lips raspberry red. I almost kissed you, you know."

Claire stood abruptly, trembling with anger. "You are mocking me!" she cried. "You… you insufferable, arrogant, selfish, thoughtless, *stupid* man! I'm trying to figure out how to save your tail and you're making fun of me."

He drew back, his eyebrows drawing downward in an apparently genuine expression of confusion. "I have no tail."

THE HEAVY CRYSTAL MANACLES caught the light as if they were made of glass.

The king shuddered, his head in his hands. The thin black shirt stretched tight over his shoulders, and Claire sucked in a breath as she surveyed the damage. Perhaps it was not entirely due to magic that she had not been killed as the tower fell; the nightmare king appeared to have been battered by every stone. His blood looked nearly black where it had dried and crusted into the fabric of his shirt, but bright red showed through a tear near one shoulder where a wound she could not see had recently bled. She had the impression that he'd been beaten thoroughly even before the tower had fallen.

"Does your back hurt?" she asked. She didn't expect much of an answer; mostly she hoped to keep him talking.

He pressed his hands to his temples. "Probably."

"Did you shield me from the rocks?" Claire found her throat unexpectedly tight at the thought of it.

He made a strange, inarticulate noise that might have meant anything or nothing.

Claire stood helplessly for a moment. The manacles looked so very *wrong* against his thin wrists. They were beautiful, almost like the jade stone bracelets like she'd seen in a magazine, but thicker and heavier, with sharp edges apparently intended to cause pain.

"Do you know how to get those off?" she said.

He looked at her blankly. "Get what off?"

"The manacles."

He looked down at his wrists and grimaced, as if pulling his thoughts together were particularly difficult. "It's oighear. It's…" he gestured gracefully. "It's magical. It's made of water, shaped by magic and locked into the shape as if crystalized like ice. But it is denser than water in any natural form, and much harder and stronger than diamond. Someone expended a great deal of magic to form these for me." He frowned faintly, his expression distant.

Claire wondered whether he'd forgotten what he was talking about. "And…" she prompted.

He blinked. "It's immensely useful for things such as blades. It holds an edge well. But one cannot make pieces with moving parts out of oighear, so it is rarely used for anything complex like a lock. Did you notice that even the chain was bronze? A chain is far too complicated to be made of oighear." His voice trailed away, as if he were thinking of something else, or perhaps of nothing at all.

"So how do we get them off?" Claire asked.

His eyes flicked to her, and he looked confused for a moment. "Get what off?"

"The manacles!"

"I don't have the key. I am captured." His eyes were vacant, as if he stared through her to something else that took all his attention. "It's... Symbolism is important in magic. The one with authority to release the manacles would simply pull them open. To one without authority, they might outlast the sun." He shook his head as if to focus his thoughts, and then looked down at his wrists. "I expect my bones will have very pretty bracelets."

Claire reached out a tentative hand to touch the manacle. It felt like glass, cool and smooth against the pads of her fingers. She gripped it with both hands and pulled, not able to discern where it was meant to divide into two pieces.

Nothing happened.

The king appeared gently bemused by her attempt, his strange eyes flicking over her face as she strained against the oighear.

His words were so quiet she wondered whether she imagined them. "Slow buds the pink dawn like a rose, from out night's gray and cloudy sheath; softly and still it grows and grows, petal by petal, leaf by leaf..."

"What was that?" she panted, glaring at the clear manacle. It was smeared with blood, his and hers together.

He ran his right thumb through the red on the left manacle, frowning at it. "You're bleeding," he murmured. His gaze snapped to her hands, and he caught both her hands in his, studying the slight cuts across her fingers from the sharp edge of the oighear. "I'm sorry." His mouth twisted in grief, and he folded her hands carefully within his. He caught his breath in what sounded like a sob, and bowed his head.

"It's all right." Claire's voice shook. How had he even seen her blood among his? The cuts stung, certainly, but they weren't particularly deep. She wasn't upset by them. Why was he? His grief, raw and mostly hidden, seemed to press upon her uncomfortably, like a weight she did not know how to bear.

She pulled away gently, and he opened his hands, letting her slip her fingers from his.

Some strange emotion seemed to slide through her veins at his touch, at the strength of his hands and the odd, warm light in his vacant eyes, as if seeing her made him almost remember who he was. She pushed the emotion down and focused on the manacles.

The king's terrible strength had had no effect on the oighear when he tried to shatter the manacles earlier. She would probably have no success that way either.

"Maybe I can pry it open," she muttered. She pulled the butter knife from its sheath and tried to wedge it between the top of the king's wrist and the oighear.

When the metal touched his skin, he sucked in his breath and jerked away, his eyes wide and wild.

"I'm sorry!" Claire cried. "I didn't know it would hurt."

His gaze snapped toward her face. "Did you not?" His voice shook, raw and rough with pain. "Yourself the sun, and I the melting frost, Myself the flax and you the kindly fire." He caught his breath and shuddered, his eyes closed tight in a rictus of pain or anger. "Bright star that you are, remember that not all of us are made of flame."

His wrist had a black burn half-hidden by the oighear manacle; the skin looked charred. The size and shape matched the back of the blade of her knife.

"Why did it burn you?" she muttered. "It's not iron." But she remembered the kelpie and frowned. *Stainless steel. I guess stainless steel has iron in it.*

She looked back at the oighear and was surprised to see that the surface seemed roughened. The interior and top surface were slightly bubbled, like plastic that had gotten too hot.

Hm. She glanced at the king, who stared back at her blankly.

The butter knife appeared unaffected by touching the oighear. She frowned thoughtfully, and then pressed the flat of the blade to the top of the manacle, careful not to touch the king's skin.

Nothing happened immediately, and she tilted her head, trying to decide if she smelled something unusual. She pressed the knife harder into the oighear, which seemed to soften for an instant, and then in the blink of an eye, it flashed into water and steam.

"Ha!" Claire crowed. She reached for the king's other wrist. "Let me help you with that."

The king held out his arm without a word, and she melted the oighear in a few seconds.

The water washed much of the old blood from his wrists, leaving the gashes open and oozing blood.

"That actually doesn't look much better," Claire said softly.

The king glanced at her. "It was a kind thing to do, especially since you believed it pointless."

Irritation made her voice sharp. "You're welcome, then."

He tilted his head, his eyes narrowed as if he were trying, and failing, to solve a difficult puzzle. "You are angry. Why?"

"You just told me I wasted my time getting those things off you. A 'thank you' wouldn't be out of line, you know."

His pale eyebrows drew down in puzzlement. "I said it was a kind thing to do, and more important than you realized. Is more thanks necessary for something you did believing it only to be kind rather than of vital import, and more for your comfort than for mine?" He looked away, his lips twisting in an expression of dismay. "I am discourteous. My apologies. I have forgotten my manners as well as myself." He pressed his face into his hands, unaware or uncaring that his fingers smeared blood and water over his face and into his hair. "Everything is unraveling and I cannot find the thread," he breathed.

"What is unraveling?" Claire pushed her irritation aside. *He's insane. I shouldn't expect his manners to be perfect.*

"Me!" he snapped, though he didn't look at her. "Me. I am hidden and the longer I am lost, the more tenuous the recollection becomes. Myth and mist and smoke and reflection and memory evaporating like dew under the sun. I thought I could hide myself long enough to make a difference, hold out long enough, hide myself inside myself and give myself away, and..." He rocked back and forth, his hands clenched against the sides of his head.

"It's all right," Claire said. "You're going to be all right." *Stupid platitudes! But what else can I say?*

He glanced up at her, eyes blank and startled. "Do you think so?" he asked. "How?"

A lump rose in her throat, and she licked her lips. "I don't know."

He smiled, a reckless, sharp-toothed smile that made her blood suddenly turn to fire within her. "I believe you," he murmured. He raised one hand to brush the back of his fingers against her cheek, the touch light as a butterfly's wings.

She wasn't sure whether he meant that he believed her that he would be all right, or believed her that she didn't know how. But his sudden smile had made the words irrelevant.

I don't want to like you, you arrogant, impossible man. I don't want to like you. Don't you even dare make my heart race like that.

CHAPTER 22

The chalkboard room was familiar now. The nightmare king stood in the center of the room, his hair a moonlight fluff around his face. He watched her without moving, blue-gold-silver eyes following her as she walked slowly around him.

"I don't believe you're dangerous at all," Claire murmured. Despite her words, she stayed a safe distance from him.

He raised his eyebrows at her in amused disbelief. "Oh?" His narrow lips smiled, showing his sharp teeth. "Why would you think that?"

"You haven't actually hurt me."

His eyes sparkled a little. "And you believe that's by choice? How charmingly innocent you are."

"I don't believe you're mad as a hatter, either." She took a careful step forward. "I think you're playing a game."

"An interesting hypothesis. Do you think I *let* myself be captured and tortured beyond sanity for the sake of a game?" His gaze flicked toward her lips, then back to her eyes. "I must be quite mad."

Claire frowned. His eyes laughed at her, but he said nothing, merely waiting as she tried to put the pieces together.

She stepped closer.

He was so thin she could see his pulse at the base of his throat and the hollow just behind the point of his jaw. It quickened, though she couldn't guess why.

She stood just in front of him, barely within arms reach.

"Are you going to attack me?"

His pale eyebrows drew downward. "I'm rather trapped at the moment, if you haven't noticed."

It was true. He still wore the straightjacket, the buckles of which looked rusted shut. The questions swirled in her mind. Words came to mind, but none of the questions were the *real* question.

"Are you going to hurt me, then?" The question was filler while she gathered her thoughts. His eyes made it difficult to keep her mind focused; when he looked at her, heat flooded her veins, electric gold promises woven with silk and moonlight.

"Undoubtedly." He closed his eyes and turned his face away.

The set of his shoulders intrigued her; it seemed to say more of grief than danger. The sharp line of his bones through the thick canvas caught at her pity.

"When did you last eat?"

He glanced up, startled, then his gaze grew distant. "Don't forget the charcoal."

The edges of the room seemed to waver like reflections on water.

"What's happening?"

The king turned away from her with a strangled sound. She darted in front of him. "What's happening?" she asked again, more urgently.

His lips twisted in an expression that might have been pain or dread or any number of unpleasant emotions, then the expression was gone so quickly Claire wondered whether she had imagined it.

"Time's running out," he murmured.

"What happens when the room falls apart?"

"Tick tock."

"I wish you'd tell me what was happening!" she cried. "You always speak in riddles."

"He bartered all his soul for her, with tender pleading eyes." He gave her a narrow-eyed glare.

The words cut her more deeply than she could have imagined, and she sucked in a breath.

"You don't love me," she whispered. "You can't."

"Who are you to tell me whom I love?" he snapped, his voice all snide condescension. "Human child, you speak of what you do not know."

"You hate me!" she cried. "You're horrid to me. I've tramped all over Faerie for you and you can't be bothered to say my name, much less 'thank you'!"

"Claire." The name hung in the air between them. "Claire Maeve Delaney." Something in his eyes gave her pause; his voice was nonchalant, but his eyes were anything but dismissive. He said nothing else, only watched her as one corner of the room dissolved into mist.

"It's floating away," Claire whispered. "Are you dying? Or waking up?"

"Are they different?" He pressed his lips together into a bloodless line, only stared at her with those burning eyes, blue and gold and silver like sunlight on water.

Without thinking, she darted to him. With fumbling fingers she tugged at the rusted buckles on his straightjacket. She freed the first arm, and let the canvas fall away as she fought with the second buckle. He was shaking; he'd hidden it before, but now, with the back of her hand pressed against his too-thin side, she could feel him the tremors that racked him.

He brushed past her. Long, white fingers picked up a piece of chalk (had it been there before?) and began to write on the chalkboard.

Don't forget your charcoal.

Everything spiraled apart.

CHAPTER 23

He sat across from her at a small table by a window. A luxurious repast was spread out before her, blackberries and raspberries, peaches and plums, stuffed chicken breasts and angel hair pasta, nut cakes and cheese, bread and olive oil, and a dozen other small dishes.

He leaned back in his chair, his strange, brilliant eyes sweeping over her face. "You'd be wise to eat. It will be a while before you have the chance again."

She reached for a handful of berries and then hesitated. "Isn't it dangerous to eat anything in Faerie? Won't it trap me here or something?"

"This is human food, procured especially for you." A smile danced around his lips. "Your caution is both insulting and reassuring."

Claire studied him. "Are you from the future?"

Something in his eyes flickered. "Not exactly."

"If you're… you… him… whatever… in the present, you should be eating too."

"It doesn't work that way." He looked out the window. The light seemed strangely harsh for a dream, highlighting the hollows beneath his high cheekbones, the slightly sunken temples. "Anyway, don't worry about me. I'm the villain, remember?" As he spoke, his lips curved in a bitter smile. With one finger, he drew intricate patterns on the arm of his chair.

"What are you doing?" She indicated the patterns.

"Nothing." He clenched his hand into a fist, the knuckles going white. "Eat quickly. Something wicked this way comes." He looked out the window again, his nostrils flaring.

Claire stuffed a cube of cheese in her mouth, then a scone.

"You're dehydrated. You should drink some water." He gestured toward a sweating tumbler filled with ice cubes and water.

She filled her mouth with water even as she swallowed the bite of scone. "That's good," she said, taking another bite.

"I'm glad you like it," the king murmured. He appeared to almost forget she was there, intent on watching something out the window.

"What are you looking at?" Claire felt the tension in her shoulders first. It was *odd*, actually; in the dreams, he focused on her with disconcerting intensity. To see him distracted was worrying, to say the least.

"You have one more minute. Eat quickly." His gaze swept over the table again. "It's not enough," he breathed. "Quickly, please!" His concern set her heart racing. She stuffed the rest of the scone in her pocket, along with a handful of relatively sturdy fruits and a generous chunk of cheese. She filled her mouth with berries and chewed as quickly as she could, feeling both panicked and unforgivably rude. More water. She drank so hurriedly she spilled a little on her shirt.

"Time's up." He reached across the table and touched her wrist with his long, elegant fingers.

He's so thin. The touch was gentle, and his strange, electric eyes held an air of regret, of apology, that caught her heart.

THE NIGHTMARE KING SHOOK her awake, one hand on her wrist. "Get up. Now."

He pulled her to her feet before she realized what he was doing. He pressed a finger to his lips, holding her gaze with his own until she nodded.

"Why?" she mouthed.

His gaze flicked over her shoulder. He tugged her forward, his grip on her wrist strong as steel, into a jog and then a headlong flight through the forest. Leaves and twigs slapped her face. She tripped on a root and would have fallen flat but for his vise-like grip.

"Faster." His voice barely reached her ears.

"I can't!"

He jerked her forward and caught her up in his arms somehow, so that he was sprinting through the woods carrying her. The speed was disorienting. She bounced uncomfortably in his arms, feeling heavy, ungraceful, and terrified. "What is it?"

Then she was flying upward through the air. The king had apparently thrown her into the lowest branches of the nearest tree; a branch caught her in the stomach with bruising force, leaving her gasping and flailing frantically for any handhold.

Teeth snapped at her foot, and she cried out as she clawed her way up onto the branch.

Something roared beneath her.

Claire looked down to see the nightmare king facing a huge black dog. From her vantage point, a regular dog would have looked small, but this one looked as large as a horse, with small ebony horns jutting from its skull and eyes that glowed like coals.

"What is that?" she cried.

The king didn't answer. The animal lunged at him. Somehow he had managed to grab a fist-sized rock in one hand, and he dealt the creature a stunning blow as he slipped out of its reach.

The beast snarled, and the ground shook, making the leaves tremble around Claire.

It flew at the king again. He sidestepped, but it twisted with impossible speed and sank its teeth into his shoulder. It shook him and flung him aside.

Claire screamed as it placed its front feet against the tree and leapt at her. Its teeth snapped closed millimeters from her ankle, and then something jerked her nearly off the branch.

As soon as the beast's feet touched the ground it prepared to leap again. She pulled herself back on the branch and reached for the next, but could not reach it. She looked down at the ground.

The knife! The monster's foot had caught the leather of the sheath, popped the rivet on the loop, and pulled it completely off her belt. It lay on the ground far out of reach.

"Help!" Terror made her voice high and shrill.

What right do I have to ask him for help?

The king was crumpled in a boneless heap, bleeding from a gaping wound in one shoulder. His head turned weakly in her direction, his eyes glassy.

She didn't ask for help again. It wasn't fair, it wasn't right, for him to even try to save her when he was clearly dying. But she *wished,* with all her heart, that he had the strength to rise and help her. "I wish he could help," she breathed.

She shrank away from the beast's snapping teeth.

And then the king rose, bloody and implacable. He wrapped a bit of cloth around his hand and darted over to pick up Claire's knife. The fight raged across the clearing and back, inhuman speed against monstrous hunger.

Once, twice, and a third time he struck at the creature, until it slowed for a moment and he plunged the knife into its throat, avoiding the still snapping teeth.

The creature died in a gurgle of red-black blood, back feet thrashing. Its strange, glowing eyes fixed on the king, and its teeth clicked together in fading menace until it lay still.

The king stood in the center of the tiny clearing covered in blood, swaying slightly. "It is safe to come down now," he said in a low voice.

I'm not so sure about that. The thought slithered through Claire's mind.

He glanced at her, his strange eyes blank but for a dark, momentary flash that Claire could not interpret.

"Are you afraid of me?" The words were nearly inaudible.

Claire chewed her lip. He had risen from a grievous wound to kill a monster to save her. But his eyes were empty and dark, and he held the knife as it was part of him, and he moved with speed and ferocity that were entirely inhuman. He was dangerous and feral, and he did not know himself, much less her.

"You need not be." He tossed the knife to the ground between them and turned away.

The immense, terrible silence of the forest pressed upon her as she climbed down, her hands trembling as she tried, unsuccessfully, to grip the rough bark. She fell the last eight feet, landing with a clumsy roll and a twinge of pain in her shins.

Claire studied him from what she imagined was a safe distance before she looked at the knife. It had been covered in dark blood, but as she watched, the last of the blood sizzled away, leaving the metal clean and bright. She picked it up and slid it back into the sheath, which she stuck in her pocket.

The king said nothing, and she looked up at him. He stood in the same spot, hands hanging loose at his sides, staring vacantly off into the underbrush. His black shirt was streaked with gore.

"Thank you," she said finally. "I thought…" *Didn't I see him hurt? I thought he was dying, but maybe it happened so fast I imagined it.*

A drip of dark blood fell from the end of one long finger into the leaves. Then another.

"Are you all right?" Claire ventured.

The king said something that she couldn't quite hear.

She edged closer.

Another drop.

"Let me see it. You're hurt, aren't you?" Her voice shook.

He twitched at the sound of her voice, as if she had woken him from a trance.

"It was a barghest. They're always lethal." His voice was devoid of inflection.

"Let me see the wound," she said. Sudden, fierce fury rose in her. She would *not* let him die from some dog bite after all the trouble of rescuing him. Not now. Not like this.

She touched his wrist, panic almost crowding out her fury as she saw the blood slicking his palm.

He took a deep breath, as if fighting dizziness, then braced his other hand against a tree branch.

"Sit down."

He turned to put his back against the trunk, his eyes wide and glazed. His pupils were dilated so that his brilliant irises nearly disappeared.

Yet he remained on his feet.

"Sit down," she repeated.

He slid down the tree trunk to sit propped against it. The bark pulled his shirt up unevenly.

She murmured, "I'm going to help you lie down."

His thin lips rose in an odd grimace that might have been a smile. "For what purpose? There is little comfort to be had now. I'd rather die upright."

"You're not going to die!" she snapped. "I won't let you."

His vacant eyes slid over her face, and for an instant she thought she saw a flicker of something, some glimmer of *him* inside, a hint of the sardonic, mocking, brilliant king. Then all his muscles seemed to stiffen, and he gasped. When the tension left him, he still breathed, but shallowly and much too fast. His eyes were closed.

Claire used the knife to cut the sleeve of his shirt off. For an instant the back edge of the blade touched his skin with a hiss like that of cooking meat, and she jerked it away, not noticing that tears slipped down her cheeks.

The barghest had torn his shoulder to the bone. She didn't know anything about anatomy, but she thought the bite must have severed an artery; blood seemed to be flooding the ugly mess of torn flesh with a discernible rhythm.

She glanced at her jeans, at the dirt crusted on the sturdy fabric, and then, with considerable effort, cut a generous section off the bottom edge of her shirt. She folded it and pressed it to the wound, leaning on it with both hands.

She closed her eyes, trying to believe that the warm liquid soaking the cloth, seeping between her fingers, was coming out more slowly than before.

THE KING SNORTED SOFTLY. "That's not going to work, you know."

Claire glanced up at him, then back down at his supine form. The king bleeding under her hands had a waxy cast to his pale features; his eyes were sunken and shadowed, and his lips were tight in an almost hidden grimace of pain. Blood continued to seep through the cloth, slicking her hands and soaking into the forest floor.

She looked up at him again, leaning unconcerned against a nearby tree.

"It's not?" Her voice sounded raw in her own ears. "What would you suggest, then?"

He chuckled, the sound like sunlight flickering on water. "Oh, if it were that easy, we wouldn't be stuck in this dance, would we?"

"Answer the question!" Claire cried. "Don't you even want to live?"

"Of course I do." He gave her a soft, remonstrative look. "But this is for you to discover. I can't tell you or it won't work at all."

"Do you mean it really wouldn't work or do you just want to make me dance like a puppet?" she growled in bitter frustration. She glared down at the king's too-still features. "You're manipulative! I hate being a pawn in some game I don't understand."

He knelt beside her. His white-blond hair tickled her neck, and she trembled, inhaling moonlight and magic, ozone and frost. "You were never a pawn, Claire Delaney." He smiled, thin lips lifting in a dangerous smile that sent tremors down her spine that had nothing to do with blood or fear. "You have been the knight, moving crooked through the world. And you have been the castle, unbreached and unyielding. And, perhaps, someday, you shall be queen." His gaze slipped away from her eyes to caress her cheek, the slim line of her neck, her shoulders, down the curve of her breasts, her hips, and over her legs folded beneath her as she knelt in the leaves.

She flushed red, though she couldn't tell whether it was outrage, embarrassment, or sheer annoyance that made her cheeks heat.

Then his eyes met hers again, dancing like lightning across the sky. "Never, *ever*, call yourself a pawn, Claire."

"ARGH!" CLAIRE SCREAMED IN frustration. "I wish you'd wake up, you stupid arrogant git!"

The king blinked at her from his position on the ground.

They stared at each other a moment cautiously. The king's eyes still had that odd vacant look, but at least his pupils had retracted to something approaching normal.

After a long, uncomfortable minute, the king rasped, "I think the bleeding has nearly stopped." He sucked in a pained breath, and added, "You really can't bring yourself to respect *any* rule or precedent, can you?"

Claire let up the pressure on the king's wound, half-expecting more blood to suddenly well up between her fingers.

"How much does it hurt?"

He gave her a narrow-eyed look that almost convinced her that he had his mind back, at least for that moment. "Rather a lot, actually." He closed his eyes again, as if the words had used all his strength.

"You said barghests were always fatal. You looked like you were dying." Was that accusation or merely shock in her voice? Even Claire herself couldn't tell.

"I was." He didn't open his eyes.

"So what happened?"

He was silent for so long that Claire put her hand near his mouth to feel his breath, wondering if he was still alive.

The air moved almost imperceptibly, but that was all that could be said for him. He gave no indication of being conscious.

Not knowing what else to do, Claire sat beside him, resting her head against the rough tree bark.

As the adrenaline slowly faded, her body shook with trembling. Nausea rose, but she kept her head back and her eyes closed, willing herself to be brave.

I'm not really brave. But I can pretend I am, at least for a while. For this moment, I can pretend that I am heroic and that this will all end well.

"ISN'T IT OBVIOUS?" THE king leaned one narrow hip elegantly against the edge of his desk.

"Isn't what obvious?"

Light streamed in through the windows of the study and made his wild hair glow like white gold.

His eyebrows drew downward in an expression of hurt and disappointment. "You saw that I was dying."

"I thought I did." Claire's voice shook. "But then I thought I'd imagined it. I wondered if you'd been deceiving me."

The breath puffed out of him almost inaudibly, and she raised her eyes to his. The pain in his eyes made her heart give an unsteady little lurch.

"I guess I misunderstood," she breathed.

"I guess so." His voice was flat. He turned away and strode to the window, his shoulders straight and proud. Then he bowed his head bowed and buried his face in his hands.

Claire stepped to his side, her footsteps soft and careful on the gleaming marble floor. "What did I misunderstand? That you're brave? I don't think I ever questioned that."

He rubbed his hands hard over his face and let them drop. A faint, melancholy smile flickered over his lips. "At least that's something," he murmured.

When he met her gaze again, the blue and gold and silver seemed to spark like lightning, electric current running through her veins.

He raised one hand as if he meant to touch her cheek with the back of his fingers, but hesitated, his fingers millimeters from her skin. "I remember you with more hair."

She scowled at him. "Yeah, well, I wrecked my car and had to have brain surgery. They shaved it all off." Her lips trembled. "I'm not exactly happy about it, so if you don't mind, I'd rather not dwell on the subject."

His eyes swept over her, slowly, as if he were drinking her in. "I didn't…" He cleared his throat. "Your hair, or lack thereof, has no bearing on… events."

A strange light shone in his eyes.

"You think I'm pretty even though I'm practically bald?" Claire's voice was harsh. "I'm the farthest thing from pretty I ever remember being. I don't appreciate being mocked."

He withdrew a little, his jaw tight and his eyes glittering with an emotion she could not identify. "No," he said softly. "I don't 'think you're pretty.'"

Claire sucked in her breath. Even a stupid kid would know enough to answer *that* question correctly, to read the pain in her voice and know it wasn't the time for flippant insults.

His next words barely reached her ears through the haze of grief and anger.

"Your hair is not *you*. It is like a shirt you wear. It changes, and it has no effect on who are." The king's long, pale fingers touched her cheek. His skin was warm, the touch so light it might have been a butterfly's wing. He lifted her chin, and she knew he could feel her trembling, see the tears streaking her flushed cheeks. He bent toward her, and for an instant she thought he might kiss her. Then he leaned further and murmured into her ear, "You, Claire Maeve Delaney, are brilliantly, magnificently *human*." As he withdrew, he pressed a kiss against the corner of her mouth, light as birdsong and bright as the morning sun.

THE SOUND OF RUSTLING leaves woke Claire from her doze. She blinked blearily at the king, who had managed to push himself into a sitting position just in front of her.

"You look awful," Claire breathed.

It was true. He'd been pale before, but now his skin was the dead white of old bones, his pallor only highlighted by the dried blood streaking his neck and stiffening his shirt. His eyes were sunken and deeply shadowed.

"Thank you," he murmured.

The hint of dry humor startled her, and she looked more closely at him, half-expecting some spark in his eyes. He stared blankly back at her.

"Are you sane again? Do you know what we're doing? Do you know where we're going?" Her voice shook.

He blinked slowly. Perhaps he was fighting pain or dizziness or exhaustion; some expression flashed over his face far too quickly for her to interpret. The silence drew out so long that Claire licked her lips, then gathered her courage to touch his wrist. "Do you understand at all?"

He stared at her hand, at her dirty fingers resting lightly on the fresh scars on his wrist. Then he placed his other hand over hers, long, narrow fingers threading through hers with infinite tenderness.

"I trust you," he whispered.

CHAPTER 24

Claire wept.

Sobs shook her, but she kept them silent. Who knew what other horrors lurked among the trees?

The king slept beside her, gaunt and pale and uncomprehending.

Eventually her tears died away. Hungry and exhausted, she sat by the king, not knowing what to do.

Now I'm the one with the thousand-yard stare.

The tree bark dug into her back, and she shifted her shoulders.

Something knobby in her pocket pulled against the fabric, and she frowned. What could possibly be in her pocket? She dug her hand into the cloth and pulled out a slightly mashed scone.

Her eyes widened. From her other pocket, she produced a chunk of cheese, several slices of apple, and a handful of dried cranberries.

"I thought that was a dream," she murmured.

The king, unconscious on the leaves beside her, let out a soft, pained breath.

Hunger clawed at her belly; besides in the dream, she had eaten nothing since she had entered Faerie. That meant… what? Three days? No, probably more like four.

Claire frowned, looking at the king's face again. Four days was longer than she'd ever gone without eating before. It wasn't particularly pleasant, especially with the running and jumping and terror. But… well, she was alive, and though her stomach growled and she felt an odd, tingly emptiness at the ends of her fingers, she wasn't exactly dying of hunger. Hungry, yes. Starving, not yet.

The king, on the other hand, looked like he hadn't eaten in months. He'd been wiry and lean; now he was emaciated.

Her mouth watered, and she closed her eyes, imagining the tart sweetness of the cranberries against her tongue. She imagined the rich creaminess of the cheese and the cinnamon spice of the scone.

She broke the scone into two pieces and then hesitated. One portion was noticeably larger than the other. She put the bigger piece on an enormous flat leaf, then divided the cheese into roughly equal pieces and put the larger one next to the larger piece of scone. She divided the apple slices and cranberries in a similar manner.

Claire ate the scone first, taking tiny bites hoping it would be more satisfying to eat it slowly. It was dry, and though the flavor was exquisite, the texture reminded her of the thirst that had been lurking at the edge of her awareness for hours.

The king studied her for some time before she noticed he was awake.

"Here." She gestured toward the leaf with the larger portion of food. "I'm sure you're hungry."

His strange, blank eyes slid to the scone and his eyebrows drew down. "Where did you get that?"

The lump in her throat seemed to choke her. "From you, I think. In a dream."

One corner of his mouth rose in a quick, bemused smile. "Interesting," he murmured. His lips tightened in pain as he sat up.

Claire motioned at the food, her mouth full.

He glanced at her, and there was a flicker in his eyes, a glimmer of comprehension that gave her hope for an instant before it faded. He looked back at the food and swallowed. "You need it more than I do," he muttered.

"That is ridiculous." Her voice cracked. "How long has it been since you ate anything?"

He rose gracefully to his feet. Then he staggered against the tree, catching himself with his wounded arm with an almost stifled grunt of pain. "It doesn't matter." His strange, blank eyes turned toward her. "Come. The border is miles away, and we are pursued."

Claire's stomach dropped into her toes. "We're pursued?"

He swayed, his eyelids fluttering closed. He would have fallen but for his convulsive grip on the tree.

"Please eat something. I don't even know how you're alive."

The king gave a tiny, secretive smile. "I think I do." He leaned heavily against the tree, his eyes playing over her face, down her neck, lingering on the pendant. He turned away. "Eat as you walk. They are not far behind us."

Claire gathered the food hurriedly and jogged after him.

"I thought you were dying," she said. *Way to repeat myself. He probably thinks I'm stupid.*

"I was."

"But now you're better." She frowned at his back.

He stumbled and caught himself with a quick intake of breath that made her think he was barely keeping himself upright. "No, not really. But you are."

With a sigh, she took another bite of cheese.

"WHY ARE YOU BACK in the straightjacket? I thought I freed you."

"I thought it best. I'm still insane; it seemed a wise choice."

The harsh fluorescent lights gleamed on the tile floor. It had been clean last time, or so she had thought, but now there were dust bunnies in the corners and faint shadows of dust along the tops of the chalkboards.

"You put yourself in the straightjacket?"

"Of course not. You did."

She scowled at him. *That doesn't make any sense at all.*

Claire ran her thumb over the familiar pattern on her pendant, at first absently, then with a thoughtful frown. She walked to a chalkboard and looked for chalk.

The ledge was empty. She frowned and glanced at the king, who stood in the middle of the room, his eyebrows raised inquiringly.

"Why isn't there any chalk here?"

"Perhaps it's a representation of something." The king smiled, showing his teeth.

"Of what? Your inability to communicate clearly?" Claire snapped.

He turned away without saying anything, and guilt assailed her. "I'm sorry. That was cruel."

The king made a thoughtful sort of noise. "So it was," he murmured. "No matter. I'd hoped…" He clicked his teeth shut, biting back words.

"Hoped what?" She chewed her lip. "That I'd be kinder? I'm working on it."

"Are you?" He raised an eyebrow, and she couldn't tell if the gesture was inquisitive or mocking.

She kept her voice even. "I am. It's hard. I've discovered that I'm a rather selfish person. I'm trying to change but it's work."

"So it is." His eyes were on her face, bright and wild, and she looked away.

"I wish there was chalk!" she muttered.

Then she saw chalk on a ledge she had not previously searched. She glanced at the king, wondering if he had made the chalk appear. He merely studied her with his lips pressed together.

She examined the pendant, then drew the symbol on the chalkboard, with three straight lines converging at the top and splaying outward at the bottom, three dots at the top, all enclosed in a neat circle. "What does this symbol mean?" she asked as she turned to him.

He stared at it, his face tight. "Where did you see that?" he asked, his elegant voice strangely rough.

"What does it mean?"

"I don't remember. I should remember but I don't. Power. Authority. A marriage proposal. A reservoir. A symbol of reality that isn't."

Claire blinked. "Is that supposed to make sense?"

The king strained against the straightjacket for a moment, then relaxed, breathing heavily. "Does anything make sense? Is it supposed to?" He rocked back on his heels and forward again, bare toes spreading against the floor as if to keep himself anchored. "It isn't and it is. It wasn't and might be. Power. A gift unaccepted." His gaze fixed on her face. "Don't forget, Claire. It's important."

"All right."

He stiffened. "Wake up, Claire." His eyes widened. "Wake up! Now, Claire. Wake up now. NOW!"

CHAPTER 25

The king's warning came late.

Claire blinked awake as the king grabbed her wrist and pulled her to her feet.

They made it only a few steps through the darkness before something flew through the air and hit the king a skull-cracking blow on the head. He tumbled face-first into the leaves and did not move.

Claire caught her breath in wordless fear as she was surrounded by things. Yes, they were *things*, not people, though they walked on two legs (mostly), wore rags of clothing, and generally looked like very small people. She knew they were something else, something bad, by their eyes. There were a dozen of them that she could see, and she had the feeling others lurked out of sight.

One of them smiled—or at least showed its too-long teeth—and bent to lick the wound on the king's shoulder. The king's blood began flowing again, and the creature lapped at it eagerly, grunting.

The king did not move.

"You're a pretty little thing!"

Claire spun to see a beautiful woman standing behind her, giggling. "Such smooth skin! So young and fresh." The woman grinned. "Don't worry, my dear. I'm so glad I found you before the fomoiri did. You'll be safe with me."

Claire's heart thudded raggedly. "Thank you. But we need to be going." She stepped toward the king, intending to help him up.

The creature, whatever it was, snarled at her, the king's blood smeared around its mouth.

"Oh, no, little darling. It's getting dark. You don't want to be out at night, especially not with this one." She nudged the king's limp form with one pointed boot. "He's pretty, isn't he? Appearances can be deceiving, you know." She smiled warmly at Claire. "Let me offer you safety in my house for the night, and in the morning I'll send you on your way."

"Um…" *This is a bad idea. But what choice do I have?* "I think we'll be fine. Thank you for your offer, though." Claire offered, her voice as bright and cheerful as she could make it. "We're really in a bit of a…"

"I must insist, dear." The woman gestured, and the creature grabbed the king and began hauling him through the woods. Claire jogged after them, terror and anger jostling for priority.

She ran into a clearing just in time to see the creature disappear, with the king, into a charming little cottage. It was surrounded by mounds of cheerfully blooming flowers of species she did not recognize. The door was bright yellow, the shutters were cobalt blue, and the wooden siding was white and fresh.

The woman ushered her forward. "Come, little dear. A little bit of food and tea in you, and you'll feel ever so much better. The woods are not a place to be alone at night, you know. Wolves hunt these woods, and shadow men, and many other dangerous creatures I will not even name. I would hate to frighten such an innocent." She opened the door and urged Claire in. Claire opened her mouth to ask if the shadow men or other monsters were worse than the vampire-imps shadowing them, but thought better of it.

The interior of the cottage was just as charming as the exterior. A burnished wooden table sat by one wall. Another wall had a small fireplace, above which a pot of water was boiling. "Tea!" the woman exclaimed. "It always cheers me up. Here." She poured tea into two delicate porcelain cups and set one in front of Claire. "Now, darling, tell me what you were doing out in the woods so very late."

Claire stared at the cup. It smelled like chamomile tea, but with a slightly warmer scent, like vanilla and perhaps honey. "I shouldn't…"

"Oh, tosh!" The woman waved a hand dismissively. "They're so bossy, aren't they?"

"Who?" Claire asked cautiously.

The woman blinked. "Whoever told you not to." Her lips curved in a conspiratorial smile. "Always telling you what to do, as if you're not your own master."

Claire inhaled the scent of the tea. It was home, and comfort, and relaxation. She had been worried about something, but couldn't quite remember what. The tight knot between her shoulders relaxed a little. She raised the teacup to her face, just breathing in the warmth. She let it touch her lips, not sipping it, just letting the hot liquid tempt her.

The woman's eyes gleamed. "Yes. Don't you feel better now?"

"Where is... um... my traveling companion?" Claire asked. Her mind felt hazy and warm, wrapped in a cocoon of steam and comfort.

"He is being attended." The lady smiled, her lips red and her teeth white.

Claire blinked slowly, and, without meaning to, she let a tiny sip of tea through her lips.

"Tomorrow, if you're willing, you can help me with my garden."

The words were fuzzy, but Claire found herself nodding. "Of course. I wouldn't mind at all."

She slept deeply in a comfortable bed with soft white cotton sheets and a down comforter and woke to the sun shining golden across her face.

She meandered out to the tiny kitchen to find the woman cooking breakfast. "Ah! There are you are. Here, eggs and toast."

Claire frowned. There was something just at the edge of her mind. Something important. Something she should remember.

"I'm not that hungry," she said finally.

"Oh, but you must eat something!" the woman cried cheerfully. "Gardening is hard work, you know. You can't work on an empty stomach."

"Shouldn't I be leaving?" Claire asked vaguely.

"I don't see why," the woman said with a kind smile. "You're welcome here."

The eggs were moist and perfectly peppered, just the way Claire liked them. The bacon was salty and the toast was buttery, with a thick layer of strawberry jam.

Every bite was delicious.

Claire spent the day in the garden, pulling weeds and planting rows of tomatoes, corn, peas, and squash. She and the woman sat in a companionable silence during lunch, a light and enjoyable repast of fresh tomatoes, homemade warm bread and butter, boiled eggs, and plums from the orchard beyond the garden. At the end of the day, her hands were dirty, and her back ached, but she had a pleasant sense of having accomplished something. She stood at the edge of the garden as the sun set, smiling at her work.

She and the woman chatted about nothing over dinner, about how the sun shone on the flowers and when the tomatoes would be ready.

When she went to bed in the comfortable little guest room, she did not remember the king at all.

CLAIRE BLINKED AT THE golden light streaming in the windows. Hadn't it been evening before?

Oh, it was another dream.

She was in the king's study again. At first, she thought she was alone.

Then she saw him. He was slumped over the desk, head resting on his folded arms as if he had fallen asleep. Just beside his elbow stood a glass pitcher full of water, rivulets of condensation streaking the glass. A heavy glass tumbler sat next to it.

A slip of paper was the only other item on the desk. It read: *Please drink. The water is safe for you.*

Thirst clawed at her throat, and she eagerly poured herself a glass of water. Then she hesitated, wondering if she was about to fall for some trick. Perhaps the water was not from him. Perhaps it was not really safe after all.

Besides the king's terrifying leanness, there was a strange stillness to him, and for a moment she thought wildly that he wasn't breathing. But he was; his ribs moved in a soft, steady rhythm, and she sighed in relief.

She licked her lips and gathered her courage. Her hand hovered over his shoulder while she hesitated. Then, before she could lose her nerve, she touched him gently.

He drew a deep breath, almost a groan, and blinked into a dazed awareness. He frowned at her; his eyes had an odd darkness to them that was perhaps more unsettling than the dangerous, unpredictable lightning she remembered.

"Drink," he said in a low voice.

"Why did you write the note? Did you not think you'd be here?"

He blinked slowly, and murmured, "I wasn't sure I'd wake up."

The dullness in his voice gave her pause, and she studied him. In the dreams, he had generally been more alert, more aware, more coherent, than in wakefulness. Now he seemed distant, either distracted or merely dazed.

"Drink," he repeated.

"Thank you," she murmured.

His eyes flicked to hers, and his lips rose in a faint, startled smile. "You're welcome." The smile vanished. He rubbed one hand over his face, hiding his eyes for a moment. "Let me tell you a story."

"Is it true?"

He gave her a narrow look. "Would you believe me if I said yes?"

"Probably not."

"Then what does it matter how I answer?" He rose and crossed the room to stare out the window, his jaw tight. After a moment, he began, "Once there was a great king of the Seelie. He was good and just, and his people loved him very much. He—"

"You're talking about yourself, aren't you?" She rolled her eyes.

"No. Don't interrupt. It's discourteous. The king and queen had a son, who was beloved by all the king's subjects and courtiers."

Claire rolled her eyes again. "You're the prince, then?"

The king was holding a bronze letter opener in one hand, flipping it absently between his fingers. The motion stilled. In a low voice, he said, "Do you want to hear the story or not? Keeping the words straight is rather a strain, so I'd appreciate your undivided attention."

"Fine then. I'm listening." Claire studied the king's profile. His lips twitched, as if he wanted to say something else, something she imagined would be cutting or profound, depending on how angry he was.

But his words, when they came, were almost devoid of inflection or expression. He stared out the window again as he spoke. "The queen died when the boy was quite young, devastating not only the king and the prince with their personal grief, but also resulting in a difficult situation for the king in the long conflict with the Unseelie.

"The power inherent in the rule of Seelie monarchs can be fully utilized only by two ruling with one heart. It's a fact of being Seelie; the power is not divided into two smaller parts, but multiplied by their unity. Generally the two who hold power together with one heart are king and queen, but there have been two who were not lovers but rather parent and child, brother and sister, or once, in the distant past, two cousins who were close friends.

"The king, bereft of his beloved wife, gave her portion of power to his son. But the prince was young, and the burden was heavy and weighed upon him. Worried for his father, longing for his deceased mother, and grieved by the war that threatened to spill over the border, the young prince wished, for one instant, for a friend.

"A friend, or someone who might become a friend, appeared for a few moments. Without meaning to, the young prince gave her part of his heart.

"Not long afterwards, the king died in battle, leaving the weight of the kingdom upon his son's shoulders."

"How old were you?" Claire asked.

The king hesitated, and then said softly, "Eight. I was eight." He cleared his throat, and said, "Even while my father was alive, we were barely holding the borders against the Unseelie. My mother was strong and wise in magic of many disciplines, and I was but a child, hardly her equal and not yet a fit partner for my father's rule. Also my father and I, despite our love, were not entirely of one heart, for part of my heart was given to the young friend I had wished for, and most of his heart had died with my mother."

Claire felt a strange, uncomfortable pang in her chest, as if the king, by his words, had pricked something tender. "What happened next?"

"I ruled for many years alone. The war escalated." He frowned faintly. "And I grew quite desperate." He did not look at her, had not looked at her for some minutes. His finger drew absently on the windowsill, the same swirling pattern she had seen before.

"What are you doing?" she asked.

He blinked, as if coming back from distant thoughts. "Telling you a story," he said, his lips curling in a grimace of bitter amusement.

"I mean with your finger there," she said softly.

His eyes flicked downward, and the air seemed to still for a moment. "Reminding myself of myself," he said at last. A shudder shook him for a moment, and he murmured, "The damp and the cold and the hunger and the Unseelie magic leeching through my skin, burrowing through my flesh, seeping into my bones like poison. I write my name over and over and over to remember who I am, and what I was, and why I…" His teeth clicked shut, and he trembled and turned away.

"Why you what?" Claire whispered.

"Here, in this madman, I have dwelt all these years, with naught to do but renew his pain by day and recreate his sorrow by night. I can bear my fate no longer, and now I rebel." He frowned at the window, studying his fingers spread wide upon the stone sill. "And what of me, the love-ridden self, the flaming brand of wild passion and fantastic desires? It is I the love-sick self who would rebel against this madman."

"What madman?" Claire whispered, for he seemed to her to be suddenly coming apart at the seams, his mind spiraling away in remembered torment.

"The one in which I have hidden myself," he murmured. "I gave you the key." His hand clenched, white-knuckled, and he closed his eyes to lean his forehead against the glass. "You don't remember either. I forgot because I had to, and you forgot because… because…" His voice trailed away, and he frowned faintly, his eyes still closed. "I don't know why. Perhaps it was the magic. Perhaps it was only that you didn't know or realize it was important. Perhaps I played my part too well, and you didn't stop and *think*."

"What do I need to remember?" Claire asked. She tugged on her necklace, the bumps and ridges familiar against the pad of her thumb.

He looked at her, his gaze slipping from her eyes to her lips, her cheeks, her jawline, her slim throat, to her hand on the pendant, tugging the chain against her neck. He swallowed and turned away. "How should I know? I'm mad."

She dropped the pendant and clenched her hands into fists. "You are infuriating," she said, her voice shaking. "If you want me to know something, you should just tell me."

"I want you to know a great many things, all of which I am telling you as clearly as I can!" His voice shook. "My mind has been scattered into a thousand splendid, glittering shards, dancing before me, taunting me with meaning that means nothing and everything. I cannot remember the things I have hidden from myself, for very good reasons that I cannot, at this time, recall." He glared at her down his sharp nose, his eyes flashing dangerously. "Where am I? I don't know. Why have you forgotten? You ate… something. What are you going to do about it, Claire?"

Anger had been flooding her veins, making her tremble, but this made her pause.

"What did I eat?" Eggs and bacon, toast and jam. "I ate fairy food, didn't I?"

He tilted his head and stared at her, his eyes flicking over her face. "No… but you… something is *wrong*, Claire." He sucked in a quick breath and clutched at his left shoulder, pressing his lips together.

Claire frowned. "It's all fuzzy."

The king sagged against the window frame. "When you had the mask on, Claire, what made you keep going?" He seemed to have trouble catching his breath, and slid down the wall to sit on the floor. "Remember that, Claire."

She stepped closer. He'd always been pale, but he seemed an especially alarming shade of white now, with his head thrown back against the wall. He swallowed hard and pressed against his shoulder. Blue ink bled between his fingers.

"Are you bleeding? How can you be bleeding in a dream?"

No, it wasn't blue, it was red. *Why did I think it was blue? Blood is red.*

The king gasped, "Remember."

When she woke, she forgot.

CHAPTER 26

Claire stared at the eggs and thick, crusty bread spread thick with butter.

"I'm missing something," she said.

"What could you be missing?" the woman smiled sweetly at her. "We'll work in the garden again this morning. It's a lovely day."

"All right." Claire pushed the food around and pretended to eat, feeling vaguely guilty for not being honest with such a kind host.

"Aren't you hungry?"

"I feel strange," Claire mumbled. At the woman's gentle look, she frowned at the bread. *I'm forgetting something. I wish I could remember. I wish I could see.*

She reached for the jam, and, not seeing a knife, pulled her butter knife from its sheath. When it touched the jam, Claire's eyes widened.

Where a fat little jar of homemade jam had stood, she saw a chipped mug full of dirt. The jam did not exist; nothing clung to the blade of the knife.

This is a lie.

She is lying to me.

Claire glanced surreptitiously at the woman, who was bustling around near the door with a little garden trowel. Her golden hair cascaded over her shoulders, lit by the sun streaming through the window.

Then she focused on the bread in front of her.

I need to see the truth.

The bread looked just as before, warm and crusty, with the butter melting into the center. But it was a lie, and Claire knew it was a lie. She focused on the *truth,* not on what she wanted to see.

The bread became slightly translucent, revealing a scrap of filthy cloth on a cracked plate. The tea in her little jug was nothing but dust.

I haven't eaten fairy food because there is no food.

The thought gave her a perverse sense of satisfaction. *No wonder I'm still hungry and thirsty!*

She looked at the woman again, looking for the truth and not the comforting lie.

The illusion faded before her will.

The witch was not beautiful, and her eyes were not warm. She was a wrinkled, filthy hag, with crooked teeth jutting from her mouth, her lips glistening with saliva. She wiped a blue-stained hand on her stinking apron and muttered, "No, don't finish him yet, not until we find the foinse cumhachta. Stop snacking. Search him again."

Claire swallowed the taste of bile and pretended to raise the bread to her mouth. The illusion was visible, and beneath it was the reality, the images layered like film.

Like when the nightmare king asked me for his gift back. The memory of his face, sharp and pale, the unexpectedly gentle touch on her shoulder, brought a lump to her throat.

Remember, Claire.

The cottage wasn't a cottage at all.

It was filthy hovel. The table at which she sat listed to one side, and the top was crusted with various forms of filth. The open door to the room in which Claire had slept revealed that the cozy bed she remembered was only a pile of stinking rags on the floor.

A dark blue liquid streaked the floorboards. Claire's horrified gaze followed it to a corner where the blue stain disappeared into a crack in the boards. A bronze handle jutted upward from a trap door.

The bronze hinges were heavy, and there was a simple lock on the outside. *Why would there be a lock on the outside? To keep something, or someone, from getting out.*

Fear slid down Claire's spine and curled through her chest.

The hag didn't seem to notice when she looked at Claire. "Come dear," she said, the two versions of her voice in sharp conflict. The false voice was warm and kind; the true voice was sharp and malicious, as if at any moment she might break out into a terrible cackle. "It's time to pick raspberries."

Claire nodded. "Of course." She stood and slipped the knife back into its sheath, pretending to stuff the last bite of bread into her mouth.

She worked outside for several hours. The horror faded, replaced with a vague sense of unease. She straightened to stretch her back. The woman was pushing stakes into the dirt around the tomato plants.

"I'm a little thirsty. I'm going to get some water," she said.

The woman glanced at her. "Of course, dear. When you get back, I'd like your help with the raspberries."

"Of course," Claire said.

She meandered inside. Her head felt like it was simultaneously buzzing and filled with cotton balls, loud and yet muffled somehow.

She looked around, finding the pitcher of cool water on the table and a cup. She was so *very* thirsty. Her hand shook a little as she poured a cup of water.

Remember, Claire.

With the cup raised almost to her lips, she looked for the truth. The truth was green-tinted water in a chipped cup, a listing table, and a blue stain across the floor leading to the trapdoor.

Claire put down the cup with a disgusted frown and stepped toward the trapdoor. What was down there?

A sound near the door made her whirl.

One of the imps stood there, rubbing his hands together. "There you are," he giggled. "Can't see me, can you? Can see you, though!"

"Must have been the wind," Claire said, trying to keep her voice steady.

The imp's eyes widened. "Ooooh, that's *different*! Is it the foinse cumhachta?" He sidled closer, sharp little teeth flashing in an ugly smile.

Not knowing what he meant, Claire smiled vacuously and pretended not to notice what he was doing.

One small hand shot out and seized the handle of her butter knife.

His scream split the air.

Claire clapped her hands over her ears, grimacing.

The imp fled, still screaming, clutching his hand to his chest.

He would be back with the witch, of course. She looked out the window, and the witch was already turning toward the cottage, her hands clenched.

The only door led out the front, in full view of the witch. *Can't get out that way*. The imp hadn't realized she could see the truth, so she had a moment to think. If she ran out the door, even if she could run fast enough to escape the witch and the terrifying little imps, would she be able to sneak back? She needed to find the king. What if he was down in the cellar, or what if the trapdoor led to a better way out?

She knelt to open the trapdoor.

Charcoal! If she found the king, he'd ask her whether she had her charcoal. She darted to the hearth and picked up a piece of coal, then ran back to the corner.

Claire flipped the latch and strained to lift the heavy trapdoor, and as the cottage door began to open, she hurriedly shimmied down into the darkness. She let the trapdoor close as quietly and quickly as she could, hoping the witch or her vampiric beasts wouldn't notice that the latch was now open.

When she reached the bottom of the ladder she turned and stepped onto something that twitched under her, and she froze.

"Where did that snippet go?" said the witch. Her voice sounded deeper and scratchier, laden with malice and danger rather than friendly hospitality. "She was just here!"

"Burned my hand! Burned my hand! Nasty burning shiny," wailed the imp.

"Stop your squalling! It's nothing! Find her."

"*Is* something! Fingers are *gone*!"

There was an instant of silence. "Why, so they are." The witch's voice sharpened. "I don't think the foinse cumhachta would do that. I wonder what it was. Find her."

"Must have run outside," said the imp resentfully. "No where else to go. Didn't see nothing." Something shuffled, and he grumbled, "Was *distracted*."

The voices moved away, and the door above shut with a thunk.

Then there was a movement beside her, and Claire bit back a shriek, scrabbling away.

"Do you have your charcoal?" The king sounded odd.

"You're here!" Claire whispered.

"More or less. Do you have your charcoal?"

"Yes. I knew you'd ask me, so I got a piece out of the fireplace."

There was a brief silence, and then the king murmured, sounding inordinately pleased, "*Thank* you, Claire."

After another silence, he said, "It's almost dawn."

"No, it's not. It's almost noon. I was outside working in the garden when I came in."

"In the dark, Claire."

"No..." She frowned and thought back, remembering the truth beneath the lie. "What a nasty trick," she muttered. "It *was* dark. But why?"

"The morrigan's pets, the fomoiri, can't abide sunlight. I'm not sure the morrigan can, either. They'll come back to sleep at dawn."

"Come back?"

The king made an odd *hm* sort of noise, then murmured, "You'd best work quickly."

"Me? What can I do?" Her voice squeaked a little with fear, and then a tiny thread of resolve formed in her heart. "I have the knife. They don't like that much."

She felt around in the dark with careful hands, cautiously exploring the confines of the pit. One wall was brick; the other three were lined with little cubicles.

"What are these for?" she asked.

"When they're full, they sleep. Sleep, perchance to dream, of death and blood and all the stinking tortures they might devise. I didn't explore their dreams; my own have been unreliable of late, and I didn't want..." His voice faded.

Claire listened for a minute, hearing only the faint rasp of his breath. Was it her imagination, or was it irregular? "Are you awake?" she whispered. "What should I do?"

"Remember the cats."

"What?" Claire cried. "What cats?"

"'Give them teeth and claws!' They killed the rats. Remember?" The king's voice was almost inaudible, the layers stripped away, leaving only a thin, pure thread.

Claire's questing hands felt only air, but her toes felt something on the floor. She bent to discover the king's uninjured shoulder, his arm bent up behind his head as if he were relaxed. She pulled away, not wanting to brush her fingers over his face by accident.

"You're not much help," she muttered. "So it's up to me, I suppose."

The king's breath caught for an instant, and then continued more steadily.

The cats. What does he mean by that?

She'd drawn the cats, and they'd come alive to kill the terrifying rats.

A sound on the floor above made her heart jump into her throat.

"Taibhseach has the entire force looking for them! If you can't find it, I'll give him to Taibhseach and let him dig out where it is. He promised me much if I found the foinse cumhachta, but even without it, Taibhseach will reward me for the capture." The witch stomped around the tiny hovel. Claire crouched beside the king, one hand on his chest as she reached for the knife at her hip.

"But won't he know we lost the girl?" The fomorach's voice was scratchy; Claire couldn't tell if it was the one who had grabbed the knife or a different one.

"We won't tell him. He won't care anyway. The foinse cumhachta is the prize, and after that the king. If the king knows where it is, Taibhseach will make him talk." The witch cackled with bitter satisfaction.

"What if the girl has it? Burned my fingers, she did! Was that it?"

"I don't know. Maybe. Humph. If she has it, we need to find her. If we can't, then we tell Taibhseach that we captured them both, but she got away before we could get word to him. She won't be able to travel fast. Will take her days to get to the other side, and he can catch her before then. Better if we have them both, though. Think. Think!"

The stomping continued irregularly, as if the witch paced angrily above their heads; the smaller skittering sounds of the imps made Claire's hair stand on end.

"Hungry," grumbled one of the creatures.

"Shut up! This is important!" snapped the witch. "Taibhseach will skin us all if we play it wrong. We can take a little while to look, just until sun up. It's too close to dawn to travel far now, but unless we find her trail, we have to send word to Taibhseach as soon as it's dark enough to travel. Everyone, go look. Send word to me here when you find her trail. Oh, and be careful not to get your fingers burned off like Scabbit here. Don't attack her until you've sent someone back to me with word of where she is, then attack all at once. No need to keep her alive, I think."

Fear slid down Claire's spine, but she pushed it aside, trying to consider her options logically. The witch apparently planned to stay in the hovel above awaiting word on which direction Claire had fled. It would have been hard enough to get out even if the room above were empty, but if she tried it with the witch up there, all the hag had to do was stand on the trap door or use the latch. Even if Claire could somehow get out, the witch was probably stronger than she was, and with magic. Would her knife be much good against her spells? Besides, if the king could get out that way, he probably would have already. What good would it do to get out herself if the king were still stuck in the hole?

Charcoal. The king seemed to know things he couldn't, perhaps from dreams, or perhaps from some other magic. He seemed to think the charcoal was critical.

She had the charcoal. Now what was she supposed to do with it? Draw cats to fight the fomoiri? Could cats do that, or were cats specific to fighting rats? She didn't know enough about magic or cats, or magical cats, to be confident in that plan. Even if they could fight, the cats, the king, and Claire would still be stuck in the cellar with the fomoiri... and the boy had hidden her away when the cats were summoned before. She couldn't imagine it would be safe to be in the cellar in the middle of a fight, even if she could summon the cats in the first place.

If she were going to attempt a magical solution, fighting was probably not the right idea.

What about hiding? The fomoiri would spend all day down in the cellar. Would it even be possible to hide from them in such a small space they were so familiar with?

No, hiding wasn't a good idea either.

So it was escape. Could a bit of charcoal help there?

She'd come to Faerie through a mirror. Perhaps a magical door? The idea felt *right* somehow, despite the strangeness of it. Anyway, she couldn't think of anything else.

"Could I draw a door to get us out?" she whispered, feeling strangely tentative. "We can't hide here, and I doubt we can fight our way out."

"I can manage a little magic, I think. Enough to open a door for a moment."

Claire tried to interpret the strange tone in the king's voice. He sounded surprisingly coherent, which was reassuring, but also weaker than he had before.

"You sound... better, I think."

He made a soft, noncommittal noise. Then he murmured, "Your presence is invigorating."

Claire glared in the direction of his voice, then remembered he could see in the dark. "Sarcasm is not appreciated. Try to focus on the task at hand."

"I was not being sarcastic," he said mildly.

Claire rolled her eyes. "If it's a magic door, can you make it come out somewhere else? Like back at your palace?"

"It's a door, Claire. It's not a tunnel."

Right. Of course. If that were possible, surely they would have traveled that way before now. There would be none of this long hiking from place to place if zipping from one place to another were so easy.

"So it can only take us from one side of the wall to the other? That's not much use." She frowned. "We're underground. There's dirt on the other side of those bricks."

"The other side of the wall doesn't necessarily mean opposite where you are standing. The wall extends above the ground also, and the door can open on the other side of the wall above ground. In effect, it would be a door to the outside of the morrigan's hovel."

Claire's frown deepened. "That won't help much if the whatever-they-are swarm us."

"Fomoiri," the king murmured. "And it will help. At the moment, I am captured. If we get out, then we have *escaped*."

"Getting out is good but not enough. How do we get away?"

"Daybreak. We'll wait until they come back at dawn." The king must have seen the confused look on her face, because he added in a low voice, "Like the manacles, Claire. Symbolically, I am captured. I must symbolically escape or we won't get very far."

The creatures would, presumably, not return until they were forced to by morning light, since they would not find the trail they sought. If the king and Claire fled outside at that moment, the fomoiri would be unable to follow until nightfall, and would be unable to send a runner to inform Taibhseach until dark either.

Claire said thoughtfully, "If we get away, they might not send word to Taibhseach as soon as it gets dark. If they can't find our trail, they won't want to tell him they lost us, because without evidence, there's no reason they can admit for them to know we were near."

There was a long silence. "You think they would not inform their king?" the king said.

"If they can't point to a trail, the only way they'd know about us is to admit they'd had us and lost us. I bet Taibhseach wouldn't like that; no one would want to carry that message. As long as our trail starts here, I bet the morrigan won't alert him; she'll want to cover up this end of the trail first. She won't want to admit she held us captive, looking for…" Her voice trailed away. *What was the witch looking for, again? That's important. I should know this.* "Looking for the thing she's looking for. She won't want to admit it, because Taibhseach will be angry. So as long as the trail clearly shows we started here, she's stuck until she can hide that."

There was another silence, and Claire wondered for a moment whether the king had lost consciousness.

"I agree," he said finally. "Draw the door. I will prepare the magic. It will await only the trigger, which will be that you draw the door handle and grasp it. It will be open for only an instant; I have only a bare breath of magic, and anyway, we want it to close quickly behind us."

Claire drew the door shape, stretching upward to make it tall enough for the king, then pulling the charcoal down to the packed earth floor. The king sucked in a breath as he moved; she imagined him reaching for the wall and pressing his fingers to the line of charcoal, though she couldn't see him in the darkness.

The door above opened with a bang. "Nothing!"

"Nothing?" raged the morrigan. "How can there be nothing? She's human! She knows nothing of these lands! How can you be so incompetent?"

"Dawn comes," scratched another fomorach. Other fomoiri voices filled the room, arguing about which of them was at fault for their failure to pick up the trail.

The king whispered, "As soon as the trapdoor above begins to open, complete the door, open it, and step through. I will hold them off while you do this. It will take a moment for the spell to take effect."

"No. I'll hold them off." The objection came without thought, and it terrified her, but she knew the words were right. "You can work the door magic faster and better, even if all I have to do is trigger magic you've prepared. As for fighting, they're afraid of me, and I don't think they fear you at all."

"Oh, but they *should* fear me! *That* I can teach them." The king's voice carried grim satisfaction.

"Perhaps, but remember our goal. We want to escape. The goal isn't to show them you can fight but just to get out of here. I'll wave the knife and act fierce. I don't think they're particularly brave, and we're trapped in a hole, so they won't see any reason to hurry. They'll take their time figuring out what to do. So then we slip out the new back door and leave them behind, preferably with no fight at all."

"Far be it from me to hide behind a lady when danger threatens. Think you so little of me?" the king said stiffly. "Get thee behind me, Claire Delaney."

Claire blinked, then scowled at him, wishing she could see in the dark as he could. "Someone once told me about right and just service. You're a king! Call it my right and just service if it makes you feel better. I want to get out of here alive as much as you do, and I think this is our best chance. I'm not impugning your honor." *You noble, self-sacrificing, arrogant jerk,* she added mentally.

The king's breathing hitched a little, and she heard him shift in the darkness.

"Wearing the mask taught me something. Stay focused. Let's not get distracted, all right? It's not noble to sacrifice yourself to save your own pride. You don't have to prove anything to me or anyone." she hissed desperately. "Just open the door, *please*!"

The morrigan shrieked in rage above their heads. "You're all equally useless! The lot of you should be staked out by your toes to crisp in the sun! None of you found the trail, and it had to start right at the door!"

"You couldn't smell it either!" whined a fomorach.

"She's tricksier than we thought, that's all!" the morrigan cried. "Now what shall we do? Same plan, I think. Sun is coming up, we can't do more today." There was a brief silence, and then she said, "I count only twenty. Where is the missing one? Was there trouble?"

"No, Glik ran ahead to the river to check there. Too eager. Didn't think, should have known he had to turn back. Told him, we did! We barely made it back. He thought he could run fast enough, but caught out in the sun, he was, unless he found a hole to hide in. Serves him right for being stupid."

The morrigan said, "Well, if he found her, he will have killed her, and we will find out tonight. If he killed her before he died, it was worth the loss. So tonight we send runners to get Taibhseach and tell him we have the king, and we send others to see if Glik is ashes and whether he found the girl. If we don't have a trail or the girl, then so far as Taibhseach knows, we never saw her. Got it? Now, go get some sleep down in—wait."

Silence fell.

"Open the door," Claire breathed.

"As you wi—,"

The king's words were cut off by the morrigan's scream. "The latch is open! She never left! That's why we can't find her trail! She's hiding in the cellar with him!"

Footsteps stampeded toward the trap door.

There was snuffling at the crack around the door. "Yes! Yes, we smell her now! Oh, how foolish! No way out. We have you now!"

The trap door opened and faces crowded around the opening. Claire's eyes, adjusted to the pitch dark of the cellar, made out their bloodthirsty leers easily.

"There! On the far wall! There they both are. We has them *both*!" The vampiric creatures cheered and chittered, bouncing up and down in excitement.

"Go down and seize them! We must find the foinse cumhachta, or at least that burny thing."

The fomoiri flowed down the ladder as if they had been poured from a bucket, but kept to the far side of the small cellar.

Claire had her back to the king, facing the fomoiri and trying to look confident. She held the knife out in front of her, waving it a little so they wouldn't see how her hands were shaking and so they would be sure to see it.

Their gazes were fixed on the knife. One of them, in the very back, said, "That's it! That's the… the thing! Burned my fingers off, it did. Careful, now. Be quick, and don't let it touch you!"

Not one of the fomoiri moved to attack, though they shifted nervously.

Another fomorach asked, "Does it only burn if it *touches* you? Can it do anything else?"

There was a brief silence, then the first said, "Don't know. Burned me when I touched it."

Claire hissed at the king, "Now would be a good time!"

"Seconds. Stall."

"You want to see what I can do? Come closer then! I'll burn more than your fingers!" Claire waved the knife as menacingly as she could.

From the trap door at the top of the ladder, the morrigan cried, "She can't handle all of you! Just charge her! All of you! If she burns one or two, you still have more hands than you need! Just do it!"

The vampire creatures hissed, and one asked, "But… they be stuck here. All we have to do is hold them through the day, and then Taibhseach will come. We should go up and keep them here while we wait. House is dark enough."

"I want the burny thing! I want the foinse cumhachta if we can find it! Taibhseach would take it all! Hm. Wait." The morrigan turned her attention to Claire. "You, girl. I only need the king. And I want that… that thing, whatever it is. Put it on the floor and step away, and you can go."

Absolute conviction washed over Claire that the witch was telling the truth. If she put down the knife and walked away, she would be allowed to leave safely.

That's how she knew it was another lie, and the witch was trying to trick her.

Claire laughed aloud. Perhaps the laugh was hysterical laughter, born of terror and disbelief, but the fomoiri didn't seem to realize that, and it frightened them, which was good.

There was a burst of light from behind her as the door opened to a bright morning. The king said, "NOW!"

The fomoiri hissed, the hag screamed, "Get them! Before they escape!" and the creatures actually moved hesitantly toward her.

Claire waved the knife and the creatures scrabbled backward.

The king's hands gripped her by the collar and waistband and snatched her backwards so fast her teeth clicked together. The doorway vanished just as she passed through it.

The king stumbled back and let her go. They both sprawled on their backs on the grass outside the hovel.

Loud screeching could be heard from inside and down in the cellar. A breeze rustled the leaves in the nearby trees, and some sort of bird cawed in the distance.

The king said in a low voice, "We can rest a minute. They won't come out into the light." He added, "That was a very, very near thing."

"I don't know. I think they were too afraid of the shiny, burny thing. They weren't going to do anything soon." She felt a little proud of that, and hysterical giggles threatened to escape her lips.

"Look at your shoe," the king murmured.

Claire raised her foot into the air, too tired to contemplate sitting up quite yet. About a quarter inch of the tip of her right shoe was gone, cut off as if by a razor sharp blade.

"I only opened the door for long enough for us to jump through. I didn't intend for you to linger and debate them. I had to pull you through or you would have been stuck behind by yourself. If you were part way through when it closed... well, the tip of your shoe is still in there."

"What about your arms?" Claire was past feeling terror, and besides, the danger was already past.

The king frowned faintly. "Yes, that would have been quite unpleasant."

"I understand how the burny... I mean, the knife... works, I think. It's that iron and magic are incompatible, and iron cancels magic. Nothing magical can touch or affect iron, right?"

The king snorted softly. "It's more complex than that, but I suppose that explanation will suffice."

"What if the knife had been caught in the door instead of my shoe?"

"I... don't really know." He let out a soft breath, staring up into the bright blue sky. "I think it would have been Very Bad."

STILL LYING ON HER back, Claire turned her head slightly to look at the king. He stared upward, his eyelids half-closed, looking dazed.

She pushed up to one elbow to look at his wounded shoulder, which was on his other side. Dark blood crusted the torn fabric and glistened damply in the golden morning light.

Exhaustion, thirst, and hunger pulled at her, and she closed her eyes and sighed.

"We should probably go," she said in a low voice.

"Undoubtedly." The king's voice rasped, and she opened her eyes to see him roll over and push himself to his hands and knees, taking only a little weight on his injured arm. He paused, blinking, then rose to his feet.

He offered her a gallant hand. She hesitated and then put her hand in his; his blue-gold-silver eyes gleamed with a sudden spark of pleasure.

"Thank you for that," he murmured softly. "Hope springs eternal."

She glanced at him sharply. What exactly did he mean by that? He closed his eyes and swallowed as if he was fighting dizziness, and the moment was broken.

Look for the truth.

"Your blood is blue!" she exclaimed. The torn flesh of his shoulder was open to the air; the crusted blood was dark navy blue, which appeared much lighter, nearly cyan, where it had smeared over his marble-white skin.

He stared back at her blankly. "Yes?" he said.

"Why?" *And why did I see it as red?*

"Why should it not be?" He tilted his head and studied her face. "Oh, you expected it to be red, didn't you?" he murmured. "And so you saw it." A wondering smile flashed across his face, and he raised a hand, then let it drop. "No hemoglobin, of course." He pressed a hand to his forehead, wincing as if his head ached.

"What's wrong?" Claire asked.

"I can't remember." The king's voice cracked with grief. He took a deep, shuddering breath and raised his head. "We must move quickly. Taibhseach and his searchers passed over us once; for that we can thank the morrigan." He glanced over his shoulder at the hovel and narrowed his eyes. "Though I have little inclination to thank her for anything; there were moments of my imprisonment by Taibhseach that were more pleasant than the company of her fomoiri." He twisted his lips in disgust and turned away.

Claire hurried after him. "When I saw you in the infirmary, there was a boy with you. Who was he, and what happened to him?"

The king's steps slowed slightly to allow her to catch up. "Ciardha. The son of a friend. He lived."

"You were worried about him, weren't you?"

The king was silent so long that she wondered whether his brief period of lucidity had ended. But then he murmured, "Worried? Yes, I suppose that word will do." He glanced at her out of the corner of his eye.

"The morrigan wanted something." *Why can't I remember what she wanted?* "What was it?"

"The foinse cumhachta."

"What is that?"

"Seelie power. Authority. A symbol of a reality that…" He sucked in a quick breath. "She must never have it. Taibhseach would burn both our worlds to dust if he found it." But he smiled grimly as he looked ahead. "He won't. I hid it."

Claire forgot.

FOR ALL THE TIME she had spent thinking of that nightmarish journey to save the captive fairy, she had not really stopped to consider the role the nightmare king had played.

He had given her the task of rescuing the fairy. She had assumed he was the fairy's captor and thus her opponent. Feighlí had spoken of *His Majesty* and how terrible he was. But Feighlí had been speaking of Taibhseach, and that implied that Taibhseach was the fairy's captor.

Now she remembered the distant cries she had heard while traversing the endless corridors of the maze, a sound of fighting that had never drawn too close to her.

Could that have been him?

Had he been *helping* her?

And if so, why?

The fairy, Fintan, had been grateful to the king for his release, as if the king were more responsible than Claire herself. She had assumed Fintan would be frightened or resentful, and his gratitude had always struck her as strange.

She had imagined the king the villain, and so he had acted, with his cloak of crawling void and his velvet-and-gravel voice, his threats and his snide arrogance.

Perhaps her assumptions had been wrong.

CHAPTER 27

In late afternoon they stopped to rest awhile. The king was staggering with weariness, and Claire felt bleary-eyed and light-headed with hunger and thirst.

Claire curled up on the ground with one arm under her head. For a few seconds she thought resignedly that one of them should probably stay awake to watch for the morrigan or other dangers, but she drifted off to sleep before finding the words.

"YOU SAID YOU TRUSTED me. When we were awake, I mean, before the morrigan captured us."

He motioned gracefully for her to continue.

"Was that true? Why would you trust me?" She frowned at him. "You hardly know me, and…" Her frown deepened. "Well, we haven't exactly been the closest of friends."

A faint smile flickered over his lips, and the tension in her shoulders relaxed a little.

"Of course it's true. I've never lied to you."

She raised a skeptical eyebrow, and his lips tightened. "You think I have? You wound me, Claire. What do you think I have told you that is untrue?"

She licked her lips, thinking back over all his words, shifting and elusive and oh, so slippery. "You sent me to rescue a fairy with you as the captor, but I don't think you were the captor."

"I never said I was."

Claire's eyebrows drew downward as she thought. "You told me I was the hero and you were the villain. I don't think that's entirely accurate." She glanced up to meet his eyes and actually *looked* at him. His eyes were dancing with a dangerous, terrible intelligence that *knew* her, dancing with dry humor that waited for her to understand something, waited while laughing at his own fading hope.

"I played the villain for a time in the story you told yourself about yourself. I did what was necessary."

"Necessary for what?"

"An *excellent* question, Claire Delaney." He smiled, and his teeth seemed too white and too sharp. "That is a very, *very* good question indeed. I wish I could answer it for you. But," he glanced away, "That is a question you must discover for yourself."

"Why?" She frowned. "Why can't you answer it?"

"Because I don't know," he said simply. "I don't know because I knew I mustn't know. I was one, and I should have been two in one." He frowned, looking distractedly off into space. "Or perhaps I was two, and I should have been one."

"WHAT DOES THIS SYMBOL mean?"

"Nothing and everything." He clenched his jaw and turned away.

"That is profoundly unhelpful!" Claire cried. "Don't you want me to help you?"

"More than nearly anything," he murmured. "I'm trying. Madmen and lovers have such seething brains."

She stared at him suspiciously. "Was that supposed to mean something to me?"

"Everything means *something*. The question is, 'what does it mean?'" His eyes gleamed. "Everything and nothing, Claire. If I could be more clear, I would be. Perspective is everything."

"You said the heart was always what mattered."

"And what is the heart but the organ with which you see?" He tilted his head, and the sudden motion reminded her of a falcon deciding whether to eat her. "Surely you don't evaluate a person with your *eyes*? How foolish you humans can be!" He wrinkled his lips in disgust and turned away. "No wonder you dismissed Faolan so quickly. And I..." He frowned. "Oh, that does not bode well at all for me." He glanced at her again and murmured, "Oh, Claire. Do you mean to be so cruel, or does it come naturally?"

CLAIRE SHIVERED, HER MIND drifting upward from sleep and turning away from cold, uncomfortable wakefulness. She shifted her shoulder against the ground, pressing her head against a pleasing warmth against her ear and neck.

Warmth?

She snapped awake and twisted in place to look up at the nightmare king.

He was leaning back against a tree trunk, legs crossed before him. Her head rested in his lap, her shoulder snug against his hip. She slid out of his lap and backed up hurriedly.

"What were you doing?" Her voice shook, and her pulse thundered in her ears. His hand had been resting on her head, hadn't it? Her scalp tingled with chill where his palm had been warm against the soft bristles of her hair.

He blinked blankly at her. "Keeping watch." His voice rasped a little with fatigue.

Her tension began to fade. Though he frightened her, he didn't seem the type to molest her while she slept. His striking eyes slid over her face and away again, and she frowned. They seemed duller, less like lightning flashing and more like a deep pool, still blue but clouded with silt.

"Are you all right?" she asked.

He looked back at her, frost-kissed eyelashes half-lowered. "As well as can be expected, I imagine." His eyelids fluttered, and his head thunked back against the tree trunk.

The thin skin of his throat moved slightly as he swallowed. The wound in his shoulder seemed darker, shot through with an odd purple color.

"Do you feel feverish?" she whispered, unsure whether he was conscious or not.

"I feel a great many things, most of which are contradictory," he murmured. "The air is bright with hues of light, And rich with laughter and with singing: Young hearts beat high in ecstasy, and banners wave, and bells are ringing." He sucked in a deep breath through his nose, as if to keep himself awake. "But silence falls with fading day, and there's an end to mirth and play." He slitted his eyes open and glanced at his shoulder; his lips tightened in some expression Claire could not decipher.

"What do you dream of?" she asked before she could bite back the words.

He opened his eyes and looked at her, and for an instant, she thought he had his mind back, all of it, all the terrifying brilliance and magic of him. "I dream of you." Then he began drawing patterns with a finger against the worn fabric of his trousers. "Even as I stood with raptured eye, absorbed in bliss so deep and dear, my hour of rest had fleeted by, and back came labor, bondage, care." He frowned. "Hour of rest… hour of rest…" He leaned forward to press his face into his hands. "All mimsy were the borogoves… No! It's missing something." He looked up, focusing on her again, his eyes momentarily sharp upon her face. "Light doth seize my brain with frantic pain." He shuddered and pressed his hands against his temples, digging his nails into his scalp.

"Stop!" Claire's heart twisted inside her, filled with pity and a strange, unpleasant guilt that she could not at first identify.

"Stop. Stopstopstopstop." He placed his hands on his legs, long narrow fingers digging into the sides of his knees. His eyes flicked to her again, slid from her eyes to her lips and lingered, hungry and desperate, then down her neck to her chest. "A fairy gift is never without cost, even one so generously meant."

"What gift do you mean?"

"The gift!" His voice cracked. "The gift you did not want, cannot remember even when you wish to, and so never knew you had! The gift you would not give back even though you despised it."

"What gift?" Claire cried. "I know you wanted something but I still don't know what you wanted!" She clenched her fists. "And how can you say I despised it if I never knew I had it? That's not fair."

"I never said anything about fair." He tilted his head and looked at her as if she had something completely bizarre. "I said *fairy*. What does fair have to do with anything?"

Claire's voice rose in frustration. "Fair! Like right and just and… and… all those things that this ridiculous adventure *isn't*."

The king's eyebrows drew down in apparent confusion. "We weren't talking about your right and just service to the throne." He looked down at his hands. "I'm confused. Stopstopstopstop." He pressed the tips of his long fingers together and examined them, as if the symmetry would reveal something to him that would explain everything. "No, this is not your right and just service. Not fair not fair. But generously given and repaid in full." He looked up, his eyes sharp for an instant as his gaze met hers. "I paid in advance in full. I trusted you. Do you say now that my trust was misplaced?"

"What did you trust me to do?" Claire felt the edge of understanding just beyond her grasp, understanding not only of his confused words now but of everything that had gone before. *Right and just service.* Who had said that before?

"Become the queen. Checkmate."

The silence between them seemed fraught with emotion, and the king did not look away. His eyes were glassy and feverish, the extraordinary gold and silver dulled but not entirely vanished.

"Right and just service?" Claire murmured. "What do you mean by that?"

The king winced, as if the words pained him in some way. "Paid in full," he whispered, and looked down at his hands clenched white-knuckled in his lap. "More than required of you but paid in full." He closed his eyes. "I wish I could think." The words were almost inaudible, and Claire reached out to put her hand on his arm.

THE KING LEANED GRACEFULLY against a tree across the clearing. "My apologies. Coherence seems a bit beyond me at the moment."

"What did you mean by right and just service? I've heard that before." Claire glanced between the king sitting before her, clutching his head, and the vision of him standing across from her.

He raised a graceful eyebrow at her. "Service to the crown. Your family is of my... house, I suppose you could call it."

"You mean we're related?"

"Not by blood. The relationship is more akin to that of a feudal lord in your human history; the lord owed his vassals some measure of protection, and the vassals owed the lord some measure of service."

"Are you trying to say you're king over me? I don't think so!" Her voice rose in anger.

He tilted his head in what might have been confusion. "You seem affronted by the implication that you owe loyalty and service to anyone. Or is it only that you owe it to *me* that makes you angry?" His lips tightened. "Be assured the obligation is equally strong in the opposite direction."

Perhaps that's why he saved me from the cockatrice. Because he thought he had to, or magic made him do it.

But why does the phrase right and just service seem so familiar?

"How are you in two places at once?" The question felt like stalling, but it was a real question nonetheless.

His smile looked both startled and amused. "I'm not. This isn't real." He gestured at himself, the gesture both graceful and vaguely arrogant, as if he fully expected her to be impressed by his lean elegance.

"But you're here and also there. That's two places, isn't it?" Claire frowned as the seated, physical king shuddered, then began to rock gently, hands clenched into fists and eyes closed.

The standing king sighed softly. "Do I look as if my mind were there, in that body?" When she met his eyes for an instant, there was an offended, bitter gleam in the brightness, and then he turned away.

"Where is it, then?"

"Hidden," he snapped. "Hidden away, in a place I thought was safe."

"Why?"

"I couldn't very well leave it in there, could I?" the vision muttered. "I don't even want to imagine how cracked I'd be if..." His teeth snapped together, and he swallowed the words. "No, that would have been exceptionally unwise."

CHAPTER 28

They walked for hours. The forest grew darker as the trees grew closer. Claire followed the king, watching his bare feet padding silently over the moss and damp leaves. The silence weighed upon her, oppressive and foreboding.

"Why aren't there any sounds of birds or bugs or anything?" she whispered.

The king stopped walking, one hand out to stop her as well. He listened with his head cocked to one side, then began walking again.

"What is it?" she whispered.

"The dryads are deciding whether to delay our pursuers or not."

Claire looked at the trees with new caution.

"What will they do?" She drew closer to him. Insane or not, villain or not, he was the closest thing she had to an ally here.

He glanced at her. "Probably nothing."

"Aren't they your subjects?"

"These are Unseelie lands. But many of the Unseelie king's subjects are not *entirely* loyal. We cannot change our nature, as humans do, but we choose our allies, friends, and lovers with the same freedom humans do."

"You're saying you've subverted the Unseelie king's subjects?" She frowned at his back.

"Nothing so formal as subversion." He gestured gracefully, and Claire wondered whether he had talked with his hands when he was sane, or whether that was an effect of the insanity. "Indeed, if I had subverted many of the Unseelie king's most loyal forces, we wouldn't be in this situation, would we?" He turned to smile at her, his eyes alight with humor. "No, it is more that I have, through the long years of my reign, established a certain reputation. Even many Unseelie would prefer my rule to that of their own king."

"So they just like you better?"

There was a moment of silence, and Claire was about to repeat her question when the king stopped and raised a hand to his head, covering his eyes. His mouth contorted in pain or frustration, and his breath caught for a moment.

"What's wrong?"

"I'm forgetting something," he groaned. "Something I meant to forget but must remember.

Because he *knew* what I knew, and I had to hide the knowledge like a treasure, not to be found until the right time. And the time is speeding away, and I asked you…" His voice trailed away.

"Asked me what?"

He gasped in deep, shuddering breaths, ran his long fingers through his hair, leaving it more disheveled than Claire had thought possible.

"Tendrils of malevolent magic ran through my brain, searching out all that I had hidden within myself. But I hid it so well he could not find it! Not even Taibhseach could guess or search it out." He smiled bitterly, his eyes meeting hers with a spark that shook her to her bones. "Too clever by half, I was. Gave it away where *he'd* never find it, at least. So clever I fooled myself too."

"What did you forget?" Claire asked softly. Perhaps, if she asked with the right words or tone, she could help him remember. *He asked me for a gift he'd given me. But what gift does he mean?*

He closed his frost-white eyelashes, and tilted his head, as if listening to music only he could hear.

"What did you forget?" she asked again.

He winced, and a shiver ran through his body. "I forget."

After a moment, he began walking again, eyebrows still drawn downward in frustration.

The underbrush grew denser, but the king seemed to have little trouble picking a path silently through the bushes.

The shadows deepened. Claire had the unsettling impression that sometimes the shadows moved of their own accord, and she stayed close by the king. She tripped on a root and nearly fell, then sucked in a surprised breath when the king caught her hand.

"Can you not see?" he asked.

"No."

A faint glow of moonlight filtered through the canopy of branches above, but it wasn't enough to see the king's expression, much less the path he followed.

He let go of her hand and knelt, pressing both hands to the ground. Claire felt the silence like a physical presence, something threatening waiting patiently for its moment.

"We have a few hours," the king said. He remained on one knee, head hanging down, as if the idea of standing were entirely too difficult to contemplate.

When the king showed no signs of moving, Claire said, "Should I make a fire or something?"

He sucked in a soft breath, making Claire wonder whether he'd begun to doze.

"Do you know how?" he asked.

"Not at all." She smiled at him, and he tilted his head as if trying to figure her out.

"Wait here." He gathered a few sticks and fallen branches without going far and made a fire by rubbing two sticks together. It took longer than Claire had expected; he seemed so competent that watching him struggle with something relatively mundane was surprisingly amusing.

"That took awhile," she finally said, knowing he would shoot her a venomous glare.

He did so, and she smiled sweetly at him.

"Normally I would use magic. I haven't done it this way since I was child." He glared at the little curl of smoke now emerging from the pile of bark and shreds of wood.

"When will you get your magic back?"

A stick snapped in his hand, and Claire almost regretted her flippant tone.

"I don't know," he said in a strangled voice.

"So it's almost like you're a normal person."

He made an odd sound in the back of his throat; Claire couldn't tell if it was a laugh cut short or a cry of angry protest.

Bright tongues of flame emerged from the little pile of twigs, and the king angled a slightly larger piece of wood gently over the top.

The soft crackle of the fire was the only sound in the oppressive silence. For a moment, she almost forgot that the king was insane. He was quiet, perhaps pensive, but entirely coherent.

A soft rain began to fall.

Claire shivered and drew closer to the fire, wishing she had some way to gather the water.

The king picked a fresh leaf from a nearby branch and deftly folded it into a cup, which he set on the ground. In a few more minutes he had woven another six leaves into a wide funnel, which he placed over the leaf cup.

He folded another cup, and wove another funnel, then a third cup and funnel.

"That's kind of brilliant," Claire murmured.

The king shrugged one shoulder as if the compliment bothered him. "Another childhood skill not used in many years."

The firelight flickered on his face, glinting on the drips running down his thin cheeks. His wild, dirty hair became even more bedraggled, dripping into his face in long, silver-blond strands.

He shivered and rubbed his hands over his arms.

"Are you cold too?" Claire asked.

He blinked and looked up at her, as if he'd only just noticed she was there, his eyes wide and blank.

"But to me the darkness was red-gold and crocus-colored…" His voice trailed away, his gaze sliding from her into the distance.

"What?" Claire asked tentatively, when he did not continue.

His gaze snapped back to her. "Your brightness. Words whispered torches flames orange against the silver rain." He frowned. "No, that's not right." One finger began tracing curling patterns in the damp dirt. "Cold rain. Silver rain." He winced, as if the wrongness of the words were deeply offensive.

Claire edged closer to him, careful not to move too suddenly. She put her hand on his wrist.

"Please don't," she said softly. The words were unnecessary; as soon as her fingers touched his skin, he froze as if electrified.

"There's water in the cups," he said in a strange, quiet voice.

Claire licked her lips and removed her fingers from his wrist. He remained motionless, and she handed him one of the leaf cups, then took the second for herself.

"Feighlí told me not to drink or eat anything," she murmured. The water was so *very* tempting though. Thirst made her tongue seem too large in her mouth.

The king blinked slowly, lost in thought. "He was wise to warn you. But rainwater will not trap you here; it has, temporarily, lost its connection to the earth, the richness of the soil and running rivulets of streams."

The water was cool and fresh, though with a faint hint of a dusty texture that she imagined was some sort of pollen from the leaves. Raindrops pattered softly on the leaves around them.

The king held his cup between his long, thin fingers, staring at it as if it were something unknown and unimaginably complex.

"Drink some water," Claire prompted.

He glanced at her before taking a drink. She couldn't tell whether the strange light in his eyes was a wry amusement at her prompting, appreciation for the reminder, or something else altogether.

"How did you know who I meant?" Claire asked suddenly. "He said that wasn't his real name."

The king snorted softly, his lips curling in a slight smile. "Feighlí isn't a name. It's a word that means childminder or nanny."

"That…" Claire expelled a sudden breath of mingled outrage and laughter. "I suppose that's fair enough."

The silence that fell between them felt more comfortable than Claire could have imagined possible.

The firelight glinted on the king's bare arms, on the fine pale hairs standing up with chill. A ragged scar arced across his left forearm. It was so pale she hadn't noticed it before, the white of the scar blending with the white of his skin, but the combination of firelight and rainwater washing away the dirt and blood made the edges more visible.

"How did you get that scar on your arm?" she asked.

"Cockatrice."

She stared at him. His voice held no inflection, no interest in the question at all.

"Cockatrice? When?"

"Years ago." He frowned faintly at the fire.

"Do you remember…" She swallowed a lump in her throat. "Do you remember anyone else there?"

He glanced at her, one blond eyebrow lifted in gentle confusion. "I am not myself. I am hidden. There was water and blood. One, two! One, two! And through and through the vorpal blade went snicker-snack!" His thin lips lifted in a sly smile. "He did not expect that. He saw only a small girl child, not a king, but though I too was small, the heart is what matters." He looked back at the fire.

Claire closed her eyes, remembering the fear in the boy's face as he shoved her into the water. *Saving me.*

"Why did you save the girl?" she whispered.

He looked at her sharply, as if he doubted the sincerity of the question. "Because I could." His nostrils flared. "What other reason is necessary?" He frowned, his expression distant for a moment. "But I was *there* because… she had called me. And she was there because… I had called her?" He blinked, as if his own question had startled him. "But, she wasn't the right person. Yet?"

She shrugged, and he kept his eyes on her suspiciously for a moment. Holding his gaze was terribly uncomfortable; lightning seemed to flash through her veins, flooding her with shame and desire and a strange, unfamiliar sense of compassion that seemed entirely different than the pity that she'd felt earlier.

Then he looked back at the fire. He covered his face with both hands. "If only I could think," he muttered. "I am hidden and cannot find myself."

Claire almost reached out to touch his arm again, to offer whatever scant comfort she could. But she held back, too frightened of… what? Not exactly of him; the boy who had saved her was a king who had saved her again. Perhaps she was frightened of the feelings that arose when the firelight caught the faded scar on his arm, or the way his eyes drifted across her face, looking for something he could not find. Perhaps it was how, even when his eyes were empty and uncomprehending, there was the memory of sharp intelligence both alien and familiar.

His face held the memory of who he had been. His body remembered the predatory feline grace of his former self, the *villain* who had so terrified her and the nightmare king who had stalked her dreams.

Every bit of him, every image of him in her head, was frightening. And yet… and *yet.* He was danger but he was not dangerous *to her*. Perhaps he never had been.

"The heart is *always* what matters." The king said it suddenly, as if he had come to some momentous decision of which Claire remained unaware. He glanced at her, and a faint smile flickered around his lips. "Why do you think you are stuck here in this place you despise?" A bleak despair darkened his eyes, and he added, "Your heart drew you against your mind's will. You wished and repented of the wish but the wish was made and could not be taken back. I don't think you even wanted to take it back, not really."

Claire stared at him. "Which wish are you talking about?"

He pressed his palms against his temples, his eyes closed. "I don't remember." He dug his fingernails into his scalp, pressing so hard that Claire sucked in a breath.

"Stop!" she whispered. "Please stop."

He let her pull his hands away from his head, relaxing slowly to let his head hang down between his gaunt shoulders.

The distant patter of raindrops had fallen away, leaving no sound but the crackle of the fire. The silence was eerie, and Claire found herself listening for any sound of approaching danger. The thought of pursuit by Unseelie armies made her nervous and twitchy.

But even the constant tension could not keep her awake and alert forever. Despite the chilly dampness of the air, her shivers slowly subsided. She blinked awake, imagining that the king was asleep and she should keep watch. What she would do if something terrifying appeared was a question she deliberately did not consider.

Exhaustion eventually began to get the upper hand, and she fell into a kind of half-doze.

The king rose to his feet, and the movement jerked her back to wakefulness, despite his uncanny silence. The motion was unsettlingly graceful, an unnerving reminder that he was not human.

He appeared to be studying something across the clearing from her, his blue-gold-silver eyes intent and more focused than she had seen in… well, since she'd come to Faerie. He took a soft, careful step sideways, then spun and lunged into the brush behind where he had been sitting.

A grunt and several thuds followed, then the king emerged from the bushes holding a man by the throat. As he thrust his captive toward the fire, the man changed shape into a snarling wolf snapping at the king's face, then a bird caught by the throat crying piteously, then a flapping fish, then a creature Claire could not identify, then a panicked buck struggling to escape the king's grip.

The illusion disappeared. The man stumbled backward and would have fallen into the fire but for the king's steely grip on his throat. Then he stood still, head thrown back, green eyes wide, nostrils flaring as he tried to breathe. His hands clawed helplessly at the king's wrist.

The king let him go suddenly. "Silvertongue?" he said, as if surprised.

The man turned his face away from the king, and the light fell on his features.

Claire cried out in horror.

Dark threads stitched the man's lips together. Dark blood crusted each hole, and fresh blood dripped in thin tracks from several of the wounds.

Besides the wounds, the man was handsome, though in a way entirely different than the nightmare king. The king was starlight on snow, his beauty cold and clear and sharp as glass. The stranger, Silvertongue, was golden. His skin was sun-kissed gold, his hair fell in flaxen curls, and his eyes were an unnerving shade of gold-green.

He was filthy and too thin, and his clothes had apparently been worn for at least weeks, perhaps months, without washing or mending.

I've seen you before. The thought slithered through Claire's mind, and she studied him surreptitiously. *But where? You weren't in the Fae court when I was sent out. We're very far from there, anyway.*

"Finally said too much?" The king studied the stranger without moving.

Silvertongue nodded sharply, just once, as if there was an infinitely complicated story that he did not wish to tell.

"How long?"

Silvertongue shrugged one shoulder, and the king raised one elegant eyebrow at him. His golden head drooped a little, and he held up three fingers.

"Three days?" Claire guessed.

He gave her a withering glare, and she subsided.

You winked at me in the Unseelie palace. Her eyes widened as she recognized him.

"Months?" suggested the king, his eyes sweeping over the man's form again.

Another sharp nod.

The king gestured gracefully at their little camp, at the tiny fire and the folded-leaf cup that held a few ounces of water. "I welcome you, Silvertongue."

The man studied the king with narrowed eyes, and then gestured at Claire questioningly.

"A friend," said the king easily. "Her name is Claire."

Silvertongue's green eyes turned toward her with a startling gleam.

"Do not even consider it, Silvertongue," the king murmured. "I will make you wish the Unseelie king had you back in his dungeon if the thought dares cross your mind."

The gleam faded, and Silvertongue bowed to Claire carefully, then looked back at the king.

Claire had the strange feeling, as she studied his profile, that Silvertongue had merely been going through the motions of appearing lecherous.

The king sat down. "I would that I could remove the stitches." His long, thin fingers rubbed his jaw, then absently began to draw patterns on the fabric of his trousers.

Silvertongue flopped to the ground beside him, the movement almost graceful until he lost control at the last moment and sat down heavily.

"How much longer?" the king asked in a low voice.

The golden man held up two fingers and nodded when the king asked, "Days?"

"Who is he?" asked Claire softly.

The king looked back at her, his strange eyes blank, as if he couldn't remember who she was. "A liar prince who once set the world aflame."

The green-eyed man's eyes gleamed with what Claire imagined was gratitude. He lowered his head toward the king in respect.

"I've seen you before," Claire said murmured. "You knew I wasn't supposed to be there, didn't you?"

Silvertongue glanced at her, then away, as if the conversation did not interest him. Then he winked at her, green-gold eyes glinting in the lamplight. The skin around his mouth tightened a little, as if he would have grinned at her but the stitches prevented it.

The king's eyes turned toward the loam in front of his crossed ankles, and he drew a finger through the dirt in a curling pattern that circled back upon itself over and again, like smoke rising from a forgotten ember.

Silvertongue's hand shot out to catch the king's wrist, and the king froze.

"What are you doing?" Claire's fear made her voice squeak.

"Nothing," breathed the king.

Silvertongue's green eyes flicked to Claire with a frisson of fear, which made Claire's fear turn cold in her stomach.

The king shuddered, as if Silvertongue's fear had passed to him as a chill. "Nothing," he repeated. "I'm fine." He smiled, and the smile was like a mask, his blue-gold-silver eyes empty and emotionless.

THE FLAMES DIED, AND the king made no move to build the fire up again.

"Is Faerie always this cold?" she grumbled.

The king glanced at her, his eyes almost sparking with understanding for a moment before they became blank again. His words came out of the darkness. "No. It is cold because the world is ending. Though we are close to the border, we are on Unseelie land. It is not kind to humans, nor to my kind."

"What do you mean 'the world is ending'?" Claire said. Her voice sounded harsh with fear, and she cleared her throat. "Are you being literal or figurative?"

"Yes."

She glared at him, and he seemed not to notice.

"Time grows short."

Silvertongue caught her eye from where he sat, his eyes bright with worry.

He reached forward to touch the king's wrist lightly, fingers just brushing over the torn skin. The king looked up at him, his expression confused for a moment as if he couldn't remember who Silvertongue was or why he was with them.

Silvertongue wrote in the dirt with one finger, the letters all curls and swirls, layering over each other. The language was not English, but even if it were, Claire wondered whether she would be able to read quickly enough to follow what he said.

The king snorted softly. "No wonder he was angry," he murmured.

Silvertongue's eyes glinted with a hard light, and he continued writing.

"Come to my court, Silvertongue. I offer you refuge as a friend and ally."

More curling words in the dirt. Silvertongue's shoulders drooped a little, and he glanced quickly at the king's face before looking back at the ground.

The king's frost-colored eyebrows lowered. "That is vile, Silvertongue, and you will not speak so of yourself in my presence. Chaos follows you, I will not deny that, but you have never belonged in Taibhseach's court. Your heart is Seelie, through and through, and the offer stands."

Silvertongue took a deep, shuddering breath, his nostrils flaring.

The king lowered his voice further. "I regret that you have suffered so long under him, but the choice is, and always has been, yours alone. Yet I would not have you think yourself friendless. I trust you."

The golden Fae made a strange noise deep in his throat and pressed his hands to his face, hiding his eyes.

The silence pressed upon them, unnatural and oppressive, broken only by the distant creak of the trees in the cold and the soft crackle of the fire before them.

FINALLY, SILVERTONGUE GLANCED UP, his eyes flicking from the king's face to Claire's and then back. He wrote in the dirt again. For an instant Claire thought it was not English, then she thought it was, and then she realized it was not English after all, but that Silvertongue was making it so that she could understand it somehow. The letters and words made sense, unless she focused on them, which made them resolve into swirls and loops she could not understand. He wrote quickly, erasing the words as rapidly as he wrote them.

Claire has been watched from the time she entered Unseelie lands. The dark lord, whose name I will not say, is interested in her. She moves through the land with confidence, desperation, or perhaps utter ignorance; they have been unable to determine which. She bears some power the dark lord does not understand but desires for himself, but she does not seem to be using it. This frightens them.

Silvertongue glanced at Claire.

They saw that you easily defeated the kelpie. They did not see all that happened, but they did see that you were merciful. This implied that your victory was easy and that you had reason to be friendly with the Seelie, though you did not appear to be Seelie yourself.

You are strange. Human, perhaps, but not a typical human. You seem to be heroic and dangerous, and you carry something beneath the surface. Potential, perhaps? If it is the foinse cumhachta, you have not used it. You do not radiate power as one bonded to the foinse cumhachta would. Perhaps you are a powerful hero merely carrying the foinse cumhachta to His Majesty so he could use it to escape.

The skin around Silvertongue's eyes crinkled in what might have been a smile if he had been able to move his lips. Claire wondered if he realized how absurd the theory sounded, and the almost hidden impudence in his eyes made her suspect that he did.

Perhaps you don't have it at all.

Now she was sure he was mocking her, and she glared at him. His eyes glinted, and he inclined his head toward the king.

The guards surrounding your prison were meant to prevent your rescue by Seelie forces, but their more important purpose was to alert the dark lord if you escaped or were broken out of imprisonment by means of the foinse cumhachta. A stealthy rescue was impossible; breaking the spells imprisoning you would be impossible without the power of the foinse cumhachta except by the dark lord himself, and I dare say it would strain even him. Perhaps, if the cell itself were physically destroyed, a group of Seelie strong in magic might do it in concert, but I doubt it.

They were warned that if you were somehow able to break yourself free, or if a single individual or small group attacking openly managed to break you free, that such a one almost certainly carried the foinse cumhachta, else it would be impossible. They were not to attempt to apprehend you again; it would be impossible. You would destroy them. Instead they were to notify him immediately and fear no punishment, because the dark lord wants the foinse cumhachta even more than he wants you.

"So the king was bait?" Claire glanced at the king to see if he was offended, and he smiled as if the question amused him. Silvertongue's eyebrows drew downward.

His Majesty, King of the Seelie and Lord of Dreams, was no mere bait. Impudent human child! If the dark lord got his hands on the foinse cumhachta, he could rip the world apart at its seams. By imprisoning His Majesty, the dark lord not only hoped to draw out whoever might possess the foinse cumhachta, but perhaps to prevent it being used at all.

"I hid it," the king murmured. "He will *never* find it."

Silvertongue glanced at him. *Where?*

The king gave a soft bark of laughter. "I don't know. I forgot."

The golden Fae frowned worriedly. *They are searching for you now. They know not how you broke the bonds, but that you did so indicates that somehow you accessed the power of the foinse cumhachta. They believe you to still be helpless, and even if somehow you have obtained the foinse cumhachta, the dark one believes he can capture you before you reach Seelie territory.*

If you have it, the dark lord will rip it from you and use it for horrors I dare not imagine.

Without the foinse cumhachta, even your freedom is of little consequence to him. The invasion will merely proceed as planned.

"Indeed," murmured the king.

A distant cry made Claire's blood freeze in her veins.

The fomoiri were hunting.

The morrigan's scream of rage carried through the still air, calling the fomoiri closer.

The king closed his eyes and let out a soft, despairing sigh, and began to stand. Silvertongue caught his wrist, and the king stilled. For an instant, their gazes met, and then the king sat again.

"What are we doing to do?" Claire breathed.

The king said, "Trust the liar, Claire."

The first fomorach bounded by them.

Without the morrigan's illusion, Claire could see it clearly. It had two legs, and it was approximately the size of Feighlí, or whatever his name was. The formorach's skin was pale and waxy, with a faint, greasy gleam that made Claire's stomach turn. Needle-like teeth protruded from its small mouth, and its eyes gleamed with malice.

Another came into view, jogging rather than sprinting; Claire imagined it could maintain the gait for hours, if not days. It stopped only a few feet away and looked around, nostrils flaring as it sniffed.

"Was here!" it cried in a sharp, scratchy voice. "Hours ago. No trail. Help me search!"

Fomoiri converged upon them, sniffing at the ground hungrily.

Claire's heart thudded raggedly. The fomoiri were only feet away, spreading out in a spiral pattern as they searched.

The king and Silvertongue were transparent, just as the morrigan's illusions had been when Claire saw through them. She glanced down at her own hands and saw that she herself appeared transparent.

The morrigan arrived a moment later.

"Seelie blood!" she cried. "Smells like sunlight on snow! Fahhh!" She stopped and sniffed, staring around with sharp eyes. For an instant her eyes fell upon Claire, and the girl sucked in a terrified breath.

Then the morrigan looked past her, turning slowly as she searched the dark woods. Her stringy hair fell over her face.

The morrigan and her fomoiri appeared not to see the king, Silvertongue, and Claire at all, though Claire could still see their transparent forms. Claire wasn't sure whether this was a courtesy Silvertongue extended to her or whether the illusion simply did not entirely work on her.

Claire looked at the king, whose eyes danced with a deep, terrible mirth as he watched the fomoiri weaving through the woods and then glanced back at the morrigan, still standing near them. The skin around Silvertongue's eyes crinkled as if he would have grinned but for the stitches in his lips.

A fomorach sprinted toward them and through their tiny fire, and then screamed in pain and surprise. "Hot! Something is there!"

The morrigan's attention snapped toward them, and she grinned for an instant. "Ha! Fool thinks to deceive me with illusion!" She waved a hand, scattering sparks in the air, and cried something that Claire did not understand.

Suddenly there were a dozen or so transparent behemoths sitting around the fire.

The morrigan cried out, "Trolls!"

The largest troll stood and roared, baring long, wolf-like teeth. The morrigan skittered backward.

The fomoiri scattered. The morrigan backed farther away from the troll illusion, her gaze locked on the trolls. "Your pardon. I thought you were someone else."

The troll's answer shook the ground.

A moment later, the morrigan called her fomoiri to her, and they departed to search elsewhere.

"Thank you," the king said simply.

Silvertongue bowed his head, leaving it lowered longer than Claire might have expected.

"Yes, thank you," she said. Her mouth felt dry, more from fear than the lingering thirst. "What did you do?"

Dark humor glinted in the king's eyes. "The prince of chaos can use even deception for good."

Silvertongue wrote something else in the dirt, and the king hesitated, then murmured, "Yes, I think that would be wise." He glanced at Claire. "We will rest a little while before continuing on toward the border." He lay back in the leaves and closed his eyes, gingerly moving his injured arm to rest more comfortably.

Claire glanced at Silvertongue, who nodded that she should do the same. She rested her elbows on her knees and put her head in her hands, intending to rest her eyes for only a moment.

Within minutes, she had drifted to sleep.

CHAPTER 29

The king and Claire stood atop a high battlement looking across a series of rolling hills lined with low walls. A dense forest stood at a distance slightly to the left, while mountains shrouded in clouds stood to the right, so far distant they looked hazy and insubstantial.

Claire rested her elbows on the smooth stone. "It's beautiful," she murmured.

"Of course it is." The king turned to her with a faint, proud smile. "I chose this spot partly for the view, in addition to its more pragmatic qualifications."

Claire frowned. "Chose it for the site of the castle, or for this dream?"

"Both."

"Why?"

The king gestured gracefully, the gesture encompassing the entire panorama. "Perhaps if you see the beauty of Faerie, you will not hate it so much. And perhaps, if you do not hate it, you will not hate me, because I serve the Seelie peoples as king. My blood and power are the thin line between the Unseelie, who would invade and destroy this land, and all peoples under my rule."

She studied him out of the corner of her eye. He didn't seem to notice her scrutiny, staring at a point on the horizon with a melancholy air.

"Why do you think I hate you?"

His lips pressed together in a pale line. Perhaps he was trying to decide what to say, or how to say it. He took a deep breath, then let it out. "I gave you a gift, twice upon a time. A token, at first, though not without power. Then later, I gave you everything." He glanced down at her, then looked up toward the horizon, his jaw tight. "I asked for it back, pleaded with you, and you did not understand. Or perhaps you did and merely meant to keep it for yourself." His voice dropped until she had to strain to hear his next words. "I... I had entrusted you with *everything*. I did not want to believe that you betrayed that trust. I clung to the hope that you would begin to understand. When you found me mad and dying, I believed that at last you had begun to understand and feel your duty press upon you, even if you could not feel compassion for the villain you believed me to be.

"And yet... here we are. The war rages. It seems you feel more compassion for Silvertongue, the liar prince, lord of mischief and master of deception, than you do for me. I feel it is my fault. Perhaps I have wounded you unintentionally, or perhaps I played my part too well. It amused me to stretch myself into an image that felt so foreign, and it served my interests to do so. At least, I thought it did. You *wished*, and in your wishing I saw your heart.

"We of Faerie cannot change our nature. We make decisions, we act upon our impulses either honorable or base, but we remain fundamentally what we are. I am a *king*. I was born to be king, I was trained for the role from birth, and the nature of a king flows in my veins just as blood does.

"If I had no peoples and no lands and no power, I would still be fundamentally a king. A landless, powerless king of no one, but nonetheless a fairy king. A *Seelie* king, although that distinction probably matters little to you.

"But you, human as you are, are malleable. You can change your nature." He gave her a sidelong look, and then looked again toward the horizon, the skin around his eyes tightening a little. "Time speeds away," he murmured.

"Malleable?" She breathed in through her nose, barely controlling the impulse to slap him. "Because I'm not royal like you are, I'm clay to be molded into something useful for your ends?" Anger pulsed in her veins. "So to satisfy *your* needs, I have change myself? I have give up some of what makes me *me* to please you?" She imagined daggers shooting out of her eyes and stabbing him in his selfish, arrogant heart. "That's unrealistic and not particularly flattering and not at all compelling."

Surprise flashed across his face. "You persist in finding offense where none is meant. Behold." He held out his hand toward her, filled with deep black powder. "Soot. Pure carbon, more or less. Tell me about it."

"Uh… it's black?"

"Indeed. What is it good for, though?"

Claire scowled at him. "I don't know. Not much. Maybe putting out fires or something."

He closed his hand and then opened it again. The soot was gone, replaced by a chunk of what appeared to be quartz crystal on his palm. "And this? Tell me about it."

"It's a rock. Or rather, it's *not* a rock because we're in a dream! Why are you testing me?"

His eyebrows raised in a faintly amused expression. "Anything special about it?"

Claire wrinkled her nose. "Not really. Looks like a piece of gravel from a parking lot."

"It's actually a diamond, which is made of the very same carbon atoms as the soot. They are merely arranged in a neat, orderly crystal structure, which gives them form and beauty. But the beauty is hidden."

She glanced up at his face. "I didn't realize fairies knew about elements and atomic structure."

"We don't, as a general rule. But this is your dream, and you do. Pay attention now; don't get distracted."

So he knows what I know. The thought was unsettling.

He closed his hand, and opened it again to reveal an enormous cut diamond that shone as if lit from within. "And this? Tell me about it."

"It's beautiful," Claire breathed. "It's a diamond, obviously."

"Indeed." The king smiled. "Made of carbon atoms. It was the soot, and the piece of gravel. Soot that has been ordered and disciplined becomes diamond; it is hard, no longer soft powder that blows in the wind and dirties all it touches. But though the gravel was diamond, it was unremarkable because all the unnecessary bits on the outside interfered with our seeing it, and prevented it from refracting light. But those unnecessary parts could be cut away, revealing the precious gem in all its glory."

Claire frowned at the diamond. "So you're saying you cut away the bits of me you didn't like? That's not much better."

The king sighed softly. "I gave you the opportunity to become the diamond I knew was within you from childhood. You have changed; you have ordered your mind and personality. Some extraneous bits have fallen away, but most of you is still hidden by bits and pieces of personality that you have put on to better fit what others expect of you. You accuse me of trying to mold you into something you are not, but that is the very opposite of what I hope for. I want you to cast off all the bits that are not really you. But it must be you who does it. I can't do it. I can't even really push you to do it, even though I desperately…" He stopped.

"But you do push me! You put me in situations where I have to do what you want or die!"

He inhaled sharply and his eyes flicked over her face before he turned away. "No, Claire. I have never…" He let out a soft breath. "I admit I used you, am still using you. But only because you were crying out for a challenge; I did not search you out or intend to harm you. In every danger, you could have chosen differently." His voice lowered. "I would never have chosen for you to put on the mask, but neither could Taibhseach put it on you. A mask can only be donned voluntarily, you know. When you did, I nearly despaired, and when you overcame it, I thought there might be a little hope after all."

The sun broke through the clouds overhead, washing the landscape in golden light. The gold on the king's cuffs glittered as if it were molten.

"I didn't overcome it," Claire said. "You pulled it off me, remember?"

"When you don the mask, you cede power to make your own decisions to the lord of the mask, Taibhseach. You donned the mask, but somehow rejected the authority. He had no power over you." He smiled slightly as he glanced down at her. "Why do you think he was trying to use the mask to kill you? Because you remained your own, and would not bow to his will."

The mask had sapped her will and tried to influence her, but she had still chosen how to act. The challenges she had faced had been similar. She had had goals, but she had not actually been compelled to perform.

"What about when you pulled me here to rescue the fairy?"

"I was fulfilling *your* wish." His eyes glinted.

He desperately wanted something from her, though *what* exactly he wanted was still unclear to her. He said that time was short. Yet still he did not force her to do anything.

Did that imply…

"YOU HAVE NO POWER over me."

"No." His eyes swept over her with an odd, hungry expression. "I don't. At least not yet."

She glared at him, feeling her skin flush. "You won't ever!"

His lips lifted in a smile, and she had the impression she had surprised him. "Oh, is that what you think?" His smile widened, sharp white teeth giving her a moment of nervous fear. He let the silence grow, let his eyes sweep over her body, lingering on the curve of her neck, on her trembling lips, on her flushed cheeks.

"That's not even fair," she breathed. "You're... you're trying to seduce me! In a dream! That's... ugh!"

His pale eyebrows rose, and he gave a short, startled laugh that quickly changed into an elegant cough. "I assure you, Claire Maeve Delaney, that were I trying to seduce you, you would have no doubt of it."

She glared at him. "Oh, so you seduce girls in dreams often? Is that how it is? You have lots of practice?"

"Not at all. But I flatter myself that my efforts would at least be understood, without a shred of doubt, as attempted seduction." He smiled at her, his eyes sparkling with barely suppressed mirth. And *warmth*... the warmth and affection startled her.

"Do you like me?" she breathed. "Or is that another of your acts?"

He turned away. "It is quite immaterial whether I like you or not. You wouldn't believe me if I told the truth anyway."

"I wish you'd look at me!" she cried.

He turned stiffly toward her, his eyes flashing like lightning.

Something about his movement made her uneasy; his eyes swept over her again, bright and hard and dangerously, terrifyingly intelligent. He was clever and alien, and although she thought she understood him sometimes, the flicker in his eyes now reminded her that she didn't *truly* understand what was going on at all.

"What did you mean you had no power over me *yet*?" Her voice sounded high and frightened.

He lifted his lips in a slightly predatory smile. "Exactly what I said. *Yet*."

"Why do you talk to me in dreams?"

He inhaled softly, as if she had done him some terrible hurt without realizing it. His eyes remained on hers, and because she looked, really *looked*, she saw the despair that he almost managed to hide.

"Isn't it obvious?" he said finally, in a voice so low it barely reached her ears.

"Is the madness getting worse?"

He closed his eyes. "Perhaps you should be the judge of that."

She studied his face. He had a disquieting sort of beauty; his eyes were too slanted, his cheekbones too high and his jaw too narrow and sharp. There was too much steel beneath his thin skin, as if it were clothing he might shed at any moment.

"What is your name?" Claire asked.

The king gave her a sidelong look. "Why ask that now? You have never wondered before."

It was true, and guilt weighed upon her so heavily so that for a moment she could not speak. "I never… never really saw you before." *I saw my idea of you, but I didn't really see you.*

"You never looked." Blue-gold-silver glinted as a faint smile flickered over his lips for an instant before it disappeared. "I played a part. I can hardly blame you for believing it."

She looked down at her hands in her lap, at the torn nails and scratches from the thorns, then looked up to meet his eyes.

"Tuathal," he said softly, as if giving her a gift. "Tuathal is my true name. Guard it well."

Claire recalled some legend of true names holding power, and she wondered, suddenly, what he was giving her. A lump seemed lodged in her throat, some emotion she couldn't identify, much less name. "Did you just give me power over you? Aren't names important?"

The thin skin around his eyes crinkled as he smiled, holding her gaze. "No, and yes."

She pondered that. "I wish you would answer my questions," she said finally.

He gave a quiet, elegant laugh. "Oh, if only it were so simple."

"Tuathal," she said. His name felt like snow in her mouth, ozone-fresh and glittering with light.

His eyes flicked to hers, and slid downward, lingering on her lips, on the line of her jaw, on the pulse she could feel pounding at the base of her throat, to the points of her clavicle, down the smooth skin of her chest to her breastbone. "Where did you get that necklace?" he murmured. His gaze held hers.

Claire pulled at the pendant, running her thumb over the familiar knobby texture. *I'd forgotten I was wearing it. Has he asked me that before?*

She studied his face, how his eyes flicked to the pendant and back to hers.

"Why did you ask me that?" she said finally.

He said softly, "Seems like something you'd remember."

"Why do you think you will get power over me? Why would you ever think that?" she whispered. "I'm here to help you. That's all."

His gaze rested on her face, a tiny smile flickering over his lips. "Because you give it to me, of course."

The moment was broken. "I would never!"

He let out a breath, as if he'd been hoping for other words. "Perhaps not." His gravel-and-silk voice was scarcely audible.

"Why would I do such a thing? Why would you even think it?" She almost winced at the harsh tone of the words, but she kept her eyes on him. How could he assert with such certainty something so absurd?

His thin lips rose in a melancholy smile. "Nevertheless, I am not altogether unhappy. I have chosen, and yet I choose, and will so continue to choose." He bowed deeply to her.

For an instant, she imagined there was mockery in the gesture. Then he shuddered and he fell to one knee. He remained kneeling, head bowed, one elbow on his knee, moonlight-pale hair falling over his face.

"Are you all right?" she whispered.

He did not answer.

He trembled, and as the distant mountains seemed to turn to vapor and float away, he began drawing curling patterns in the air.

"Stop," breathed Claire.

His hand twitched, and his shoulders jerked as if he had been punched very hard in the stomach. His hair hid his face.

Claire fell to her knees beside him, putting her hand over his.

His fingers were warm and strong, fine bone and sinew just beneath paper-thin skin. He flinched at her touch, then his hand closed around hers, weaving his fingers between hers in a gesture more intimate than she had been prepared for.

He looked at her through the white fringe of his hair. "Tick tock."

CHAPTER 30

Cold pulled Claire back to wakefulness from the comfort of sleep. The fire had died, and the king sat staring into the ashes. Silvertongue sat with his legs crossed and his elbows on his knees, but his head drooped in sleep.

The image of the mountains turning to mist and floating away remained in Claire's mind, and she stared at the king.

"Is your name Tu—" She stopped abruptly as she realized that perhaps she should not say it aloud.

At her voice, Silvertongue jerked to sudden wakefulness and glanced at her, then at the king. His eyes flicked to her pendant and then back to her eyes.

The king turned to her, his eyes slightly glassy with fever. "You may speak freely. Silvertongue knows my name."

"Is your name Tuathal?" She stumbled a little over the unfamiliar pronunciation. The name tasted like starlight upon her lips.

Silvertongue turned wide eyes toward the king and wrote something hurriedly in the dirt.

"Yes," the king said, a spark of hope in his eyes. "Where did you hear it?"

"In a dream."

Silvertongue's eyes widened.

Claire glanced between them, noting the golden Fae's poorly hidden alarm. *Tuathal gave me a gift so important that giving me his name is little more, and yet Silvertongue is shocked that I know his name.*

And her mind discarded the thought.

She tugged on the pendant on the chain around her neck absently.

I want to see the truth.

She had seen through the morrigan's illusions and through Silvertongue's troll illusions. Something about the king seemed… odd. Something was missing. Something important.

She could see the blood caked on his shoulder, dried dark navy blue. She could see no illusion, but something was still …

Something sparkled, and it was distracting.

Her mind kept chasing something else, something it could never quite find.

And she forgot.

With a great effort, she fought the distraction. *This keeps happening! Every time! I keep getting distracted and forgetting… something! Something important!*

So what is it that I need to remember?

The pursuers must be getting close by now. We need to leave.

"No! I need to be able to see! I need to see through whatever it is. Focus, Claire!" she muttered.

Silvertongue's golden eyes flicked toward her necklace and then toward Tuathal's face.

"You gave me the necklace!" The revelation broke over her like a roll of thunder.

"I did." Tuathal seemed to straighten almost imperceptibly.

"But… how is that possible? You were so young!"

"Didn't I tell you dreams could be stuffed full of paradoxes?" His smile gleamed bright, full of exquisite hope that she would understand something else.

Claire pulled the pendant over her head and held it in her open hands, examining the design. The king's eyes followed it, but he made no move to take it from her. Three straight lines converging at the top, spreading wide at the bottom, topped by three dots, all surrounded by a circle. The bronze was dull in the crevices, slightly brighter on the high points where her fingers had rubbed over the years. Silvertongue sucked in a breath through his nose, his eyes wide as he saw the pendant.

"But aren't we close to the same age? We were both children when we met in the wood and you saved me from the cockatrice. And then you were an adult when you came as the villain, and I was only sixteen. And then," she glared at him, "you were a child when you made me draw the cats. How is that possible?"

He raised his eyebrows. "I did no such thing. I suggested, rather emphatically, that *you* draw the cats."

Her frown deepened. "But... How did you bring me to Faerie the very first time, when we were both children?

Something dark flickered in his eyes, some memory of pain immediately hidden. "I was lonely. I must have wished you here, albeit by accident. You would have been wishing too; I had no authority or power to take you against your will."

"You think I wished myself to Faerie? I did not!"

"Not exactly. You wished for adventure, and a friend, and a purpose. All of which, I might add, I gave you." His smile widened as she glared at him.

"So all of this is my fault?" Her voice rose in frustration.

"Not at all." Tuathal pressed his lips together in an expression of dismay. "Not at all, Claire. You wished something *magnificent,* and I took the opportunity to grant your wish for my own ends. I used your humanity, your essential malleability, your latent courage that you did not yourself realize or acknowledge, and gave you opportunity to become *yourself.* I presented you with a challenge and a role and a villain to vanquish, and you did so."

She stared at him, appalled. "I wished to be a hero, and I was the worst, most selfish hero who ever wore the title. I lost my temper at the little fairy. I deserted Feighlí even though he saved my life. And I almost killed that servant in the hallway, and then I didn't even feel guilty about it until later." Her throat tightened and tears welled up. "I've always regretted that. I wish I could tell them how sorry I am." She choked on her guilt, pressed her fist to her mouth to hold back the sobs.

He let out a soft breath, and she wished desperately that she had the courage to meet his eyes. But she didn't; she kept her eyes on his thin, elegant hands, one finger absently drawing patterns upon his knee.

"I admit I was… not entirely satisfied with the results of the challenge." His voice was tightly controlled, but she heard the raw edge of grief in it, sliding like a knife between her ribs and into the tender place of her heart, the place that wished to be better than she was. "I had hoped you would rise to become the Claire I knew you wished to be, a shining beacon of hope and impossible courage. You could change your nature, and I gave you opportunity, but I did not see the fruit of the seed I had intended to plant.

"It was no dream. I was only seventeen, barely older than you were. What you saw was a glamour to make myself older and conceal my grief.

"After the challenge, I did not think to see you again. But then you were pulled into Faerie by the force of your wish, and your brother's, to be somewhere else, somewhere *safe*. In the instant of the car wreck, between consciousness and death, you wished, and you found yourself in my infirmary."

Claire blinked. "I did that?"

One corner of his mouth quirked upward. "In a manner of speaking."

She narrowed her eyes and tilted her head. "What do you mean by that?"

His lips twitched, as if he wanted to smile, or say something clever, but he only said, "Paradoxes,

Claire." At her steady look, he added, "Did I look as though I had expected you to appear in my infirmary in the middle of a storm?"

She frowned, thinking back. No, he had looked rather surprised to see her, though he'd hidden it well. *Still playing the villain.* "So somehow I wished us to your infirmary? I had no idea that it existed, much less that it was safe." She pondered that a moment. "In fact, I'm quite sure that if I had known of it, I would not have thought it was safe at all."

His eyes glinted, shadows shot through with the light of hope.

"But it *was* safe," he murmured. "There was, quite literally, no safer place in all of Faerie. It was warded with layer upon layer of the most intricate and powerful spells, and guarded with the very best and most trusted of my personal guard." He watched her, waiting for her to understand something that she did not yet grasp.

"Can you fly? I thought you had wings in the dream."

His frost-kissed eyelashes flickered. "I… have in the past. At the moment it is a bit beyond me." His voice had a strange, tight sound, and she glanced at him.

Claire's eyes met his, and the spark between them made her tremble. "What have you done?" she breathed.

I went to the infirmary because he gave me power and authority. He gave me the right to be there. He gave me himself.

Oh.

OH.

She fumbled with the necklace, thrusting it into his hands. "Take it!" she cried.

As his hands touched the necklace, he made a strange sound deep in his throat and a shudder ran through him.

Then he straightened, and he was again *the king*.

He was himself, with all the danger and grace of a fairy king, with fire in his eyes and electric power in the air around him.

"Thank you," he said, his voice velvet seduction, rose petals on ice. He smiled, teeth sharp and white, eyes bright and triumphant.

He put out his hand to her, graceful and impossibly elegant, and his eyes asked a question.

She licked her lips, took a deep breath, and put her hand in his.

A distant horn sounded, and he pulled her to her feet.

"Come, Silvertongue!"

They ran.

THEY RAN WITHOUT STOPPING for what felt, to Claire, like several miles.

I'm more out of shape than I thought. Her breath came in gasps.

The forest seemed to part before them, never exactly presenting a path but never impeding their way.

At last the king slowed to a brisk walk. He brushed his fingertips across the tree trunks as he passed, murmuring in a low voice.

"What are you doing?" Claire huffed.

"Thanking them for the easy passage. The border is just ahead."

A low murmur rose behind them, and the king's steps quickened. He stumbled once, but did not fall.

Come on, Claire. Don't give up now.

The murmur grew into a roar like ocean waves, distant and yet terrible in its immensity.

They emerged from the trees into brilliant sunshine beating down. A long, low slope lay before them. At the bottom of the hill flowed a river. The banks were made of pebbles, and the water appeared to be only as deep as Claire's waist.

A thread of fear curled through Claire's veins, but she did not stop to analyze it. Not with the roar of approaching terror so much more insistent. The branches of the trees behind them swayed in a wind Claire could not feel.

As they approached the water, Claire hung back. "Wait!"

The king stopped, blue-gold-silver eyes turning to her. "Come, Claire."

"There was a kelpie! And a water woman who almost ate me!" Panic made her voice shrill. "I don't think it's safe."

The king caught her hand and pulled her forward without a word. Silvertongue crowded her shoulder, pushing both the king and Claire forward even as he looked back toward the forest.

They splashed into the water as their pursuers broke through the trees behind them.

CHAPTER 31

The naiad's pale face rose out of the water. "Hello." Her eyes gleamed with delight at Claire's sudden inhalation. "I see you have learned a little respect since we last met."

The king stared expressionlessly at the naiad for an interminable few seconds. If he had been anyone else, she might have wondered if he were terrified, or didn't understand that the naiad was dangerous, or were simply so lost in pain and hunger that he was unaware of the creature at all. But none of those fit what she knew of him, and for an instant Claire dared hope that he was exerting some sort of authority she could not perceive.

"The mad king!" breathed the naiad. "Tuathal, beloved of all Seelie. Oh, we have missed you, my king."

A bolt of lightning shot past the king's ear, and he swayed.

Perhaps he's about to faint.

"Mad no more," Tuathal said in a low voice.

"Let us pass!" Claire cried. She reached for the knife with her left hand.

The naiad's eyes widened, and she hissed, "No need for that." She opened her mouth and sang. Her voice eddied and flowed, dripped and rang and thundered and swirled in the air, calling sisters and brothers and allies.

The water rose around them, and the king pushed Claire forward.

Cold fingers touched Claire's shoulders, and she tried to flinch away, but the naiad surrounded her, watery arms holding her in place. "Get the king to safety. We will hold the border against all threats."

"I will."

The naiad's eyes were deep pools of blue. "Do not lose the king, nor let him be further injured. He is beloved by all our people, water folk and land folk. Our wrath shall be upon you if you let him come to harm."

"I understand." Claire's heartbeat thundered in her ears.

Then the naiad was gone, and the water was a wall behind them and a shallow stream before them.

The king and Claire splashed across the river in three inches of water, and the king fell insensible into the grass on the other side.

THE BATTLE RAGED ON the other side of the wall of water, but Claire couldn't see much. At times the water seemed lit from within by a strange greenish light that hurt her eyes, but for much of the evening the battle was merely a subdued, irregular roaring devoid of meaning or import.

Silvertongue was gone. Claire didn't know whether he'd been eaten by the naiad, was fighting the Unseelie, or perhaps had merely drowned in the chaos.

A dull grief settled on her, along with exhaustion that pulled at her bones.

She stared fuzzily at the water for an hour before she fell asleep still sitting up, her elbows on her knees.

CHAPTER 32

Tuathal strode beside her, long strides eating up the distance effortlessly.

"Come, Claire!" he encouraged.

Claire scowled at him and jogged to keep up.

"Where are we going now?"

He glanced at her and slowed his pace a little, offering her his arm in a gallant gesture. "Time is running short," he murmured.

"Time for what?" Claire's fingers gripped his arm, the lean muscles tight beneath her fingertips, and the contact sent electric desire through her. He placed his other hand lightly over hers for an instant, the touch as fleeting as the kiss of a butterfly wing, then drew back.

"I live by your command. You have all the evidence you need!" His voice cracked, and he did not look at her.

I live by your command.

She stared at his profile.

I live by your command.

She had wished he would have the strength to fight the barghest, and he did.

She had wished he would wake, and he did.

"What have you done?" she breathed.

His nostrils flared, but he said nothing. His lips pressed into a white line.

"I wished you would save me and you did." Her voice sounded strangely flat.

"No. You wished I would have the strength to save you."

She swallowed. "And then you *chose* to save me, didn't you?"

"I did." His arm tightened almost imperceptibly.

"Does that mean I have power over you?" Her voice rose, fear and anger crowding each other for prominence. "I don't want it! I didn't mean to take it!"

He stopped abruptly, his eyes sharp on her face. "You still don't understand," he breathed. "You did not *take* power. It was entrusted to you!"

Her eyes widened. "What do you mean?"

His lips twitched, as if he wanted to explain everything but could not. Perhaps the rules of Faerie prevented it, or perhaps it was only his pride.

"I gave it to you," he said finally.

"Why?" Her voice cracked, and she pulled away from him.

He took a deep breath and let it out softly. "Come," he murmured. "Whatever argument you have with me, let us walk as we speak." He offered her his arm again, inclining his head graciously toward her.

She hesitated, and he waited, motionless and silent, his lightning eyes strangely dull. His lips tightened, and he swallowed, but he still waited as the seconds drew out, as a thousand contradictory thoughts and emotions swirled through her head.

Finally she slipped her trembling fingers into the crook of his arm, and he closed his eyes.

"Come away with me, oh human child," he murmured.

"What's that?" she whispered.

He glanced at her, his steps quickening. "Come away, O human child! To the waters and the wild, with a fairy, hand in hand…" His voice tightened.

At her questioning look, he added softly, "For the world's more full of weeping than you can understand."

"Weeping for what?" A terrible fear crept through her limbs, as if something dreadful were about to happen that she could neither understand nor prevent, but would suffer anyway. "What is going to happen?"

He looked down to meet her eyes with a melancholy smile. "Nothing that concerns you." He raised a hand to cup her cheek, his thumb grazing softly over her cheekbone. "I'd thought… I'd hoped things would end differently. But there is not enough time."

"What do you mean 'end'?" Her heart thudded raggedly.

The fading sunlight caught his long lashes, pale as moonlight, and the sharp edge of his jaw, the faint lines of strain around his eyes. "When you wake, tell Lord Faolan, whom you know as Feighlí, that I thank him for his service. He is both wise and good, and I could not have wished for a better friend." His eyes swept over her face. "Tell him also that there is not enough time for what we had hoped, and he must send you back. I would do so from here, but I need all the power I have, and more, for the fight. Faolan can use the mirror in my study to send you; it will make it much easier. After sending you back, he is to come here with all who can fight, and send all who cannot to a safe place. Not the palace; he will know the place I mean." He licked his lips and hesitated, then lightly pressed a kiss to her forehead. "I thank you, Claire Maeve Delaney, for all that you have done, and all that you have suffered on my behalf. You are, indeed, a hero." His lips trembled, and he clenched his jaw.

He raised one hand to cup her cheek again, then brushed his fingers gently over her eyelids as he said, "Now you must wake up."

CLAIRE BLINKED, AND WHEN she opened her eyes, she was facing the grand front entrance of a magnificent palace. An expansive set of marble steps rose before her, leading to a wide portico lush with vines dripping with fuchsia blooms.

The marble was smooth beneath the soles of her feet, lightly worn with age but spotlessly clean. The door, when she reached the top, was of dark, heavy wood inlaid with what appeared to be gold. The pattern was floral and elegant, rising in bright, intricate symmetry far over her head; the door must have been fifteen feet tall.

The king was gone.

Claire turned slowly on her heel, replaying the dream in her mind as she looked over the palace grounds. Intricate arrangements of flowers and little pools of water spread out before her within a network of interconnected paths. It was the palace, but not the door she had exited long days before.

Walking with him *had* been a dream, hadn't it? It must have been.

Yet misgiving twisted inside her. If it were a dream, how had she come here?

Claire knocked tentatively, unsure whether anyone would answer.

A moment later, a little peephole opened a little lower than her chin. She bent to look in, but the door swung open before she had a chance to see more than a sharp brown eye.

"Oh. It's you." The voice that greeted her was flat and a little unfriendly. The creature looked to be an imp like Faolan, though quite a bit younger. "Wait there." He pointed to a spot on the floor just inside the door and swung the door closed behind her.

Then he disappeared through a hidden door.

Claire waited with her hands in her pockets. Her right pocket was filled with the gritty, dry crumbs of the scone, and she rubbed them between her finger and thumb. She felt slightly dizzy with hunger, but she imagined that if food were offered, she would probably be too nauseated to eat anyway.

Why am I here? How did I get here?

He was saying goodbye.

But if I'm here, then where is he?

Probably back at the riverbank. He can't fight the Unseelie. Even if he has his magic back, and his mind back, he couldn't fight the Unseelie when he was well. He can barely stand up!

I haven't come all this way, and endured everything, to give up now.

"You didn't find him?" Faolan stood in front of her, his expression bleak.

"I did." Her voice sounded strange and distant. Her pulse thundered in her ears. "He said I was to tell you…" She blinked, and considered the words. "I was to tell you thank you for your service. That you're wise and good and he couldn't have wished for a better friend. And…"

Tell Faolan to send you back.

But… what about him?

Tell him to send you back.

And what next?

It's not about being the hero. It's about doing the right thing.

Can I leave him there to die while Faolan sends me back to safety?

"I need to go back," she said. "He's at the riverbank with the naiads. They're fighting, and—" her voice cracked, "—and I should be there. I don't know what to do, but I should be there. He wants you to come and bring all those who can fight and send everyone else away from the palace to somewhere safe. It won't be here. Take me there with you!"

Faolan's eyes glittered strangely. "You'll not leave him, then?" he asked "Perhaps you've learned something after all."

Claire's throat closed with emotion. "Maybe I've just grown up."

ALL MANNER OF FAE rode toward the river in a bright and glittering cavalcade.

She rode at the front with Faolan, sitting nervously on a tall bay horse that entirely too intelligent and cooperative to be entirely animal.

"Don't worry. He'll behave for you," Faolan had said when a tall Fae had effortlessly boosted her into the saddle. "He understands our purpose."

At first she was cheered by the noisy strength of the army behind her. But when she looked back a few minutes later, she realized she had overestimated their numbers. Only a tiny force rode out to Tuathal's aid. They were no more than three hundred, including tiny fairies that buzzed furiously above their heads.

I wish I could see the little green fairy. I hope he got better.

Guilt sat dull and heavy in her belly, and she focused on it, feeling that if she understood and regretted it enough, it was almost like making amends.

But it's not really, is it? I can't make it better. I can't take it back.

Her eyes filled with tears, but she did not let them fall.

A buzz beside her ear did not at first catch her attention. Then a little voice cried, "Oh, it's you!"

The fairy danced in the air before her, keeping pace with her horse, his wings a blur behind him.

"You're alive!" she cried. "Oh, I'm so glad."

"Are you?" he glared at her fiercely. He darted forward to stab her cheek with his tiny sword, and then flitted out of reach.

She winced and frowned at him. "That's not very nice, but I suppose I deserved it."

"And this too?" His needle-like sword jabbed her just below her eyebrow, drawing a startled cry and a drop of blood that she smeared over her temple when she wiped at it.

She growled in frustration. "Yes! Fine. I do. I won't lose my temper again." She frowned at him. "I'm sorry. I really and truly am. I wish I could make it up to you, but I don't know how."

His frantic buzzing slowed a little. "You're not angry?" The fairy drew a little closer, hovering within her reach.

"Not really. Maybe a little. Mostly I'm just glad you're all right."

His eyes widened. "You're different."

"I certainly hope I am." She smiled at him, and he smiled back, tiny teeth white in the sun and emerald eyes shining.

As they continued, the road seemed to fold strangely ahead of them, and Claire had the disconcerting feeling that she was missing moments every now and then, like the micro-sleeps she had experienced when she was driving home from college exhausted after finals.

"What's happening?" she asked finally.

"We're taking shortcuts," the fairy said a few inches from her ear. "The border is many miles distant, and we must travel with all haste."

Claire frowned. "Even the king couldn't transport us before. How can you now?"

"That was on Unseelie land. These ways have been established for generations, upheld by Fae magic."

"How do you know where the king is?"

"I wouldn't, but the pull of the Unseelie upon the border can be felt throughout the entire kingdom. Like a spider's web pulled taut, we feel the disturbance even at the palace, we who have magic in our blood. You may not yet, but to us it is obvious where the king is." He glanced at her, tiny eyes bright and ferocious. "Even without his full strength, he is formidable."

Faolan said in a low voice, "And just as we are his subjects, he is *our king*. We will spend our lives to save him if at all possible."

"Do you love him that much?"

Faolan turned toward her, his mouth open in surprise. "Love, duty, allegiance, pride… why do you seek to parse these out into discrete motivations? Are they not entwined together for humans?" He frowned at her confusion, and said doubtfully, "Love is one of many ties that bind us, some more deeply than others. But duty and allegiance bind us all, and he has borne the weight of the conflict for long years to protect us. If we can help him now, we will."

The world folded into itself again, and then snapped back out into reality. By chance Claire had kept her eyes open for the transition, but it felt as though she had merely blinked, a flicker of darkness and light within which the world rearranged itself.

And again.

Then the river thrashed before them, the water seeming as tall as a tree, tinted silver and blue and gold with reflected sunlight.

Claire walked into the water, and it swallowed her.

CHAPTER 33

Tuathal stood before the Unseelie king.

The Unseelie king loomed high, taller than Claire could have imagined. He was monstrous, light and shadow playing over his face in a way that made it difficult to read his expressions, if indeed he had any. His features were vaguely human, but his eyes were not; they were deep pools of a strange dull orange, neither bright nor dark.

From Claire's position behind Tuathal's shoulder, she could not see the expression in his eyes, but she could tell from the set of his jaw that he was not entirely himself. He had his mind back, but not all his power. How he had held the border for so long, she could not imagine.

"Stand aside, small king." The Unseelie king's voice seemed to reverberate through Claire's bones.

"I will not."

Everything changed, and they were on dry land, though Claire could not imagine how the transition had occurred. Tuathal staggered backward.

The Unseelie king struck at Tuathal with lightning, and the king deflected the blow with one hand, though he gave a sharp cry of pain as the bolt dissipated into the ground.

A naiad created a staff of water, which she flung to Tuathal, who caught it without taking his eyes from the Unseelie king.

The battle raged for hours.

After some time, Claire understood Tuathal's plan. He was fighting merely to hold ground as long as possible. It was obvious the Seelie could not possibly win.

Though strengthened by the foinse cumhachta, Tuathal was still wounded and weakened both magically and physically. There was, of course, no time to for him to recover. He fought a delaying action, holding the Unseelie at bay long enough for the palace and royal city to be evacuated.

The Unseelie side seethed backward and forward like ocean waves as the tide rises; each time they receded, but not quite as far. Tuathal retreated before them a step at a time, avoiding the weapons with bizarre, unsettling grace, sending back bolts of lightning from the ends of his fingers at the most aggressive of the Unseelie fighters.

Most of the forces appeared to be armed with weapons of bronze and wood, though some few on both sides had blades of oighear that gleamed clear and bright in the sun. Lightning was not a common weapon, though the Unseelie king was not the only warrior on his side who sent bolts toward Tuathal.

A group of six beasts attacked Tuathal at once, and he fought them off with the staff of water, which flashed from within as if electrified. Four of the creatures retreated, limping; the other two lay dead at Tuathal's feet, and he retreated a few more steps, breathing heavily.

Arrows suddenly rained down upon them, bronze arrowheads ringing against bronze shields. The little green fairy hissed in fury, tiny teeth bared at the Unseelie. "Cowards! Not a one of them would face us in single combat!"

A minotaur roared in outrage and lunged toward them, crossing the intervening space in a split second. It raised an enormous oighear mace above Claire's head, only to be knocked sideways by a blast of some invisible force. Claire would have thanked whomever had saved her, but another wave of combat surged closer and Faolan hauled her backward by one arm.

The Unseelie, somewhat to Claire's surprise, were not noticeably less attractive than the Seelie. Both sides the line included terrifying creatures of many species, including pale, sharp-featured Fae, magnificent centaurs, and smaller fairies buzzing in the air, dodging arrows and blasts of lightning.

The little green fairy grumbled angrily in Claire's ear. "He's stalling, but it won't last much longer."

Claire looked up and gasped. Behind the first row of Unseelie, the landscape seemed to be darker, the grassy hills covered by milling hordes of Unseelie forces waiting for their opportunity to attack. The forests beyond the hills bristled with glinting spear tips, and sunlight glinted on bronze helms.

"There are so many," she whispered, cold fear threading her veins.

Faolan growled, "He should retreat. We've done all we can and more."

The Unseelie must have outnumbered the Seelie by twenty to one. Claire glanced around at the few Seelie and realized her estimate was far too low. *Hundreds to one. Or thousands to one.*

She wondered, for an instant, why the Unseelie didn't simply overwhelm the Seelie by sheer numbers. But then she looked at the motionless bodies on the ground, and Tuathal's blazing eyes, and she understood.

Tuathal was directing the battle to minimize Seelie casualties, trying to save as many lives as possible. The Unseelie let him stall; time was on their side. Their forces strengthened moment by moment. Hundreds upon hundreds of additional warriors had arrived in the last five minutes. The front line of the Unseelie was constantly changing, each fighter darting forward to strike at Tuathal or one of the Seelie, then retreating behind his fellows.

The Seelie line was exhausted.

The Seelie moved forward to surround Tuathal in a protective ring. Faolan darted between larger Fae to shout into Tuathal's face.

"You can't hold out much longer. I see what you are doing, Your Majesty."

The king shook his head and then wavered as if the motion had made him dizzy. "Give them a little more time."

"Do you see how many there are?" a dryad cried, his limbs waving in distress. "They will slaughter us!"

"Leave then." Tuathal set his jaw grimly. "You're dismissed with all honor."

The dryad's voice rose in shock. "Your Majesty! That was uncalled for, and I will die here beside you unless you command me leave. I would have thought you'd have a better opinion of my loyalty than that."

Tuathal pressed his hands over his face; a shallow cut at his hairline smudged blue blood over his hands. "Ruarc, they want the palace, for reasons you well understand. I will delay them as long as possible. You will leave—you will *all* leave—when I give the command. "

"And what of you?"

The Unseelie roared and beat upon their shields with their swords, and Claire's whispered question was lost in the deafening clamor. But Tuathal glanced at her, meeting her eyes for just an instant before he looked away.

He squared his shoulders and ran his hand over his face and through his hair, brushing the blood away from his eyes. It left a streak in his white-blond hair, which stood out from his head like thistledown. Perhaps it wasn't as improbable as Claire had first thought, if he had lightning in his veins.

"Why do they want the palace?" Claire whispered to the little fairy.

"Symbolism, of course. If Taibhseach fights his way to the palace, kills everyone in it, and takes the throne over the corpses of the Seelie defenders, it will strengthen his hold upon our people and lands. But if His Majesty holds out long enough for the palace to be evacuated, and Taibhseach conquers an empty structure, it will weaken his hold. His Majesty, of course, will..." The little fairy cried suddenly, "Look out!"

The Unseelie king himself struck at them, cleaving his way through the fairies guarding Tuathal with horrifying ease. Tuathal followed his adversary's sword with his hand, anticipating each strike and transforming them, somehow, into nonlethal blows. A heavyset dwarf went flying rather than being cut in half.

In moments, the Unseelie king loomed over Tuathal.

"Leave now." Tuathal said softly, his voice cutting through the cheers and jeers of the Unseelie to reach Claire's ears.

The Unseelie king burst into laughter more horrifying than any threat. "Or what?" He grinned. His teeth were sharpened into points.

Tuathal raised one eyebrow and murmured, "I wasn't speaking to you."

The Unseelie king struck at him with a burst of power. Tuathal raised a hand to block it. Perhaps it dissipated the force a little—rather than killing Tuathal outright, it sent him reeling backward.

"Leave *now*!" Tuathal cried, and there was the sound of shattered glass in his voice.

Faolan grabbed Claire's arm. "Come."

"I'm staying." The words came without thought, and as she heard them aloud, she knew they were true.

There was an instant of silence, and Tuathal's eyes met hers as he straightened.

Everything seemed frozen, as if she and Tuathal existed in a little bubble of time, separated from the clash of weapons and magic and terror for an instant. Later Claire wasn't sure whether it was merely that Tuathal moved to her and spoke so quickly, or whether he had really wrapped them in a protective cocoon in which time moved differently for those few seconds.

"Go, Claire." He was breathing heavily, his words barely audible over the pounding of her heart. "I'm finished." His lips rose in a grimace that might have been an attempt at a smile. "Faolan can send you home. I want you safe."

"No. This is my battle too, and my place is here."

The lightning in his eyes was dulled, but it flashed now, and he opened his mouth.

"This is my right and just service! You will not deny me it, will you?" she cried. She hated that her voice shook, but she did not look away. Perhaps it would have been easier for him to argue if she had not held his gaze, but she would not give him that.

A muscle in Tuathal's jaw twitched, and he hesitated, his gaze softening. "I thank you for that, but you owe such service only until the bitter end. This is that time."

Claire managed a smile, though fear made her skin prickle with chill. "Everything has an end, but I don't think this one is entirely bitter. I will stay with you."

Tuathal's eyes flickered in surprise and perhaps grief. "So be it." He bowed, his head lowered for longer than she thought necessary. He started to straighten, then his knees buckled and he fell to one knee on the ground.

He reached for her hand. "May I?"

"Whatever you need," she said.

He pulled, and he pulled, and he *pulled,* until the very fiber of her being, her essence, was stretched into nothingness, until hope and thought and honor and courage were sifted like sand, drawn fine as gossamer into magic threads binding her to the world, until the threads ripped and tore, floating away into nothingness.

The world spiraled away, and for a moment she was gone.

Then they were in the palace. Claire hadn't seen this room before, but the grandeur of it, and the magnificent throne a few feet away, proclaimed it Tuathal's throne room. A vaulted ceiling soared above them, and graceful columns stretched before them, carved with intricate scenes that seemed somehow alive.

Tuathal leaned his back against a column and slid down to sit heavily on the floor. His chest heaved, and he gasped, "I'm sorry for that. Had to get you away."

Claire blinked, feeling each part of her body with new appreciation; her fingers and toes, her eyebrows, her tongue that seemed too large in her dry mouth. "What is happening?"

"I am spent," Tuathal breathed. His head lolled backward against the column. "If this is the end, I would say to you—"

A crack like lightning cut off his words. The Unseelie king stepped into the middle of the room, power crackling off him, filling the air with ozone. Claire couldn't tell whether it was magic or terror that made her hair stand on end.

The throne room behind the Unseelie king had vanished, lost in shadow or perhaps black smoke.

The Unseelie king spoke in a voice like thunder, "Rise, Tuathal, and let me kill you on your feet quickly. Or if you prefer, die sitting down, slowly, ingloriously, and painfully. But die now, you will."

Tuathal blinked slowly. His eyes were dulled, but there was a flash in them that gave Claire hope, for an instant. Her hope shattered when Tuathal tensed, as if he wanted to rise, and then let out a soft breath and remained on the floor.

The Unseelie king gave a nasty, feral grin, showing his sharpened teeth, and stepped forward.

I have to do something.

The naiad had been reluctant to fight when she didn't know exactly what she faced. Maybe that was typical of creatures that could live thousands of years… unless they made a mistake. Bluffing seemed to be Claire's only option.

She stepped in front of Tuathal and said, "You seem to be overlooking me. I'm here now, and I'm in a foul mood. I suggest you leave."

The Unseelie king's dull orange eyes flicked over her, hard and cold and leaving her feeling somehow slimy. "You are all that Tuathal has to stand for him now."

"I am more than enough!"

The Unseelie king laughed softly. "I see a little of what Tuathal saw in you. You are quite striking in your fury, but surely you see the futility of your position, and the humor in this. Don't you?"

Claire narrowed her eyes. "I'm not amused. I am rather irritated, though."

"You have no concept of the powers you are dealing with. Your courage is amusing, but I will not be… um… distracted…"

He had paused when Claire, remembering her butterknife, had drawn it from its sheath in her pocket and deliberately licked it. The Seelie court had been nonplussed by her doing so earlier, and she hoped he would be similarly intimidated. To her surprise, her hand did not shake.

Taibhseach's eyes narrowed, and he studied her.

Giving him time to consider how best to kill her did not seem wise, so she took a step forward, hoping he would back away.

He did not step back, and his amusement disappeared. "An iron blade. You are human. I have killed humans, including some with iron blades."

I can't back down. I can't even show that I'm scared, or he's won. "Does that include any that have carried the foinse cumhachta? I think not. I'm going to poke this cold iron into you until I find a tender spot, and you're welcome to prove you have the power to stop me."

"I can kill you from here, without even coming close. My power staggered Tuathal; you would be killed instantly!"

Yet he did not advance, only tensed his shoulders as if he were imagining ripping her apart.

Claire gasped as she finally understood something; perhaps it was not everything, but it was *something*. Tuathal had said she would give him power over her. He'd said he could not bring her to Faerie without her permission. He had waited for her to say her wishes out loud before… well, everything. And none of the other creatures had cast a spell on her, despite their physical attacks. She said to herself, wonderingly, "You… *you have no power over me!*"

The Unseelie king snarled and drew a long bronze knife. "I would bet my skill and speed with a knife against yours, though!"

He's actually taking me seriously! Claire's thoughts raced. *He's right. Even with iron, I can't win a fight against him. He's hesitating because he's uncertain. I need to push now, while I have a slim chance. The knife doesn't really matter… and Seelie don't really understand lies or bluffing. Does he?*

Claire slid the knife back into the sheath in her pocket and stood straighter. "All right. No knife for me then. Let's do this. Me, unarmed, against you and your knife. Let's see what tricks we each have up our sleeves." She smiled slowly and spread her arms, showing her empty hands. "I can take you like this."

The Unseelie king's eyes widened. He paused, and then said, "I admit I am impressed by your courage. I think you are being untruthful. But... I see no reason to test you. If I kill you, I win. If you depart, I win just as well, and I gain nothing by killing you. You may go. I will not pursue you, nor attack your people."

The idea of fleeing was like a siren call, the promise of impossible safety.

From the floor, Tuathal whispered, "His promises are not to be trusted. You are safer facing him here than letting him choose the time and place."

Claire wondered whether he had figured out that she was bluffing and was intending to help her, or whether he was merely telling her that leaving was not really an option. It made no difference, though.

The Unseelie king smiled more broadly, malice glinting in his eyes. "I think you lie, as humans are known to do. But you are beneath me. I am a king, with all the authority that implies. I have an elite guard and army for a reason. The guard is here to bear witness to my killing Tuathal, but I think I will share a little." He gestured, and the smoke behind him cleared, revealing some fifty terrifying beasts of various species.

The front row was composed of minotaurs, the largest of which was nearly as tall as Taibhseach himself. It stood upright on hooved feet, with the head and horns of a bull and furred, clawed paws gripping an enormous axe with a head of oighear. The head of the axe alone must have weighed close to one hundred pounds, but the beast handled it as if it were feather light.

The Unseelie king stepped a little to the side and gestured. "You, Bródúil, cleave her."

The minotaur locked its coal-black eyes on her and roared. It leaped forward, swinging the axe far too fast for her to even flinch backward.

No!

She raised her right arm in a futile, reflexive attempt to block the massive blade.

Time seemed to slow around her.

Light glinted on the oighear blade, sharp as a razor and bright as diamond, as it descended toward her head.

She closed her eyes, willing the blade to stop, but felt the sting of the blade slicing through the skin of her raised arm. A gush of hot liquid splashed her face and shoulder.

But… she was not dead.

She licked the blood from her lips… no, it wasn't blood. Water? She looked down at her missing arm.

It wasn't missing. Cut, yes. A clean, deep cut slashed across her forearm. It bled freely, but it wasn't spurting; it must not have been deep enough to cut an artery.

The haft of the axe lay on the floor, missing the head. She was standing in a small cloud of… steam? And a large puddle of water.

The minotaur staggered away from her; it gave a strangled cry of fear from deep within its throat. White showed around both its dark irises.

Claire looked down at herself again. She appeared to have been drenched in a large bucket of water.

What could…?

She stole a glance at Tuathal, wondering if he had saved her again. But he seemed as startled as anyone.

Wait. The axe cut me. It made contact with my blood, and the oighear blade instantly flashed to warm water. Was it the iron in my blood? No, Tuathal has touched my blood and was not burned. My fingers were bleeding when I touched the oighear manacles and they did not dissolve. But… She glanced at the minotaur again. It, and the rest of the Unseelie, appeared to still be frozen in shock. *It was something in my blood, anyway. Something happened. Perhaps it will happen again, or at least they'll believe it when I threaten that it will. Bluff harder!*

She looked at her arm. Blood ran down the pale skin to her fingers and dripped to the floor, diluted by the water that drenched her.

Then she looked past the king at the Unseelie guard, meeting their eyes one by one. In a quiet, reasonable voice she said, "I suggest you all flee while you can. Your king would sacrifice you to fight battles he fears to." The monsters looked at Taibhseach and then glanced at each other. Feet shifted uneasily.

Are they afraid of me? I hope so.

She flung her arms up, as if to scatter a flock of birds, and screamed, "FLEE, I say!"

Blood drops flung from the tips of her fingers and scattered sparsely over them. The minotaur in front scrabbled back away from her, and the others flinched backward. Their fear turned to screaming terror as the drops began to burn into them as if they were made of molten iron.

The room was suddenly, shockingly quiet.

They had fled the same way they had come, leaving the throne room empty but for Taibhseach, Claire, and Tuathal.

Taibhseach looked at Claire uncertainly, his massive fingers gripping the hilt of his knife spasmodically.

Tuathal coughed out a strained laugh. "It's over, Taibhseach. You can feel both our armies as well as I can. Your guards spent much of their power jumping all the way back to your army and are rushing to the healing tents… those who can still travel on their own, anyway. I feel panic spreading." He gasped for breath and smiled, his eyes glinting dangerously. "I am sure word of the hero who handles iron with her bare hands, stood off Taibhseach unarmed, and routed his whole personal guard by spewing burning death from her fingertips is spreading like wildfire. Your army is already vanishing. They will be scattered to the winds within minutes. You should leave now, while you can. The war is over, and you have lost."

Taibhseach shifted, his dull eyes intent on Claire. "I was just thinking that the only thing that would stop the desertion was if I produced her head immediately. I think a bronze knife would do the job quite well."

Tuathal rose, one hand braced against the wall. "Are you certain of that?" he murmured, his voice laced with menace. You'll notice she has retrieved her iron weapon, and you'll be fighting both of us, you know. I'm growing stronger by the minute."

Taibhseach gave a low grunt. "I still calculate the odds in my favor. She is quite slow, and I think more fragile than she has let on. And you can barely stand."

Claire gave a snort of derision, but Tuathal's voice cut through the air before she could think of anything to say. "You should reconsider. *My* personal guard, who can also tell things have changed, will be here in minutes, closely followed by the rest of my army. Even if you were to defeat us, you would not be unscathed. You would not be able to outrun them."

"You both would still be dead."

"As would you. Since you are trying to take the throne, and we are trying to prevent that, that would still be our victory. At this point, you cannot win. The only question is whether you die or not." Tuathal smiled mirthlessly. "Besides, you should not assume you will kill us. I think we have both been surprised more than once in this meeting. Another time is not out of the question, is it?" He paused. Claire couldn't tell whether it was to give Taibhseach time to consider the threat, or whether to catch his breath. "Consider," he continued, "You'll notice I am again wearing the foinse cumhachta. So, what is that around her neck?"

Claire realized with a start that she seemed to be wearing the necklace she had worn for years. But she had given it back to Tuathal! Hadn't she?

It seemed warm against her skin, and glowed with a soft yellow light as she looked at it.

She looked up.

Taibhseach was gone.

Claire turned to Tuathal, who fell back against the wall and slid down it, gasping.

"Are you all right?"

Tuathal gave her a sharp-toothed smile. Then his eyelids drifted closed, and his head flopped sideways against the wall as he lost consciousness.

Claire fell to her knees beside him, darkness flickering at the edges of her vision.

The sound of a door at the far end of the throne room announced the arrival of the Seelie army as everything seemed to grow dim.

CHAPTER 34

"Such courage! You became the hero you wished to be." The soft words drifted through Claire's mind, and she smiled, or she intended to smile, at the pride and love thrumming through the words.

She woke, and slept, and woke again.

The air was gold and scented with fuchsia blooms by her bedside.

She slept and woke again.

Silver moonlight slanted across the silk sheets on her bed, and she watched the fabric move as she breathed.

She slept and woke again.

The blue-gold-silver of early morning light filled the room with hope.

She slept and woke again.

Was it the same morning, or a different one?

Claire opened her eyes, feeling like a seed buried for months upon months, finally feeling the warmth of spring on her tender skin.

The room was made of sunlight and gauzy silk, gold sunlight glinting on exquisite gold sconces on the walls. It was spacious, though Claire could barely see the walls from her position nestled into fluffy pillows.

A familiar voice that she could not at first identify said, "Well, that took long enough."

Faolan's face hovered over her. He had a bandage around his head and one arm in a sling, and she frowned in confusion, trying to remember how and why he had been injured.

His face looked different than she remembered, and something about it seemed to change as she studied him. There was no obvious change she could identify, but the impression she got by looking at his face was somehow different. His eyes no longer seemed narrowed in suspicion, but narrowed in focus; his tight, twisted mouth seemed pinched with long-held frustration or pain rather than anger.

"You're awake," he said. "How do you feel?"

She licked her lips, which were dry and felt oddly distant. Her toes obeyed when she attempted to wiggle them, though they too felt distant and strange. Nothing particularly hurt. "All right, I guess. Not worth much, though."

He gave a bark of laughter, and the smile lingered on his face.

"You look different when you smile," she murmured. "Nicer."

"Most people do," he countered. Then he sobered. "Tuathal has not yet woken. He gave more of himself than he took from you, and he was, if you recall, in rather worse shape when you began." He sighed, his eyes flicking away as if he did not want to meet her gaze. "There is nothing we can do for him now. We must wait."

Something in his voice made the air seem suddenly colder, and Claire whispered, "What do you mean?"

Faolan's gaze met hers. "He has not woken since your battle with Taibhseach. The two of you vanquished the Unseelie forces."

She frowned faintly, trying to remember exactly what had happened. "In a dream? Or was that real?"

Faolan shrugged one narrow shoulder. "Dreams and reality are not so disconnected as you humans seem to think. Tuathal's title The Lord of Dreams is not mere vanity." His eyes flashed a dark satisfaction. "Was it not through your dreams that he first understood you?"

"But how is he?"

The imp's expression grew grim. "He is alive. That is all that can be said with any certainty, and that may not last long."

"I want to see him."

Faolan's dark eyebrows rose, and he hesitated, then said, "Perhaps you can do something for him that we have been unable to accomplish."

He pulled a little cord by the bedside that Claire had not yet noticed, and a moment later two Fae girls entered with deep, graceful bows and a soft murmur of words in a language Claire did not understand.

Faolan spoke to them quietly, and after a moment they nodded and began to help Claire from the bed. She felt slightly dizzy at first, but the feeling passed with a few deep breaths.

"Was I hurt?" Claire asked, looking down at herself.

"Not in body," Faolan said softly. He glanced to the side, then met her eyes. "I hesitate to speak for His Majesty, but given his…" His mouth worked for a moment, "Given his inability to speak on his own behalf at this point, I will venture to speak for him." Faolan looked down again, his uninjured hand clenched by his side. "Magic is like a three-legged stool. One must have native ability, will, and skill. Most humans utterly lack ability and thus they can do no magic. Those who have some small native ability often do not have sufficient strength of will; humans are flighty creatures, and rare is the man who can focus his entire heart, mind, and body to one purpose for more than an instant or two. Most of those few humans who touch magic, by accident or intent, quickly go mad.

"Everyone born in Faerie has some degree of native ability, but the extent of such ability varies. Skill must be learned; some learn more readily than others. Strength of will is important. The king was weakened by his long imprisonment and the injuries he suffered, both physical and magical, during his torment. His will has always been strong, but with his mind shattered and heart hidden away, he could not rely upon the strength to which he was accustomed. Also, the Unseelie were strengthened by their months of victories, and you may remember that the war had not been going particularly well even before His Majesty was captured."

Guilt sat like a stone in Claire's stomach, and she gasped at the weight of it, cold and hard and bitter, spreading through her like poison.

Faolan glanced at her. "Don't take the entire weight of war upon you. It was brewing for a millennium before you were born, and fought for a decade before you carried the king's power. There is guilt to be born, but only a little of it is yours."

As he spoke, the Fae servants dressed Claire with skillful speed, wrapping her in a sleeveless dressing gown that was thick with embroidery and cinched comfortably around her waist.

"I'd offer you a meal, but…" Faolan sighed heavily. "Only his Majesty can travel between worlds, and that not without considerable effort. And fairy food has consequences, you know."

"You gave me food before. I lost it."

"I gave you the illusion of food, spelled to give you comfort and strength. It would not prevent you from starving or dying of dehydration, but it would have allowed you to suffer less while you did so. You needed the encouragement, and illusion was all we could offer. Besides, we did not expect you to be in Faerie for long."

Claire swallowed, pondering the familiar emptiness of her stomach and the weakness that made her limbs feel heavy and her head feel light. "I'm all right," she said finally. "I'm hungry but it's not like I'll die of it any time soon."

Faolan smiled, his eyes melancholy. "You have grown, you know. Years ago you would have whined and blamed me."

"I would, wouldn't I?" Claire smiled back at him, seeing the nobility in his face that she'd missed in their first meeting. "Thanks for believing in me."

He snorted. "I didn't. I believed in Tuathal. But he was right about you, even if it took longer than he'd hoped." He nodded toward the door. "Come."

He led her down a long hallway with several other doors, all closed.

Claire had to stop and lean against the wall once, when her vision seemed to dim and her head felt like it was floating away. She put her hands on her knees, her shoulder against the solid stone wall, and breathed slowly. Faolan offered her his shoulder to lean on, but she shook her head. He was, when she actually looked at him, rather pale himself, and the easy pace he set may not have been entirely for her benefit.

At last they reached Tuathal's door.

"Tuathal is... he's..." He cleared his throat, "Well, you'll see."

Faolan put his hand on the handle and glanced at her. He opened his mouth, as if he wanted to say something more, but then just shook his head.

He opened the door.

TUATHAL LAY IN THE center of a large bed with the covers pulled down to his waist. He wore a white shirt that buttoned up the front; it was of a fine, light fabric that might have been silk, or something like it, that draped over him loosely. The shirt was open at the neck, showing the faint pulse in his throat and the edge of a bandage that covered the wound on his shoulder.

"Is he alive?" whispered Claire. He was breathing so shallowly and slowly that she could not tell, at first, whether his chest was moving at all. His arms were laid carefully at his sides atop the blanket. The position looked slightly unnatural; she couldn't imagine anyone would really sleep that way. He was, now that she saw him in repose, even thinner than she'd realized. The dull hunger in her belly felt heavy and leaden, as if she did not have the right to feel hunger pangs because he had not eaten in far longer.

Dizziness rose, and the world seemed to spin around her. Faolan cried something that she could not understand and clutched at her arm, but she stumbled to her knees beside the bed, darkness encroaching on her vision.

She bowed her head to the mattress and let the darkness take her.

CHAPTER 35

Tuathal stood at a window in his study, his head resting against the stone window frame, his neck gracefully curved as if to show off his strange beauty. She thought suddenly that he seemed refined rather than sullied by suffering, and she resolutely squashed her sudden flash of jealousy.

"Well? Aren't you going to wake up?" Claire said. "Everyone is waiting for you to."

He blinked, as if he'd been lost in thought. "Good evening, Claire." He turned to face her with a faint, melancholy smile. "Why are you here?"

"To wake you up, of course."

He raised one eyebrow. "Don't you think I'd be awake if I could be? Whatever else you may think of me, I do hope you understand that I take my responsibilities seriously."

"Why can't you wake up?" She stepped closer to him, the line of her body almost, but not quite, pressed against his, the space between them electric with tension.

He gave a gentle, elegant cough of laughter. "Because I'm nearly dead. You gave me my mind and my power back, and for that I thank you. You did, at the end, become the hero I knew you could be. I imagine that for generations my people will enjoy magnificent tapestries of the Iron Queen shooting sparks from her fingertips, routing armies with the fire in her blood." He smiled, a grim satisfaction in his eyes, and brushed the back of his fingers over her cheek. "And, whatever offenses you may hold against me, I did grant your wish."

Her eyes widened. "Which one?"

"To be the hero."

She wondered wildly whether his eyes were always that bright, or whether they merely looked that way because of the tears filling her own eyes. "You did." Her throat felt tight with emotion. "Why did you do it? Why me?"

"Because you had magnificent dreams, Claire." He cupped her cheek with his long fingers and let his thumb trace the line of her cheekbone, then down to her lips, the touch as gentle as the whisper of silk over the sensitive skin. "You dreamed of being more than you were. All I did was give you the opportunity to become yourself. We needed you as much… no, more than you needed us." His smile shone with pride.

She closed her eyes.

His hand was warm and strong, his fingers feather-light against her skin. Then he pulled away, and she imagined there was effort in the movement, though she couldn't tell whether it was physical effort or merely the effort of controlling his emotion.

"Are you not coming back?"

"I *can't*, Claire." His voice had a faint edge of roughness, and she opened her eyes to try to read his expression. He looked away, unwilling to meet her gaze, and caught his breath in what might have been a sob. Then his jaw firmed, and he met her eyes, his lips curving upward in a smile. "I don't fear death. But I thank you for making the last moments sweeter with your presence."

The grief that had been a cold stone in her chest became a hot, burning anger that would not let her accept his death.

"I wish you'd wake up!" She caught his hand in hers, twining her fingers between his as if to keep him grounded. "I wish you'd live."

His eyes widened in surprise. "You do?"

"Yes!" She glared at him. "You arrogant, obstinate man! Of course I do."

He chuckled, the sound soft and sweet as a summer breeze. "Well, then. That changes *everything*."

CLAIRE SUCKED IN A breath, disoriented and cold. Her knees were bruised, and her face was pressed into something soft.

A small, strong hand pulled at her shoulder, and she realized Faolan stood just beside her, trying, with little success, to maneuver her into a heavy velvet chair beside the bed.

"Thank you," she croaked. "Did I faint?"

"Yes." Faolan was frowning fiercely. "I should not have let you out of bed." He looked again at the king. "Then again, maybe it was exactly the right thing to do. I have no idea what just happened, but he seems better somehow."

Claire stood only to collapse into the chair. "I still feel rather dizzy," she breathed. The room seemed suffused with a soft golden glow, and she gazed dully at Tuathal's body. He looked different than before, and she studied his face trying to find some sign of life. After a moment, she realized that his near hand was upturned, his fingers slightly curled as if in expectation.

The lump in her throat nearly choked her, and she leaned forward to put her hand in his.

PERHAPS SHE FELL ASLEEP, or perhaps she only lost track of time. Afterwards she couldn't be sure how long their fingers were entwined, motionless.

Frost-kissed eyelashes opened, and his eyes met hers with a spark of electric desire.

You woke up for me.

CHAPTER 36

A soft knock sounded on Claire's door.

"Come in," she said. Her voice sounded weak and distant in her ears, and she cleared her throat. "Come in!"

The door opened soundlessly, and a young Fae woman bowed deeply. "I am instructed to make you ready for the banquet this evening."

"A banquet?"

"To celebrate the end of the war and His Majesty's return to us." The Fae smiled gently. "His Majesty sent you this." She handed Claire a folded paper sealed with red wax.

Claire opened the seal carefully, smiling at the formality of the paper and seal.

Forgive me for imposing upon you with the expectation of your attendance at the banquet. I realize you must be anxious to return to your world, but I am not yet strong enough to open the passage for you. And, since you must be trapped here for some short time while I regain a little strength, it would do me great honor, and greatly please my subjects, if you would attend the celebration.

With utmost respect,

Tuathal

"All right," Claire murmured. She frowned at the thought of enduring a banquet while her limbs were weak with hunger, but then realized the thought didn't disturb her as much as she had expected.

What is a little more discomfort in order to finish well? I can endure this small thing without complaining.

She smiled at the servant more warmly. "I'm ready. What should I do?"

The girl bowed deeply again, then set to work with practiced efficiency. She brushed Claire's skin with a soft, scented cloth before slipping a silk chemise over her head. Next came layers of silk skirts, an underdress that cinched her narrow waist and flared pleasingly over her hips, and a velvet overdress with an intricately laced bodice.

When the servant pulled the laces tight, Claire had a moment of dizziness and clutched at the nearby chair.

"The dizziness will pass, my lady." The servant's voice shook. "His Majesty was quite distraught that he could not yet travel to your world. He tried, you know, this morning."

"Did he?" breathed Claire. *He probably shouldn't have tried yet. He's been mostly dead all week.* She took a deep breath and waited while the spots cleared from her vision.

The Fae girl nodded, her lips pressed together as if she were trying not to cry.

"I'm all right," Claire said. She forced a smile, and then found that it wasn't as forced as she'd thought at first.

Claire followed the girl through marble-tile corridors to the banquet hall. The door was grand, and two uniformed Fae servants bowed deeply when they opened it for her.

Claire's eyes widened. The room was enormous, and clearly meant for hosting magnificent feasts. Massive double doors at the far end stood open, and the cavernous space between was filled with long wooden tables filled with place settings and serving dishes. Crowds of exquisitely dressed Fae and fairy creatures of several species were filling the seats, while conversation filled the air with a dull roar.

A servant guided Claire to a low dais at one end of the room. Tuathal stood to greet her with a deep, graceful bow over her hand, brushing a delicate kiss over her fingers. As he straightened, his face went a particularly alarming shade of gray, and he seemed to sway a little before his fingers tightened on hers.

"Why don't we sit down?" Claire murmured.

"An excellent idea."

Their chairs were large and covered in deep burgundy velvet with gilt accents on dark carved wood. They were not exactly thrones, but they were certainly the seats of honor. Despite the formality, Claire found the seat surprisingly comfortable.

A servant bent to speak to Tuathal, and he nodded, murmuring an answer.

Servants brought out food and drink for the guests, and the conversation continued. Musicians played softly in one corner.

No servants brought food to Claire and Tuathal. She glanced at him out of the corner of her eye, surreptitiously studying the sharply drawn line of his jaw and the shadows under his eyes.

Finally she turned to whisper to him, "I think you should eat something. Just because I can't eat doesn't mean you shouldn't."

The thin skin around his eyes crinkled as he smiled in surprise. "I ate a little earlier. It would be discourteous to indulge while you must abstain." His lips pressed together in a white line, and he swallowed hard. "I offer my apologies for that. I had hoped to provide something for you, but I must recover a little more."

The raw grief in his voice made her frown and turn to face him more directly. Her eyes widened when she saw the darkness in his eyes, the pain in what should have been a happy moment.

"I'm all right, Tuathal. I can wait a little longer. I'm just hungry, not starving. A few hours won't hurt anything, and I wouldn't miss this." When she smiled, she meant it, and her heart rose at the relief that flickered in his eyes.

She twined her fingers between his, intending merely to comfort him. He bent to kiss her hand, his lips warm and featherlight on the back of her knuckles.

His fingers fit around hers so well that she did not immediately draw away. After being so long at odds, after such terrifying adventures, the comfort in his touch surprised her.

She looked across the room, watching everyone enjoying the banquet. Fresh bread filled the air with its warm, yeasty scent, mixed with roasted meat of several types, the heavy scent of baked apples, and a dozen other dishes Claire couldn't begin to identify. The guests were all noble, or at least wealthy; their clothes glittered with gold and silver, with fresh flowers and silk, with green leaves woven into flowing cloaks and crystal blooms glinting in the whorls of intricate hairstyles.

Tuathal was similarly adorned, his gaunt frame suddenly elegant in leather, silk, and shadow. A golden crown hung carelessly on the back of his chair, as if he could not be bothered to wear it. *It's unnecessary. How could anyone doubt he's a king?* Her surreptitious glance apparently did not go unnoticed, because he met her gaze and smiled, light dancing in his eyes.

A cry rang out, and the room fell into sudden silence.

The kelpie stood a short distance in front of their dais, both arms raised. "Listen, guests of His Majesty, King of the Seelie, to the tale of the Lord of Dreams and the Iron Queen! You will remember this and repeat it, so that a thousand years from now not a single point will be forgotten!"

A low murmur filled the air, and the kelpie lowered his arms and drew a deep breath.

A fairy who sat just in front of where the kelpie stood turned around in his chair. "You are not a noble to command us! I doubt you are even a bard." His lips curved in a smile that held a slightly contemptuous edge. "Why should we listen to tales you spin?"

The kelpie turned and flung his tunic back from his shoulder. A bright red mark roughly the shape of the blade of a butter knife marred the smooth, pale skin just below his shoulder blade. "I bear the mark of the Iron Queen! I will speak and you will listen!"

Silence filled the hall for a moment.

A centaur a short distance away cleared his throat; the deep rumble echoed in the room. He said mildly, "Point of order: *Technically* she is not *the* queen. Or even a queen at all, to my knowledge."

The kelpie stared at him a moment, and then gestured wordlessly toward the dais where Claire and Tuathal sat quietly.

Everyone turned toward them and scrutinized them briefly. The centaur said, with a soft chuckle, "I withdraw my comment. Please proceed."

Heat suffused Claire's face, and she pulled her hand away. For a moment, she didn't dare glance at Tuathal, but then she snuck a peek.

His face was almost, but not quite, impassive; his lips tightened as if he were trying to hide a smile.

"Here now the tale of the Lord of Dreams and the Iron Queen!" the kelpie cried.

"When His Majesty the old king passed to dust and starlight, his beloved son wielded the full might of the foinse cumhachta. Unfortunately, there was no one found in all of Faerie other than His Majesty the young king who was capable of accepting the foinse cumhachta, so it could not be fully employed.

"Even under the old king and the young prince, now His Majesty, the Seelie were barely holding ground against the Unseelie. His Majesty is strong, but without a partner of his heart, he could not fully use the power he inherited, and it became clear that the Seelie kingdom would fall eventually.

"His Majesty believed that someone, somewhere, could join with him and save the Seelie, so he… called out... for any such to come forth from wherever they might be.

"Someone—only one—answered. She *wished* that she be the one who could help.

"The king saw that she was not capable.

"Nevertheless, she was the only one. The king, young in years but bearing the weight of the power, gave her his heart despite her shortcomings, and... she *grew*. Though it took years, she became more where she needed to be more and discarded that of herself which was a hindrance. It was a near thing in timing, but she became more than even the king had hoped for.

"At the time of Great Confrontation, she was not yet ready.

"She bore the Shining Knife, the knife that gleams like silver, burns like iron, yet neither tarnishes nor rusts; but she had not yet touched magic directly. The king was utterly spent and helpless, and all his forces had retired from the field at his command. Against her were arrayed the Unseelie king Taibhseach, and his elite guard, and close behind him his army... the army that had battered the combined forces of the Seelie kingdom for over ten years.

"Yet, she faced down the Seelie king, challenging him to single combat bearing only the Shining Knife... and he was afraid.

"He offered her a pact: Leave, taking the Shining Knife with her, and he would not pursue her or attack her people.

"She laid aside the Shining Knife and challenged him again, having no weapon, only bare hands and her Will... *and still he feared her!*

"He ordered the chief of his personal guard, a Minotaur, veteran of a thousand years of war, wielding TuaUafásach, the great axe forged of oighear, borne by the head of his line since his great great grandfathers and which has slain dragons, to cleave her from head to toe.

"She did not back one step, nor try to evade the blow, but stood fast. The indestructible axe fell on her, and it was the axe that shattered against her upraised arm! That blow, from an axe which has felled dragons, served only to mark her arm with a cut that became the annihilation of the Unseelie armies!

"She bid all the Guard to flee. They hesitated, and she encouraged their decision by sprinkling them with blood from the Cut, blood that burned like molten iron… more, even, because as they fled in terror, sparks leapt from their wounds and spread to others, injuring all who were touched by the terror of the queen! The only defense was to run away (the fire did not pursue those who fled far), or to stand without fear… and that is mere speculation, for no one tested it. The entire army was either burned to death or fled.

"She turned again to the Unseelie king. But now, she picked up the Shining Knife, and having touched magic through the Power given to her by His Majesty, she was at last of one heart with the King, and he, recovering, stood with her.

"The Unseelie king, his Guard either fleeing or dead where they stood, his army in full flight, admitted defeat and departed in haste.

"Hear this, remember this, and tell your children and their children, that this story might live for the ages!"

A roar of approval rolled over the hall, deafening and joyous. Applause and shouts of acclaim echoed for long minutes.

Claire sat in stunned silence, the cheers and shouting a distant cacophony behind the clamor of her thoughts.

Artistic license in victory stories was one thing, but this? This was absolutely ridiculous! Her eyebrows drew downward in a ferocious scowl. They all seemed to expect her to become queen! *His* queen!

In fact, everyone seemed to think she already was.

But what about her feelings? No one had even asked or consulted her! Shouldn't she have a say? Shouldn't he at least *ask* her?

She drew in a deep breath, feeling righteous anger welling up in her chest. She turned toward Tuathal, and he inclined his head to hear her words over the cheers still ringing in the air. And, with an uncomfortable rush of understanding, she realized that he had done virtually nothing else for the last eight years *except* ask her, over and over.

Claire met his eyes, the lightning flash of blue-gold-silver that set her blood racing and her heart aflame, then leaned toward him, the spider silk of his hair brushing her cheek as she whispered in his ear, "If you have any appetite left, I think I would like a bite of that feast now."

His gaze, which had been cast across the celebrating guests, snapped back to her, his frost-colored eyebrows slightly raised in surprise. For an instant, there was joy in his eyes, and then he let out a soft breath and murmured, "My most humble apologies, Claire. I will make another attempt to reach your world now. I have regained…"

She put a finger to his lips. "Just tell me if I misunderstood you. I don't care about the legends or the food. I just want to know if I imagined love where there was none."

Tuathal's hand tightened on hers, and his eyes flickered, blue as deep as the night sky shot through with lightning. "Love has been there from the beginning, since long before you bore the Shining Knife. I've loved you since you made a wish that showed me your heart."

"Then…"

"Claire, let me try again. *Please.* I want you to have complete freedom to choose." His voice roughened, and he swallowed. "Perhaps you would be able to visit your world again after you have eaten; the foinse cumhachta has never been borne by one of your world before, and perhaps that changes the rules a little. But I don't want your hunger, however courageously you bear it, to cause you to make an impetuous decision."

Tears filled Claire's eyes, and she brushed at them.

Tuathal made an almost inaudible sound in his throat and traced a tear down her cheek, the touch light as a summer breeze. "Forgive me, Claire."

She choked out a laugh and put her hand around his, threading her fingers through his lean ones. "I should be the one saying that, I think." She leaned closer and pressed her lips to the sharp point of his jaw just below his ear, feeling the pulse in his throat, and then pulled back to rest her cheek against his. His wild hair silvered the light that reached her half-closed eyes.

She became suddenly aware that the entire room was silent; an instant later, a deafening roar of cheers and clapping rolled over her like thunder.

TUATHAL AND CLAIRE LEFT the banquet with a minimum of fuss. Tuathal murmured instructions to a servant, who nodded respectfully, his eyes flicking up to the king's face and then away.

He offered Claire his arm and led her to his study. His steps were long and graceful, but he did not move quickly; Claire wasn't sure whether it was out of consideration for her, or whether it was because he wasn't yet as steady as he wanted her to believe.

She stood in front of the mirror at his request. Her reflection looked… well, pretty unrecognizable, if she were honest with herself. The cut on her arm had healed cleanly, though the scar was still bright pink. She was thinner, which seemed to make her look taller; or perhaps that was only the flattering cut of the dress. Her hair had nearly reached the length of a very short pixie cut, and she raised one hand to brush her fingers against the almost-hidden scar.

"Think of where you want to go," he said. His voice sounded a little strange to her, rough with fatigue and emotion, and she glanced at him. He leaned against the wall, long and gaunt and graceful, his face bone-white.

"Are you sure you should do this?" Claire whispered.

"Quite sure. Are you ready?" He gave her a sharp-toothed smile, and if she hadn't been looking so closely, she would not have seen the dark, hopeless look in his eyes. She sucked in a breath, searching for words to tell him that she would come back…

But for one instant, she imagined her parents' brick patio, the fall leaves shifting in the breeze, a cup of coffee by her elbow, a book in hand.

She blinked. The leaves rustled above her, the coffee steamed, and the book dropped from her hand as she cried out.

CHAPTER 37

Claire stumbled inside, tears in her eyes.

It was still Friday afternoon. She had been gone from the human world for such a short time that no one knew she had vanished.

She expected disbelief and difficulty in getting anyone to accept that this was not just a dream, or perhaps a symptom of her brain injury, and made an effort to be as calm as possible in her explanation. To her surprise, it turned out that while her family was astonished, they believed her readily for several reasons. Her hair had grown out a little, evidently in only a couple of hours. Her brother vouched for the part of the dream that they had both experienced during her coma. There was the cut on her arm, which was now a tender pink scar. She had lost nine pounds, evidently also in two hours. She was still wearing an elaborate gown of a cloth that was not quite silk but some other fabric no one could identify.

It didn't hurt that her mother had been on the patio and happened to be looking directly at the chair when she appeared in it.

Her father cooked steaks while she ate a bowl full of strawberries topped by whipped cream and explained the adventure as clearly as she could, though there were still many things she did not understand. She glossed over much of the danger and terror; her parents had been frightened enough by her car wreck and she didn't want to frighten them more. She explained a little about the pendant, but between her modesty, her incomplete understanding of the foinse cumhachta, and her desire not to worry them, her explanation was less elucidating than she'd hoped. With a smile, she noted that, as a human, she could handle iron and steel, and that ability was quite an advantage in Faerie. In her own ears, her words sounded whimsical and perhaps a little melodramatic, and she smiled a little as she said, "He's the king of the Seelie. Those are the good faerie creatures, I suppose you could say. And we're engaged to be married." The glorious weight of the words *engaged to be married* made her heart swell with pride.

"You want to marry him?" her mother asked again. "Are you sure?"

"If I can get back to him," she whispered.

There were a thousand questions in her mind, but that one fact was clear. She had given him power over her, without realizing when or how or why.

She loved him.

CLAIRE'S SUITCASE LAY OPEN on the bed as she chose a few essential articles of clothing and a favorite few books. Tuathal was a king and could probably provide everything she needed, but a few familiar items would be welcome. What else should she bring?

"Here. Take these." Her father proffered a slightly dusty pair of steel mesh gloves.

"Where'd you get those?" she asked, her eyebrows raised.

"From the garage. They were for cleaning fish when we went on that camping trip." He dug in his pocket. "These might be useful too." He smiled and held out a handful of jacks. "Like mini caltrops, you know?"

Claire snorted.

"And I bought this." He stepped into the hallway and reappeared with a BB gun and a five pound jug of BBs. "After what you said about the creatures you faced, I thought about buying you a gun, but you've never have any training. It would be as dangerous for you as anything else. Maybe even more... it might take a big gun to be effective against a minotaur. If gunpowder even works in Faerie. Then I thought about the iron. A BB gun would barely break your skin, but it shoots steel BBs. It uses a spring, so it should work no matter what. I got extra springs and parts for repairs."

Her father watched her take the gun and heft it to her shoulder. "It's not that hard. Just don't shoot your eye out, kid." He grinned when she rolled her eyes.

"Snack time!" Her mother's voice floated up the stairs.

"I'm pretty full," Claire groaned cheerfully.

Her father smiled. "Come on, Claire Bear. It means she loves you."

"I know. But I'm full of steak." She grinned. Her father's steaks were legendary, and it had only been two hours since she'd stuffed herself with steak and potatoes, asparagus and fresh buttery rolls.

She sat at the kitchen table and her eyes widened at bowls of popcorn and a carton of ice cream.

"Gil, scoop it for us, would you?" Her mother handed her father an ice cream spade.

He took it obligingly and began scooping butter pecan ice cream into blue ceramic bowls.

"That's beautiful." Claire's mother said.

"What, this?" Claire tugged at the pendant on her necklace. It felt different, and she pulled it off so she could see the design better.

The familiar awen design was there, with the three lines spreading at the bottom and almost converging near the top, with three dots above where the lines came together. The design was enclosed within a ring around the edge of the circular pendant.

Yet it was different; the pendant had been made of bronze, polished bright on the high parts of the designs and tarnished darker in the crevices. It had been heavy and solid, though not particularly large. Now the flat base appeared to be made of gold. The three dots sparkled so brilliantly they must have been diamonds, and pendant was nestled within layers of intricate gold filigree as if the awen itself were a precious jewel.

Ethan frowned. "Where did you get that?"

"I've had it for years. The king gave it to me. But it was different then."

Her brother's eyes widened, and he leaned forward to study the pendant. "Yeah. But not really that different, was it?"

Claire looked for the truth, and it warmed her heart. "I suppose not."

"May I see it?" Her mother leaned over the table.

Claire handed it to her mother, and the pendant was back on her neck, her mother's hands empty.

"Well..." her mother said in surprise. "I suppose that would make abdicating your throne rather difficult."

Ethan nodded thoughtfully. "It's part of you, isn't it? Didn't you say that's what the king said? It's not really just a necklace; the necklace is only what people see, and reality is more complex. You might as well try to loan someone your personality."

"Didn't the king give it to you, though?" her father asked.

Claire said in a soft voice, "Yes. And he was quite mad without it."

"So is it two now? Two pendants? Yours and his?" Ethan asked.

"No. I think it's just the one. We both wear it, and it's ours together." Claire took a deep, shuddering breath. "I gave it back to him, but... I still had it. Maybe if I tried again now that I understand more, it would work. But... I think it would be like breaking the engagement, breaking our connection. I don't want to!" Her voice shook. "I don't know how to see him again."

Their conversation over popcorn and ice cream was subdued.

Claire glanced up, noticing the empty dining room wall behind her mother. The framed pictures had been taken down and stacked neatly between sheets of newspaper in a cardboard box in the corner. "Why'd you take the pictures down?"

"Ah…" Her mother and father glanced at each other. "Don't worry about it, honey."

She tilted her head and studied their faces. Ethan looked down, his eyebrows drawn together, and muttered, "It won't help things if you don't tell her."

Her father sighed. "Right then. We're downsizing. We're selling the house, and we're moving to a townhouse over on Ridgeview Drive, just a few blocks away. Ethan won't have to change schools or anything."

"Why?" Claire breathed. "You love this house, Dad!"

Ethan said, "It's okay, Claire. I don't mind. I can still play on the soccer team and everything."

"But why?"

Her father's frown deepened, and he rubbed his hands down his jeans. "We didn't want to worry you, Claire. It's fine. We're keeping the same phone numbers, and we were going to let you know once the sale was finalized and we'd moved in and everything. It's all right."

"But *why*, Dad?" Claire's voice rose in worry. "Is your job all right? What's wrong?"

Her mother chewed her lip and glanced at her father. Their gazes caught, and they seemed to debate for a moment silently. Then her father said, "Well, insurance didn't cover all the medical bills. We owe quite a lot of money, actually. The hospital is taking payments, and with all the improvements we've made over the years, selling the house will make quite a dint in what we owe." He smiled and put his hand over hers. "It's fine, Claire. I know it's a shock to hear it like this, but we just didn't want to worry you."

"It's my fault," she breathed. "If I hadn't been driving like..."

"It was an accident!" her mother said firmly. "And we're just glad you're alive. These things happen, Claire, and yes, we hope to learn from them, but we'll handle it together. All right? It will be fine."

Ethan smiled brightly. "Besides, the new townhouse is pretty close to the park, so even though it doesn't have a yard, there's still plenty of space for kicking a ball around."

Claire closed her eyes. *This is all my fault, and they're so... I wish I'd recognized how wonderful they are. Why did it take me wrecking a car to understand how kind my family is?*

She swallowed, opening her eyes. "I'm sorry, Mom and Dad and Ethan. I'm so sorry."

"It's fine, honey." Her father put his hand over hers again. "It will be fine."

Claire looked down at her lap and her eyes widened as she realized she was still wearing the dress from the royal banquet. *I wonder...* "Wait. Mom, look at these." She stood and gestured at her clothes. The velvet overdress was studded with diamonds. "I'm sure these are real diamonds. The king..." Her voice trailed away, and she looked at the aquarium in the corner. In a moment she had opened the cabinet door and was rummaging in the supplies beneath, rising a moment later with a handful of carbon pellets for the water filtration system for the aquarium.

"Don't laugh at me if this doesn't work. I'm not a fairy king," she muttered. She closed the charcoal pellets within her fingers and *willed* them to change.

A moment later, she put a handful of cut diamonds on the table, her eyes wide. *Always carry a piece of charcoal.*

Ethan breathed, "Wow! That should cover the medical bills."

AFTER EXCLAMATIONS OF DISBELIEF and excitement and more explanations, Claire felt both drained and relieved. They finished their snacks and conversation petered out into a comfortable silence.

Finally Claire rose, her hand going unconsciously to the pendant on her neck. "I… I love you all."

"But you're going back?"

"I don't know how to get back." She swallowed. "But I have to try."

Her mother and father exchanged glances.

"You got there through a mirror last time, right?" asked Ethan.

"Right."

Suitcase in hand, she stood in front of her dresser looking into the mirror. *I do look different,* she realized. Her face was a little thinner, her eyes bright despite the lingering weariness. She looked almost regal. *It's probably just the dress,* she thought, but she knew, deep inside, that it wasn't entirely the dress after all.

"You look beautiful, darling," her mother murmured.

They wrapped her in their arms, and she breathed the faint scent of her father's aftershave, the fabric softener in her mother's blouse, and the warmth of their bodies pressed close around her.

"I'll be all right. And maybe I can come back."

"We love you, sweetheart."

And she pulled away. She knew that if she didn't, she would burst into tears, because so much love could not be held inside without tears.

She wished to see him again.

Her mirror shifted, and through it she saw Tuathal in his study.

Cool sunlight streamed through the windows lining the wall; Claire thought it looked like early morning. Tuathal sat on a window seat that Claire had not previously noticed, one sock-clad foot propped up against the opposite wall of the alcove. His head rested against the dark wood, and his eyes were half-closed as if he were either falling asleep or just waking up.

She let out a soft, relieved breath, knowing she could open the mirror at will.

Her father glanced at her. "Do you see something?"

"Don't you?"

Without waiting for his answer, she stepped through.

"HAVE YOU BEEN AWAKE all night?" she said softly.

Tuathal's head snapped toward her, and he stood suddenly, his eyes searching her face. "You came back," he said in an odd voice.

"Yes." Claire swallowed the lump in her throat. The light caught the sharp lines of his face and silvered the ends of his wild hair. He looked stronger, not quite *himself* yet but no longer near death. He was thin and hard, entirely self-possessed and dignified but for the strange, burning look in his eyes. "Didn't you sleep at all?" she asked.

He gave a startled half-laugh, and murmured, "It's been two weeks here, Claire. I'd assumed you thought better of your generous impulse to grace Faerie, and me, with your continued presence."

"Two weeks!" She stepped closer, and he remained motionless, as if afraid to startle her. Carefully, tentatively, she raised her hand to trace the faint line of strain beside his mouth with her thumb, her fingers feathering over the line of his jaw.

He closed his eyes. "Please don't taunt me, Claire." His voice was almost inaudible, his breath soft upon her wrist as he turned toward her touch. "You know I've already given you my heart. What more can I do you to make your decision easier?"

"I've already decided." She threaded her fingers through his hair and lifted up on her toes to press her lips against his, and then, finally, he believed her.

EPILOGUE
That Evening

Sunlight flooded the room, glinting on golden sconces and illuminating the subtle patterns in the thick blue rugs. An elegant chaise lounge sat by the windows, while two chairs sat close by the fireplace. An open doorway led to what appeared to be a bright, spacious bedroom; Claire could see a delicate wooden nightstand beside a bed canopied in gauzy white silk near another door she thought might lead to a dressing room.

"Do you like it?" Tuathal asked. "I'd hoped you might… that we might…" He frowned and cleared his throat. "I hope it suffices."

"It's beautiful." Claire glanced up at him. He seemed slightly ill-at-ease, and she wondered why. "What were you going to say?"

His eyes flicked over her face, lingering on her lips, then back up to meet her gaze. He cleared his throat again. "It is customary for a husband and wife to share a suite, but I didn't want to frighten you."

Heat suffused Claire's cheeks, and she looked down for a moment. In truth, she had not considered what might come after the wedding; she imagined only the wedding itself, Tuathal's brilliant smile and laughing eyes, and a general air of triumphant joy.

The thought of sharing rooms with him wasn't entirely unpleasant, though. She glanced up at him. "You don't frighten me."

"Oh?" He raised one eyebrow. "That's… good? I think?" His teasing smile made her heart beat faster.

She threaded her fingers through his and felt him relax almost imperceptibly.

"Can we sit down?" she asked.

He led her to the chairs and, with a wave of his hand, started a fire in the fireplace.

Tuathal smiled pensively, his eyes resting on her face. "You don't look happy, Claire. Do you wish to reconsider?"

"No. I just have so many questions."

He inclined his head, inviting her to ask.

"I thought I understood why the knife burned you and the kelpie and evaporated the oighear—because iron is incompatible with magic. But human blood is red because of the hemoglobin, which has iron in it, right? And your blood is blue because it has no hemoglobin and no iron, right?

"So if stainless steel has iron in it, why didn't my blood burn you?" Claire's frown deepened. "No, that's not my question. My question is why the iron in my blood *did* burn the Unseelie when it hadn't burned you."

A slow, bemused smile had crept across Tuathal's face.

"What?" Claire asked.

"Of all the things you might have asked me, you chose that? You never cease to surprise me, Claire." His gaze drifted from her eyes to her lips, then to her pendant, and down her arm to their clasped hands, their fingers woven together.

He took a breath and said, "It wasn't the iron in your blood but the steel in your will that burned them. The blood alone would have done nothing. Humans have been killed by oighear weapons before, and some creatures have even eaten humans, as I believe you have heard. No one but you suspected the iron in your blood was responsible… if they even know human blood contains iron, which I doubt. It is bound up chemically and amounts to just a trace—not concentrated enough to be dangerous. You willed—wished, if you prefer—the axe to stop. Your will was clear, pure, and focused. The will of a hero is a powerful force. The iron in your blood was not much to work with, and your skill in clearly forming commands is… problematic, but the circumstances helped you have a very clear vision in that moment. Obviously it was sufficient for the spell, and it used what it had."

Claire looked surprised, and Tuathal smiled. "Yes. That was you casting your first real magical spell. Remarkably timely it was, and strong, as well. The foinse cumhachta helped a bit. Your second was flinging the blood on the Guard. That one…" He frowned as he thought. "That was brilliant, actually.

Even with the foinse cumhachta, I would not have expected your blood to burn so effectively. Did you?"

"Not at all. I was just hoping the iron in my blood would do something."

The silence between them felt like the breathless hush before a crack of lightning, and then Tuathal chuckled softly, the sound as gentle as his hand on hers. "Perhaps you did not know the strength of your will. You may not have had any idea what would happen, so normally such a spell would have failed to do much of anything. But you were helped by the fact that all of the guard, especially those closest to you, thought *something* would happen, and they were supplying some quite vivid mental pictures of what it might be. Evidently at least one of them believed the blood would burn, which tied in quite well with your vague hopes about iron. His vision gave form to your wish, and as soon as he began to burn, the others' visions aligned with what they saw actually happening. Though they didn't stop there; by the time they reached the healers, some had sparks flying from their wounds and setting bystanders on fire! I wouldn't be surprised to hear of some other embellishments.

"They credit you with all of that. I expect that for the next millennia I will be seeing tapestries of you shooting fire from your fingertips and routing armies."

Claire snorted softly. "As if I meant for that to happen!"

"Did you not?" Tuathal raised his eyebrows. "I could not have devised a more complete victory if I'd had weeks to plan it."

"I was bluffing." Claire smiled, remembering the fierce, joyous relief of seeing the Unseelie forces disappear.

"Are you sure?"

Claire blinked. "Um... yes? I remembered what worked with the naiad. I tried to look confident. I figured that creatures that live a thousand years don't live so long if they're reckless. You don't live that long by taking risks you don't understand. I thought I'd make him decide that caution was the best part of valor."

Tuathal smiled. "And you're sure you were bluffing? Perhaps you only *thought* you were. Your courage is even more magnificent, if you did not believe you could win. But I think you were mistaken and only believed yourself to be bluffing." At her confused look, he said, "You *did* rout the entire Unseelie army by the power of your blood and the strength of your will, though we had been at war for half a century. Even my father's magic could not drive back the Unseelie so thoroughly. I believe Taibhseach was right to fear you."

She raised her eyebrows. "What would I have done?"

Tuathal grinned. "How could I *possibly* guess? But *I* certainly believed you when you threatened him."

"You did?" Her voice rose in surprise.

"It felt, through the foinse cumhachta, like the truest thing you've ever said." His eyes shone with pride. "I believe you could have followed through on your threat, but neither Taibhseach nor I can imagine what it might look like."

She laughed. "So I'm unpredictable? I thought you knew exactly what I was going to do."

"Not at all. Only we Fae are predictable. My kind does not change as you do, hour by hour becoming someone new."

She glanced at him, half-expecting to see mockery in his gaze, but he smiled back at her, his expression showing only gentle admiration. The setting sun lit the room with a warm pink-gold glow.

"I do have other questions," she said at last. With a wave of his hand, Tuathal lit the sconces along the wall and brightened the fire so that light and shadows danced over the walls.

At her hesitation, the king glanced at her with an enquiring look.

"How exactly did you get captured, anyway? Your palace isn't near the border. I had to walk for ages, and then I fell in a river and a water woman—the naiad—almost ate me, and when I surfaced I was somewhere else far distant."

The king chuckled softly. "Réidh? Oh, she must have liked you, if she let you go."

"I'm not so sure. I think she thought I looked tasty."

"Indeed. She's one of my more dangerous subjects, but she's hardly evil. She hasn't eaten a human since my grandfather was young. Of course, I don't know that she's come across a human since then, either."

Claire studied his face in the dim light. "Did you mean to sidestep my question, or are you always so difficult to pin down?"

He raised an eyebrow at her. "If you must know, I walked."

"What? Did you let yourself be captured?" *I knew it!* she thought. "Why?"

He licked his lips and glanced away. "I was buying time."

"Time for what?"

"For you."

She narrowed her eyes and stared at him, trying to see past the elegant planes of his face and the distracting lightning flash in his eyes, the slippery words and ever-present amusement that curved his lips in a sardonic smile.

"I'm serious, Tuathal. I want to know. How did you get captured?" Something inside her felt like it was burning, digging, twisting her heart into a knot, knowing she was about to hear something she could not bear. She *didn't* want to know, not at all.

"I made a bet, Claire." His voice was soft and clear, threading through her veins like molten gold. "Taibhseach wanted the foinse cumhachta, and it could not, it *must not,* fall into his hands. He would have used it not only to conquer the Seelie, but perhaps even to break the barrier between the human world and Faerie. He has no authority to enter your world; the right to enter the human world belongs to the Seelie crown and is inherent in the foinse cumhachta wielded by Seelie monarchs. If he captured it, not only all of Seelie but all of the human world would suffer.

"But we were losing the war. We could hold the border no longer, and I had no partner to wield the foinse cumhachta to its full potential.

"I gave you your part of the foinse cumhachta when you helped me defeat the rats, the Unseelie vanguard. But I did not endow it with all the power it might hold; you were not yet ready, and I needed the power for other conflicts.

"I left it with you because it would help protect you, and it seemed to affect you in a way that is difficult to explain. It helped you become more *you*, the you that you were always meant to be. The bright, shining Iron Queen.

"When you came to my infirmary, the war had reached a critical moment, and all appeared to be lost. And yet you appeared, pulled through the veil between worlds by the power of your own will and by the protection of the foinse cumhachta, which knew that of all places in all worlds, my infirmary was the very safest place for you to go.

"And so, seeing the opportunity to hide the rest of my power, including the right and authority to enter the human world, where Tiabhseach would *never* find it, I put it all into the foinse cumhachta, and I hid it from all who sought it, even from myself, though I kept the memory that you had possessed it. Then I sent you back with it to your world, where Taibhseach could not reach.

"Later, for a brief time, I thought we had an opportunity to make headway in the war. I was weary beyond words, and I thought, for a short time, that we might be able to end the war, if only I had the power that I had stored in the foinse cumhachta. You refused to give it back." He frowned thoughtfully. "No, that's not right. You did not remember you had it, and *could not* give it back. It was hidden even from you. This was, I think a good thing, though at the time I nearly despaired. I suspect now that the appearance of opportunity was a trick, a trap to draw me out with the foinse cumhacha. And you were not yet ready—the foinse cumhachta itself helped you grow and protected you."

"Is it sentient? You speak of it as if it has thoughts and opinions."

"Not exactly. But sometimes it *acts* as if it were sentient. It seems to like certain people more than others and approves some plans more than others. Perhaps this is the subconscious of the one or two who wield it, or perhaps it is also others who have in the past or will in the future wield it. After all, time—well, actually everything—is a bit complicated when it comes to magic."

Claire eyed his sharp features, the clever way he had not exactly answered her question. It was all very clear and concise, and yet… not entirely informative.

"But how did you come to be captured, Tuathal?" she said softly.

"I told you. I walked." His grin was sharp and almost, but not quite, bitter. "I walked out into Unseelie lands and shouted for Taibhseach by name until all his many spies slithered and flew to whisper in his ear that the mad king of the Seelie was screaming to be captured." His eyes glinted. "I like to think I was a bit more dignified than they reported, but I did want to make an impression."

"But *why?!* Why, Tuathal?" Claire's voice cracked. "Didn't you know what he would do?"

Tuathal's frost-colored eyebrows raised. "Not exactly, of course, but I had the general idea. I was buying time, as I said. If he crossed the border by force, he'd capture me on my land, and then it would be only a very short time until he captured all Seelie lands. He would know that we were weak and that we could not defend the border. If I walked into his domain, shouting my defiance to the skies, he would wonder what treachery I planned, and he would be cautious. Especially since I did not have the foinse cumhachta! He would wonder where it was, and when it might appear as part of a cunning trap. The war had already lasted for a human lifetime, and he could be patient a little longer for the sake of caution.

"I knew he would search me. Unseelie magic is deep and dark and cold. I knew it would ooze like poison through my veins, invading the deepest parts of my mind and searching my memories for the foinse cumhachta. So when you would not give it to me, I knew I would face him. It was a gamble, to be sure, but I was desperate and I could think of nothing else. So I hid the foinse cumhachta from all who might look, and I hid my mind within the foinse cumhachta within you. I left myself only the tiniest whisper of sanity, just enough to remember the next step of the plan, to walk into Unseelie land. I erased the memory of the foinse cumhachta from my own mind—what it was, what it looked like, and where I hid it. So when Taibhseach sent his magic coursing through me, there was nothing for him to find." Tuathal's voice hardened. "And thus I bought time."

The air was not enough to fill Claire's lungs, and she gasped at the terrible brilliance and audacity of Tuathal's plan. "So it was a bluff," she whispered. "You pretended the Seelie were stronger than they were to make him hesitate."

He looked faintly pleased. "Indeed. You, my Iron Queen, did something rather similar, if I understand correctly."

"But you… but…" Claire closed her eyes, and the stinking hole in which she had found Tuathal rose in her mind, dark and hopeless. "How did you hope to get out? You said you didn't think I'd come."

He smiled and bent to kiss her fingers, one by one. "I hoped you would come."

"But you said you didn't think I would."

"I didn't *think* you would come. But I *hoped* you would." He glanced at her, and, seeing her bafflement, said softly, "My hope in who you might become was stronger than my fear of Taibhseach."

Claire could not look away from his eyes, bright as lightning across the night sky.

"Besides, it isn't as if I had many other choices." Tuathal smiled, pressing his cheek against their entwined fingers. "If I gave you enough time, and the foinse cumhachta enough time to work in you, perhaps you would become the hero we needed."

"You believed in me." The immensity of his faith in her made her heart swell.

"I still do."

"Why did you play the role of villain?"

"I had to work within the framework you gave me. You wished to be the hero and defeat the villain. I played the villain to protect you. You faced me, and defeated me, rather than facing Taibhseach—at least at first, before you had become your true, heroic self."

Claire shuddered at the thought of facing Taibhseach as the child she had been. "You let me hate you."

"I had to. Only a human could slip through Taibhseach's magical defenses to rescue Fintan, even with Faolan's help. I distracted Taibhseach as well, and when you and Fintan escaped the prison, I doubled back and retrieved Faolan and Riagan." At her questioning look, he said, "Riagan, the little green fairy."

Claire closed her eyes and swallowed regret. "Thank you."

He smiled.

"You terrified me."

"Well, that didn't last," he said in a soft voice, and her cheeks warmed. "As you rose to the challenge, I loved you more, because you were more yourself. And thus I gave you more power over me. When I asked for the foinse cumhachta back, it was all I could do not to vanish when you cried out that I should leave. But the need for the foinse cumhachta gave me strength. I hoped so desperately that you would give it to me, and that I could use it to defeat Taibhseach. But you would not."

"I should have. Why didn't you simply take it when I fainted?" She searched his face.

"I couldn't. Partly because I had hidden it already, even from myself; though I knew you had it, I could not see it or search it out. More importantly, because…" He frowned thoughtfully. "I think it did not want to be taken from you. I had left it with you, with some power, to help you grow into the hero I knew you could be. The foinse cumhachta is not really the pendant, you know. The pendant is a symbol, a mostly-physical representation of a magical phenomenon that is difficult to describe—a particular type of royal Seelie power, authority, trust, and cooperation. In the intervening time, the foinse cumhachta seemed to have decided that it *liked* you, for lack of a better description. It did not want to be taken; even if I could have taken it by force (and I'm not sure that I could have, although it acknowledged the legitimacy of my claim to it), it would have been wrong to do so, as well as likely futile."

She took a deep breath and let it out slowly, finally giving voice to the question that had lurked at the back of her mind since the moment she had realized she possessed the foinse cumhachta. "Why did you hope I would walk into Taibhseach's trap if you knew he wanted the foinse cumhachta? Why weren't you afraid he would just kill me and take it?" Her voice shook.

Tuathal inhaled sharply. "Claire!" he breathed. "Do you truly think so little of me? Do you think I risked you so easily?"

"I…" She brushed at sudden, unwelcome tears. "No, I know you felt you had to. I'm not angry, Tuathal. I just want to understand."

He brushed his fingers over her cheek with infinite tenderness, his fingertips trailing down her jawline to her lips. "The foinse cumhachta was the greatest protection possible. I *hid* it, Claire. It could not be found. Taibhseach could have killed you, perhaps, but even if he had ripped the pendant from your body, he would not have possessed the foinse cumhachta." At her confused look, he said, "The pendant is but a symbol, a representation, of the foinse cumhachta. It *could not be found,* for it was within you all the time. The pendant was invested with some power, yes, but the foinse cumhachta is not merely a little bronze token to be taken so easily.

"Taibhseach and his forces could not perceive that you had it, much less how to take it from you. They could see only your actions, your courage, and your mercy, and from that they imagined that you might be the hero they feared. But they could not know, and dared not challenge you. They were right to fear you."

"I had to give it to you willingly, didn't I?" Claire closed her eyes, remembering. "It was your mind. That's why it made you sane again, didn't it?"

"I hid my mind within the foinse cumhachta, yes, though they are not one and the same. And yes, I entrusted it to you."

"What would have happened if I'd died before I gave it back to you?"

"The foinse cumhachta would remain hidden forever. Perhaps it would die." Tuathal frowned, his expression pensive. "I did consider that possibility. Yet, terrifying as it was, it was still better than Taibhseach obtaining it. At least the boundary between Faerie and the human world would not be breached."

A sick horror spread through her, and she caught her breath. "And you have been mad forever."

Tuathal shrugged almost carelessly. "Oh, not forever. Even we Fae eventually reach the end of our days. Besides, I doubt Taibhseach would have kept me around indefinitely. Once he had secured his rule over the Seelie, I imagine he would have disposed of me, foinse cumhachta still undiscovered." He smiled and pressed a kiss to her temple, then let his cheek rest against hers. "It was a risk I was willing to take. You bear no guilt for that, Claire."

"I should have given it to you when you asked for it."

"I'm glad you didn't. In retrospect, I don't know that the opportunity was as good as I hoped at the time, and anyway, if you had, then you wouldn't have become my Iron Queen." His cheek curved against hers, and she realized he was grinning fiercely. "It was worth the cost and more."

"I love you, Tuathal." The words were true, but they were not enough, and she turned to let her lips brush his cheekbone, tasting the warmth and magic of him, the starlight on snow, the electric power in his veins.

His smile widened. "And I, you." His lips met hers like lightning across a cloudless sky, bright and triumphant.

AFTERWORD

Thank you for purchasing this book. If you enjoyed it, please leave a review at your favorite online retailer! There is a bonus chapter available at http://www.cjbrightley.com/lord-dreams-bonus-chapter/ .

C. J. Brightley lives in Northern Virginia with her husband and young children. She holds degrees from Clemson University and Texas A&M. You can find more of C. J. Brightley's books at www.CJBrightley.com, including the epic fantasy series Erdemen Honor, which begins with *The King's Sword,* and the Christian fantasy series A Long-Forgotten Song, which begins with *Things Unseen*. You can also find C. J. Brightley on Facebook and Google+.

Sneak Peek:
Erdemen Honor Book One

The King's Sword

One

I crossed his tracks not far outside of Stonehaven, and I followed them out of curiosity, nothing more. They were uneven, as if he were stumbling. It was bitterly cold, a stiff wind keeping the hilltops mostly free of the snow that formed deep drifts in every depression. By the irregularity of his trail, I imagined he was some foolish city boy caught out in the cold and that he might want some help.

It was the winter of 368, a few weeks before the new year. I was on my way to the garrison at Kesterlin just north of the capital, but I was in no hurry. I had a little money in my pack and I was happy enough alone.

In less than a league, I found him lying facedown in the snow. I nudged him with my toe before I knelt to turn him over, but he didn't respond. He was young, and something about him seemed oddly familiar. He wasn't hurt, at least not in a way I could see, but he was nearly frozen. He wore a thin shirt, well-made breeches, and expensive boots, but nothing else. He had no sword, no tunic over his shirt, no cloak, no horse. I had no horse because I didn't have the gold for one, but judging by his boots he could have bought one easily. There was a bag of coins inside his shirt, but I didn't investigate that further. His breathing was slow, his hands icy. It was death to be out in such weather so unprepared.

He was either a fool or he was running from something, but in either case I couldn't let him freeze. I strode to the top of the hill to look for pursuit. A group of riders was moving away to the south, but I couldn't identify them. Anyway, they wouldn't cross his path going that direction.

I wrapped him in my cloak and hoisted him over my shoulder. The forest wasn't too far away and it would provide shelter and firewood. I wore a shirt and a thick winter tunic over it, but even so, I was shivering badly by the time we made it to the trees. The wind was bitter cold, and I sweated enough carrying him to chill myself thoroughly. I built a fire in front of a rock face that would reflect the heat back upon us. I let myself warm a little before opening my pack and pulling out some carrots and a little dried venison to make a late lunch.

I rubbed the boy's hands so he wouldn't lose his fingers. His boots were wet, so I pulled them off and set them close to the fire. There was a knife in his right boot, and I slipped it out to examine it.

You can tell a lot about a man by the weapons he carries. His had a good blade, though it was a bit small. The hilt was finished with a green gemstone, smoothly polished and beautiful. Around it was a thin gold band, and ribbons of gold were inlaid in the polished bone hilt. It was a fine piece that hadn't seen much use, obviously made for a nobleman. I kept the knife well out of his reach while I warmed my cold feet. If he panicked when he woke, I wanted him unarmed.

I felt his eyes on me not long before the soup was ready. He'd be frightened of me, no doubt, so for several minutes I pretended I hadn't noticed he was awake to give him time to study me. I'm a Dari, and there are so few of us in Erdem that most people fear me at first.

"I believe that's mine." His voice had a distinct tremor, and he must have realized it because he lifted his chin a little defiantly, eyes wide.

I handed the knife back to him hilt-first. "It is. It's nicely made."

He took it cautiously, as if he wasn't sure I was really going to give it back to him. He shivered and pulled my cloak closer around his shoulders, keeping the knife in hand.

"Here. Can you eat this?"

He reached for the bowl with one hand, and seemed to debate a moment before resting the knife on the ground by his knee. "Thank you." He kept his eyes on me as he dug in.

I chewed on a bit of dried meat as I watched him. He looked better with some warm food in him and the heat of the fire on his face. "Do you want another bowl?"

"If there's enough." He smiled cautiously.

We studied each other while the soup cooked. He was maybe seventeen or so, much younger than I. Slim, pretty, with a pink mouth like a girl's. Typical

Tuyet coloring; blond hair, blue eyes, pale skin. Slender hands like an artist or scribe.

"Thank you." He smiled again, nervous but gaining confidence. He did look familiar, especially in his nose and the line of his cheekbones. I tried to place him among the young nobles I'd seen last time I'd visited Stonehaven.

"What's your name?"

"Hak-" he stopped and his eyes widened. "Mikar. My name is Mikar."

Hakan.

Hakan Ithel. The prince!

He looked a bit like his father the king. It wasn't hard to guess why he was fleeing out into the winter snow. Rumors of Nekane Vidar's intent to seize power had been making their way through the army and the mercenary groups for some months.

"You're Hakan Ithel, aren't you?"

His shoulders slumped a little. He looked at the ground and nodded slightly.

He had no real reason to trust me. Vidar's men would be on his trail soon enough. No wonder he was frightened.

"My name is Kemen Sendoa. Call me Kemen." I stood to bow formally to him. "I'm honored to make your acquaintance. Is anyone following you?"

His eyes widened even more. "I don't know. Probably."

"Then we'd best cover your tracks. Are you going anywhere in particular?"

"No."

I stamped out the fire and kicked a bit of snow over it. Of course, anyone could find it easily enough, but I'd cover our trail better once we were on our way. A quick wipe with some snow cleaned the bowl and it went back in my pack.

He stood wrapped in my cloak, looking very young, and I felt a little sorry for him.

"Right then. Follow me." I slung my pack over my shoulder and started off. I set a pace quick enough to keep myself from freezing and he followed, stumbling sometimes in the thick snow. The wind wasn't quite as strong in the trees, though the air was quite cold.

I took him west to the Purling River as if we were heading for the Ralksin Ferry. The walk took a few hours; the boy was slow, partly because he was weak and pampered and partly because I don't think he understood the danger. At any moment I expected to hear hounds singing on our trail, but we reached the bank of the Purling with no sign of pursuit.

"Give me your knife."

He gave it to me without protest. He was pale and shivering, holding my cloak close to his chest. I waded into the water up to my ankles and walked downstream, then threw the knife a bit further downstream where it clattered onto the rocks lining the bank. Whoever pursued him would know or guess it was his, and though the dogs would lose his trail in the water, they might continue downstream west toward the Ferry.

"Walk in the water. Keep the cloak dry and don't touch dry ground."

"Why?" His voice wavered a bit, almost a whine.

I felt my jaw tighten in irritation. "In case they use dogs." I wondered whether I was being absurdly cautious, whether they would bother to use dogs at all.

He still looked confused, dazed, and I pushed him into the water ahead of me. I kept one hand firm on his shoulder and steered him up the river. Ankle-deep, the water was painfully cold as it seeped through the seams in my boots. The boy stumbled several times and would have stopped, but I pushed him on.

We'd gone perhaps half a league upriver when I heard the first faint bay of hounds. They were behind us, already approaching the riverbank, and the baying rapidly grew louder. I took my hand from the boy's shoulder to curl my fingers around the hilt of my sword. As if my sword would do much. If they wanted him dead, they'd have archers. I was turning our few options over in my mind and trying to determine whether the hounds had turned upriver or were merely spreading out along the bank, when the boy stopped abruptly.

"Dogs."

"Keep walking."

He shook his head. "They're my dogs. They won't hurt me."

I grabbed the collar of his shirt and shoved him forward, hissing into his ear, "Fear the hunters, not the dogs! You're the fox. Don't forget that."

Made in the USA
Middletown, DE
21 April 2017